FIT
for the
THRONE
II

THE ROYAL GAMES

S. MCPHERSON

FIT FOR THE THRONE: THE ROYAL GAMES

Book 2 in the Fit for the Throne series
Published by S. McPherson
ISBN: 978-1-9163026-6-2
Copyright © 2023 (eBook)
Copyright © 2023 (Paperback)
All rights reserved.

To learn more about the author visit:
Instagram:
https://www.instagram.com/smcphersonbooks/
Tiktok: https://www.tiktok.com/@s_mcpherson_books
Bookbub: https://www.bookbub.com/profile/s-mcpherson
Facebook:
https://www.facebook.com/Smcphersonbooks

For those who like their villains dark and their hero's morally grey…

ARE YOU
FIT
for the
THRONE?

1

VARIALLA
HIS PAWN

I always imagined hell with more fire. Not the scorching sun that currently baked my battered skin. Not this sweltering heat that made breathing virtually impossible and had sweat coating my upper lip. But actual roaring flames that reeked of brimstone and had some red git holding a pitchfork. Yet here I was…in hell.

My back struck the ground. Air rushed from my lungs. I groaned as I rolled onto my knees. My arms almost gave out beneath me. Everything hurt, right down to the edges of my teeth.

We'd been at this so-called training for hours, but Loch showed no signs of stopping. Not until he'd beaten me down. Not until he'd reminded me and everyone watching that I may be powerful, but he was invincible. He wanted them to see that even the heir to the Coral Court, with the might of a dragon, buckled before him.

Not that anyone knew I was part dragon. I hadn't been able to conjure that side of me since the night of the ball. I wasn't sure if it was because it had taken a lot out of me, or because Loch still kept a tight grip on that ability. Although I didn't understand why he would.

Originally, he'd claimed he hadn't wanted me to discover my own power before he was sure our bond was intact. However, lately, he'd proven that bond was well and truly intact. With every graze of his fingers that sent pinpricks of desire across my heated skin and every brush of his lips that left me panting, he proved it. I was tethered to him like a worm on a hook. If I fought, he forced his words and will to seize my mind until they somehow became my own.

Thankfully, Loch only exercised that power in public, where he made me obey his every command. In private, my mind was my own. It was like the sick bastard enjoyed the fight.

However, bond or no bond, Loch hadn't tried to fuck me yet. Not because he was a good man, but because he wanted me to admit I wanted him. He wanted me to beg for it.

"Is that all you've got?" he bellowed now as he stood over me. He flung his arms out wide to the cheers of his people.

His foot connected with my side and I bounced across the sand. Before I could blink, the bastard was on top of me. Straddled across my waist, Loch grasped my wrists in one hand and pinned them above my head. His other hand with its webbed fingers curled around my neck. He sneered. His ice blue eyes were unhinged. He dragged his thumb along my jawline.

"I win," he purred, then crushed his lips to mine.

Shit! I bucked my hips to throw him off but Loch pressed closer and cut off my air with a tightening of his grip. His cold tongue pushed inside my mouth. He groaned. Tendrils of desire and disgust shot down my spine.

The sirens around us, who'd temporarily traded their tails for legs and gathered to watch me train on this small sandbank, howled their approval. They were thrilled to see their new rulers getting along so well—unable to keep our hands off of each other. Or so Loch would have them believe.

I never thought I would crave someone's death this much but with him, I longed for it. The only thing that stayed my hand, aside from the control he had on me, was the fact that he was a symbol of hope to my people. The Rebel King. They respected me but they worshiped him.

Loch was the one who'd taken care of them for centuries. Who'd kept them from starvation. Who'd assembled their armies and put regimes in place to make sure they survived in exile. And now he'd brought them the promise of a better future through me.

A reluctant whimper slipped from my lips as his tongue slid across my own. I welcomed it. Unable to resist, I matched its deep, probing strokes. Even as a small part of me screamed, I drew him closer. Loch grunted and rocked his hips. His hand trailed down my neck to curl around my breast. I couldn't help but moan.

At the sound, his kiss grew hungrier. He didn't care that I despised him, that I'd never trust him or give him more than my body. He only wanted to see me on the Eternal Throne so he could rule at my side. All he cared about was revenge on those who'd wronged him centuries ago and on freeing the Outer Isles.

I gasped when his fingers teased my nipple. My heart raced faster than I wanted to admit. Colette once said that the bind between us grew stronger over time, especially the more we were around each other, and fuck, I felt it now.

Fight it, Varialla. I whispered in my mind. *Fight him.*

There was only one male's lips I wanted on mine and Loch wasn't him. Thoughts of the Shadow Saint invaded my mind and cleaved through the twisted bind. The rising lust I felt for Loch vanished. I wrenched my mouth from his. My chest heaved.

Loch grinned at the torment in my stare. My hunger and hatred for him.

"You lose, Princess." His lips brushed mine once more.

Then the asshole hopped to his feet to the applause of my people.

Anger seared through me. My back itched with wings that begged to be set free. The threat of fire simmered in my throat. But it would never be more than that. Not until I ripped my power from his hold.

Inhaling deeply, I pushed to my feet. The sirens gathered around Loch. They patted him on the back and congratulated him on being the undefeated champ. My scowl deepened. I'd gotten stronger in the six weeks since he'd brought me to the Coral Court, but Loch was still faster. Still had centuries of training on me.

"That's not the face of a blushing Mate-Sworn."

I swiveled to where Colette strode towards me. She didn't have much practice on her human legs and wobbled as her feet sunk in the sand.

I smiled tightly. Not for the first time, I wished I could tell her everything. Loch had used our bind to stop me from saying a word about what had really happened the night of the ball. He said it was so the sirens didn't discover I'd betrayed them. That I'd killed three of our own to save their enemy. He wanted them to follow me blindly to the Throne. I wanted them to know the truth.

Exekiel was my mate, no matter how much I wished he wasn't. I would never be able to kill him or stand back and watch him die. More importantly,

Loch wasn't who they thought he was. He was a snake in siren scales.

I sighed. "I'm just frustrated he keeps winning, that's all."

Colette bunched her lips. "Are you sure?"

I wiped my hands on my shiny black leggings that were made from the smooth hide of some water beast, and fiddled with the shells at the end of my cornrows. I couldn't look her in the eye.

"Has something happened between you two?" Her brow creased with genuine concern.

"No," I lied. "I'm just nervous about the summer solstice celebrations." This was true.

In a few days, I was headed back to the Five Isles. Back to the brutality of the Games and the assholes who ran them. I was headed back to Exekiel V'alin.

To say my feelings were conflicted when it came to the Shadow Saint would be an understatement. A part of me was head over heels, writing-sappy-love-songs, crazy about him. But another part of me couldn't stand the bastard.

It'd been easier to deny the damage of his barrier when I'd been in the Five Isles. Over the last few weeks, however, the repercussions of it had been rammed down my throat. Meagre meals often had to be rationed or skipped entirely. The sick got sicker. Children collapsed from hunger. And thirst was a constant threat, even though we were surrounded by water.

"Nervous?" Colette shrieked. Her voice pulled me from my thoughts. "I can't wait." Her grey eyes danced. "An entire weekend of being in the Isles. And on *legs*!"

She whooped and did a little jig, then quickly lost her balance and fell on her ass.

I snickered. "You're a natural."

"Shut it," she huffed around a smile.

I laughed and offered her a hand.

Despite everything, I was glad that Loch had agreed to let Colette come with me. Every contestant was allowed to bring a guest to solstice. The Rebel King thought taking a siren with me was the perfect middle finger to the Royal Court. I had to agree. Plus, it let me get Colette out of this place. To treat her to a proper meal and a warm bed with woolen blankets. Assuming we found a nice place to stay.

Eternal City had been closed until the Games resumed. This meant Colette and I would have to spend the weekend among the locals. That thought was as exciting as it was terrifying.

"Come on." Colette looped her arm around mine. "Let's get to the ward before Pearl goes to sleep."

"If she's asleep, I'm waking her up," I huffed.

I didn't care if Pearl was a sweet and sickly siren who needed the healing of the Conduit and plenty of rest. She was an excellent storyteller and I needed to know what happened after she realized a shark that had been chasing her was actually a shifter.

Colette cackled. "You'll hear no argument from me."

Her limbs morphed to fins, then together, we plunged into the ocean.

2

EXEKIEL:

GOBLIN'S GORGE

ates fuck me. I was going to die out here. My skin was rubbed raw and blistered from where tentacles grabbed and sucked at my flesh. My hands were slick with blood and oil. Tentracores were the worst.

I held my breath as it once again dragged me into the raging sea. Waves crashed over my head. The frigid bite of the water cut into my lungs. Between bursts of bubbles and frothy white foam; I snatched gulps of air.

"*Uliu—.*" My summons for the Fate of Strength was cut short as the creature's mammoth tentacle tightened around my torso and wrenched me back below.

The symbol of a green trident glowed on the back of my hands. The Fate had heard me. I tunneled into that strength and punched one arm through the tentacle. Black blood spilled and spread through the churning sea.

I punched until my knuckles split. The monster's flesh turned to pulp.

Above the water, I heard its piercing cry. Its other fourteen tentacles swung towards me. Its giant, bulbous body spun in maddening circles.

I clenched my fist and punched through the final string of flesh that held the tentacle together. Its end tore off. As it sank into a pool of black, I kicked towards the surface.

Air. I needed air.

My lungs ached as I crested above the water. I drew in a deep gulp of salty morning air.

Over on the shore, the goblins bellowed and readied their crossbows from the top of the Goblin Gorge fort. Their arrowheads were set on fire. At the base, they loaded catapults with weighted boulders.

The Tentracore screeched and surged towards them. The goblins attacked. The bastards hadn't lifted a finger when I was being pummeled, but when it came to defending the Isle of Goblin's Gorge, they were relentless.

The Tentracore swung its large conical head and shook out its tangled mane. Countless flaming arrows sailed through the air. They met their mark. The beast reared back with an ear-splitting shriek. Boulders came next.

With the creature distracted, my shadows rose. They plumed higher until the milky light of the overcast morn was deepened to black.

The symbol of every Fate shone brighter on my skin. I threw my shadows over the beast and squeezed. They mimicked the movement of my hands as my fingers interlaced and my palms clasped together.

Within my grasp, the Tentracore writhed and howled as its bones were crushed and its flesh melted. The waves swelled with the force of its undulating mass.

"Retreat," the goblin commander roared.

The sea rose up and slammed against their walls. I leapt up onto what remained of the Tentracore's limp body and raced across its rubbery corpse.

When I was close enough to the rocky pier, I leapt. The goblins bellowed orders and readied to shut the large iron gates.

"Wait," I shouted.

Two of the guards ran ahead of me. Neither one looked back.

"Wait, damn you!"

If those gates closed, I was stuck. They wouldn't open again until another attack. There was no telling when that would be.

Each goblin threw me a look that clearly said, "Fuck off."

"I need to find someone."

"You mistake us for someone who cares," the stockier of the two grunted.

Before I could argue they bustled through the gates. Those stationed in the parapet aimed their flame-tipped arrows down at me. Others pressed poisonous dart throwers to their lips. I stopped and watched as the gates groaned shut.

Fuck! I kicked at the ground and looked back across the ocean. The Tentracore's corpse was almost sunk. The water an inky black around it. In the distance, I could make out the other Isles and the shimmer of my barrier around the Inlands. I couldn't have come this far to go back empty-handed.

Something whistled overhead. It was the sound of a Periquin bird, but they didn't live in these parts. I bowed to the fuckers that regarded me with their beady eyes and poised weapons.

"As you were, goblins."

My wings unfurled. I shot into the sky. My shadows swirled around me and I used them to cover me as I doubled back.

Suspended in the air, I listened for the call again. It came from the fort's flame tower. I swept towards its glassless window and perched on the ledge.

A different goblin to the one I'd expected glared at me. He stood beside the smoldering stone basin of oil. It was recently ignited as a warning to others that the Isle was under attack.

All the Outer Isles had them. Ever since the monsters infested their waters.

"You're not Reek."

The stout goblin shook his head. His large bat-like ears and drooped nose swung with the movement. "No, I'm not," he huffed. "Because Reek is dead."

I stiffened. "What?"

"That's right." He wagged a long, bony finger at me. "What exactly had you gotten him into?"

My mind raced. Who would do this? Who had known?

Reek and I had forged an alliance, decades ago out of necessity. I'd needed eyes I could trust in the Outer Isles. In return, I'd carved a tear in the barrier and looked the other way when his daughter snuck through to visit her mother and bring back resources. Over time, he'd become a friend. I didn't have many of those.

"I imagine it had something to do with this?" The goblin pulled a rolled parchment from the back of his torn shorts.

I slid from the window ledge and held my hand out. "Did he manage to break the seal?"

"I don't bloody know," he snapped as he shoved the parchment in my hand. Like all goblins, his muddy-green skin was coarse. "All I know is he died to protect it."

I tucked the sheet inside my cloak pocket and nodded. When it came to picking locks and breaking seals of any kind, goblins were the best. They were famed for their ingenuity and craftsmanship. It was that skill that kept many of them employed from beyond the barrier. Ships were often sent out to collect the wares and weapons they made in exchange for food and other resources.

If Reek hadn't managed to break through the ward around this parchment before he died, I would have to find another goblin who could.

"You say, Reek gave his life to protect this."

The goblin shoved past me to look out the window and scan the area. "That he did."

"Who killed him?"

He scoffed. "Whichever noble Inlander has our leader in his pocket."

"Was there a siren involved?"

The goblin sneered at me over his shoulder. His yellowing teeth bared. "Isn't there always?"

He stepped back from the window and jerked his head. "All's clear. I think it's best you take your leave."

"Thank you."

"I didn't do it for you. Reek was a good one." He grumbled, "For whatever reason, he claimed you were a good one too. And I trusted him. So, I'm trusting you."

"What name do you go by?"

He shook his head and stepped back. "Oh no, Shadow Saint. You won't make a friend of me. They have a habit of ending up dead."

He levelled me with a look that dared me to deny it.

I pursed my lips. "We all die, eventually."

Despite himself, he grinned.

Sopping wet, I waded through the ocean until I reached the barrier of the Five Isles. It parted for me like water. I welcomed the rush of power that hummed in my veins as I stepped through.

"I was starting to think you'd never come back."

I turned. Vladimir strode across the sand towards me. His pale green eyes glinted in the dawns light.

He smoothed his bone white hair behind his elfin ears. "The Council want to see you."

"I'm sure they do."

The Council liked to keep an eye on their unruly pet and I'd been gone for an entire night.

I stepped out of the water and onto the beach. "I'll be there once I repair any tears in the barrier."

"Alexov said not to bother today."

I shook my head. Of course, he'd say that. That bastard wanted the sirens to get in.

"Very well." I flipped up the collar of my trench coat to fight the chill coming from the sea and strode across the sand. "Fates forbid we keep Alexov waiting."

Hands tucked into my pockets and wings loose at my back, I stood in the center of the domed Council building. Sunlight streamed in from the high windows and bounced off the red marble and ivory pillars.

Alexov thumped the dais where he sat on his green-cushioned throne. "Damn it, Bravinore, are you listening?"

I blinked. "Were you saying something?"

His pale cheeks turned ruddy and he blustered over his words. Beings aged painstakingly slow in the Isles, but whenever Alexov spoke to me, he seemed to age decades.

I grinned.

"Did you or did you not spend last night protecting Goblin's Gorge from a Tentracore attack?" He spoke slow like he was dealing with some petulant child.

"I did." I looked at each council member in turn. "Is that a problem?"

"As a matter of fact, yes." Alexov drummed his fingers on the dais. "Whilst you were away, the guards were attacked and more sirens got through the barrier."

I choked back a laugh. By attacked, he probably meant he'd paid them to look the other way.

I bared my teeth. "Then perhaps we need better guards."

He sat straighter and clasped his hands in front of him. He looked down his fucking nose at me, like I was supposed to be intimidated.

"Maybe you've forgotten your role here, Protector. You guard *our* shores. You serve us."

My wings twitched. Shadows I couldn't sheath weaved between my fingers and curled around my neck. They rose in response to my ever-present rage in his company.

"I serve no one."

Symbols of the Fates lit up on my skin and emphasized my point.

Alexov snarled, "Do not breach your jurisdiction again."

The fucker needed to know where I was at all times. He couldn't have me sneaking up on them and discovering something I shouldn't.

"I vowed to protect the realm. The Outer Isles are a part of that."

"We tell you where to protect," Alexov snapped. "We are the Council. Not you."

"And why is that?"

His jaw clenched. The Council members may have looked down at me from their podium of perceived power, but the only true power in this chamber was me. It was why I wasn't on the Council. Everything on the Council had to be equal. Public rank, housing, funds, and power level.

Alexov glared daggers at me. The poor bastard looked like he wanted me dead, which he did. Me and anyone else who threatened his seat of power.

"Remain within the Five Isles," he finally bit out.

My answering chuckle was cold. I bowed exaggeratedly low at the waist, then turned and left the chamber with the eyes of my enemies at my back.

3

VARIALLA:
BALLROOMS & B.S

Everything was different now. I wasn't going back to the Five Isles the same girl I'd been before. The girl who'd trusted blindly and had the naïve hope of getting out of this unscathed. That girl had died with Exekiel. The girl that was revived when his heart had beat again was someone who finally saw the truth.

I was the enemy of everyone—the Royal Court, Exekiel and even Loch. All they cared about was revenge and power. Which meant I didn't have anything to lose by pissing them off. This time, when I returned to the Isles, I was going to fight for myself, Lucinda, Colette, Max and all those I called family in the Coral Court and beyond.

Thunderous applause cut through my thoughts. Blinking, I took in the crowd of sirens gathered before me in the glass sphered ballroom. Their shimmering tails whipped around them, whilst I stood on a raised glass platform. Behind me were two grand thrones crafted from pearls, soft sand-filled cushions and haphazardly placed shells.

Loch pressed a kiss to the back of my hand. I wanted to pull away. I hated how my skin tingled beneath his lips. I hated him.

"Soon we will sing, *Sonu di Carghel,*" he roared. The Song of Change.

Loch hoisted our clasped hands in the air. "Hail the Queen of the Isles!"

"And hail her King!" someone shouted.

Loch's answering grin was savage, complete with fangs and icy-blue eyes. He looked every bit the manipulative monster he was, but all the people saw was their leader. The man who'd saved them from destitution almost two centuries ago and who hadn't stopped saving them. I supposed for that, Loch was admirable in a psychotic sort of way.

Sirens rushed to the dais to wish me well and praise Loch. I fought the urge to roll my eyes. The bastard kept our fingers entwined. More than once, he kissed my neck. I tried to pull away but the bind yanked on my resolve. His fingers tightened around mine.

Finally, the last of his sycophant's bowed their heads and took their leave.

I snatched my hand away from him. "An heir? Seriously?" I bent and untied the buckles that had attached my feet to the platform to keep me from drifting away. "Mention putting a baby in me again, asshole, and I will remove your favorite appendage."

I turned but he caught my fingers and tugged me back to him.

"You forget your place, Princess." His lips were sickeningly close to mine. He planted a hand on the small of my back and drew me closer until my breasts brushed his chest. "Perhaps I need to remind you."

I bucked as he yanked on the bind—on my power and control. Pain shot from his hand and up my spine. I hissed and bared my teeth.

"As far as everyone is concerned, you can't wait for me to empty my seed inside you." I shivered when he licked my neck. "For me to fuck you so thoroughly, you carry the echo of it in your womb. You want it."

His siren gift slammed into me. It was enhanced by the press of my own magic working with his. I tasted the bitterness of his power with the sweetness of mine. He knew magic better than I did. How to manipulate it; wield it. Now he used my own against me.

"Do as you're told, Princess." He brushed his lips across mine. A spark of electricity crackled between us. He grinned. "Obey your master."

Rage rattled in my bones. He let me go. I glared at him, so tempted to gouge out his fucking eyes.

"One day, I will make you regret this," I hissed.

He smirked. "That day is not today. Now, run along."

A part of me wanted to stay just to defy him but the thought of being near him for a second longer made me sick. I smothered a growl and swam away.

Head down, I crushed through the crowd and found the three sirens I was looking for. The ones who reminded me that there was still some good in the world. Something left to fight for.

Orla, who I'd met on my first foraging expedition to help find food in the outer sea—the ocean beyond the dome of the Coral Court—was doing a strange dance that involved flapping her arms like some demented pigeon. Colette was beside her. She tried to mimic Orla's moves.

As always, Nile was doing his own thing. His maroon tail swished, and he rolled his ridiculously stacked abs. Muscles upon muscles that made him look like a bar of milk-chocolate.

That was one thing I'd come to appreciate about the Coral Court. The men were usually shirtless. The women wore shells or flower petals over their breasts. Since I didn't have the luxury of the tail, I was currently in a flowing white skirt with oyster shells clamped over my tits.

I swam up to join them.

"Princess," Nile cried fondly.

He swiped a chalice from the bar beside him and pushed it into my hand. I downed the drink in one gulp. A large seahorse bobbed past with a trey of drinks balanced on his head. I took another two. I drained one then savored the other.

Whilst the others continued to dance and twirl, I shimmied up to the glass bar and held onto it so I didn't have to tread water. I didn't know how the sirens stayed steady down here. It was something to do with their tails. Meanwhile I was constantly doing the doggy paddle or hanging onto surfaces.

When the song ended, Nile slumped beside me. "You've cleaned up well, considering all the blood you were covered in earlier."

I shuddered at the memory of the wounded I'd tended to in the ward this morning. They'd been out foraging when a Tentracore had found them. I'd been on the inside of the dome but I'd seen its massive silhouette surge over us. It had looked like a giant squid with a lion's mane.

Those outside the Coral Court had been fast enough to outswim it and get under the cover of the dome but its tentacles had done some damage.

I hadn't realized there were so many sea monsters in the waters around the Outer Isles, but the longer I stayed, the more I saw.

"Messengers reported that the Shadow Saint took care of the beast," Orla announced as she swam up to join us.

I hated the way my heart leapt at the mention of him.

Colette scoffed. "All hail, our jailer and our hero."

"At least his barrier's stopped incinerating everyone who touches it." Orla laughed.

Colette rolled her eyes. "Yes. After leaving us to rot for a hundred years, he finally built a doorway."

She swiped a red worm from a passing seahorse and sucked it into her mouth.

My eyebrows rose. "A hundred years?"

I looked between them.

I'd known that Exekiel's barrier had been impenetrable for a while. Anyone who tried to pass through had apparently suffered a slow and excruciating death. Now their charred skeletons were nailed to spikes at the base of the barrier as a warning…and a threat. But I didn't know it had lasted a century.

Nile folded his arms across his broad chest. "Some say it was a manifestation of his grief. As long as he couldn't get through it, neither could we."

Colette scooped up her chalice from the bar. "Don't make excuses for him." She swallowed a mouthful. "That Fae is a killer. End of story."

I wanted to agree with her. To see Exekiel, the Protector, and not the man. It was easier to detach that way. To forget how he made me feel and the things I'd felt for him.

My chest tightened. There were reasons I never asked these questions. I didn't want to feel sorry for him. I didn't want to feel anything for him.

Unable to stop myself, I asked, "What exactly did he lose during the Brutal War?"

My friends exchanged a conflicted look.

Nile sighed. "Everything."

"There's a rumor that one member of his extended family survived. She was the mate of his brother." Orla bobbed her head to the music. It was like she didn't know how every word she said affected me. "However, after she witnessed the murder of her child and mate, she apparently lost her mind and has never been the same."

My inhale was sharp. I blinked back irrational tears.

"It's believed that the one who killed his nephew—who was about two years old at the time—had been his friend." Orla continued to rock to the music. "Wade Rorqueth. A soldier of the siren army."

I felt like I'd been punched in the gut. Exekiel once told me that some of the sirens he'd killed had been his closet friends. I clutched my cup tighter and took a deep swig. That was the exact type of information I hadn't wanted to know.

"Anyway," Orla straightened. "Here's to you breaking the barrier!" she crowed, and shook back her dark curls. Her round cheeks flushed.

With a chorus of cheers, we each raised our chalices and downed the bitter wine. My face crumpled and Colette's eyes watered as she choked. The wine tasted like piss, but they saved the good stuff for smaller parties and for schmoozing with the other Isles. I called this one, Siren Sauvignon. It was a blend of fermented grapes, magic and seawater to help it go further. Completely awful but it got the job done.

A hand rested on the small of my back. My entire body tensed. I didn't have to turn to know who it was. The bastard moved as silent as a shark but I recognized his touch. His presence.

Loch slid his hand around my waist and drew me back against him.

"Princess," he murmured and caught my earlobe between his teeth. My breath hitched. My skin crawled. "Could I steal you away for a minute?"

I tilted my head, and slid my lobe from his mouth. "You've stolen so much from me already. What's one minute?"

His eyes flashed in warning, but I met it with my own venomous glare. When I glanced back at the others it didn't seem like they'd heard. They were too busy trying to balance the chalices on their heads, which of course just toppled and floated away. I threw them an apologetic smile and let Loch lead me from the glass-sphered ballroom.

4

Varialla:
His Plaything

Loch didn't speak until we'd swum deep into the labyrinth of glass corridors lit by luminous fish. There we were away from eyes that didn't know just how much of a monster he was.

"I want to make sure your head's in the right place going into the Games," he said as we rounded a corner.

"And where would that be? Up your ass?"

He grinned at me over his shoulder. I frowned when he veered down a glass tunnel that led to his private chambers. The hairs on the back of my neck rose.

"Please tell me you aren't imagining some torrid goodbye in your bed, Lochness."

Just like that, the mask of the honorable warrior king, vanished, and the true bastard emerged. Loch didn't understand my nickname for him, but he didn't like it.

He swiveled and slammed me against the wall faster than I could blink.

"Watch that mouth of yours, Princess, or I might just fuck it." His serrated teeth flashed.

I tried to shove him away, but he used his arms to bar me in. His hands braced at either side of my head.

"You still don't get it."

He moved closer until my body was wedged between his and the hard, cold wall. I sucked down a gasp.

"We are destined, you and I." Loch gripped my jaw. He forced me to meet his cold stare. "I would have no need to use your power against you if you weren't using it against us." A familiar bite of rage filled his words. He was still furious that I'd killed three of our own to save our enemy. My mate.

He stroked his hand down my neck and over my breast. I trembled; powerless to stop the heat his touch evoked. The wave of lust that crashed into me.

"Go fuck yourself," I snarled.

"Oh no," he shook his head. "I'll be far too busy fucking you."

He pushed his hand between my legs. Heat flooded my core. I jerked into him. *Fuck.* I was starting to think the bastard was part incubus. He drew a yearning out of me even when I didn't want it.

"If you stopped fighting me for one second, you might realize we could actually be happy together."

I gritted my teeth and panted through the flame of desire his touch ignited.

"What difference does it make if the way we feel about each other was manipulated?" With his other hand, Loch yanked on my hair and wrenched my head back. His tongue trailed up my neck. My body burned. "What matters is that we feel it."

I shook with rage and desire. "One day, I will kill you for this."

He chuckled. "One day you will be on your knees with my cock in your mouth."

His magic crashed into me. I gagged as I felt the tug of my own power suckled into his. My muscles seized up. My thoughts, my will became tangled with his.

He dragged his nose up the side of my cheek. His breath was a warm flutter on my jaw.

"You can't fight this, princess." He kissed the corner of my mouth. My pulse skipped. "And you know it."

His lips captured mine. My mind short circuited as he curled his other arm around my waist and pulled me to him. His other hand still rubbed between my legs. My heart thrashed wildly in my chest. This wasn't what I wanted but I couldn't pull away.

He moved faster. Instinctively, I widened my legs for him. I should have been grateful he didn't go inside my panties but a part of me desperately wished he would. He pressed closer and brushed his thumb over my clit.

"Fuck," I gasped when the kiss broke.

Arousal ricocheted through my skin.

"No matter what happens, Princess, you belong to me." He ground his hips into me, pushing his fingers deeper. "Me."

He hiked up my leg and thrust harder. His tail furiously thumped the wall. My head spun.

Shit! I didn't want this…did I? Flashes of Loch holding me as a baby and singing me to sleep, filled my mind. A familiar surge of twisted emotions swept over me. Nausea climbed up my throat. In so many ways I hated this man to the depths of my being. In other ways, he was my father, my protector, and now, my lover? What fuckery was this?

"Sworn at birth by the bind." I didn't know when his hand had climbed up my shirt. Now Loch's thumb moved over my nipple in rough circles that had me panting, whilst he continued to pump his hard cock between my legs. "I own you."

There was no mistaking the threat in his words. But the more he pushed into me, the less I could focus on them.

I swallowed a whimper, grasped his shoulders and pulled him closer. Fuck, I was losing this battle. He moved against me and I matched each thrust. He gave me just what I wanted—even if I didn't want to want it.

"And remember, whatever you do, do not mention your dragon abilities or what happened between us to Colette whilst you're away." He lifted his head and looked deep into my eyes. I felt the compulsion of his power puncture my lungs.

"I hate you," I panted, even as my body ached for him.

He saw the loathing in my eyes and grinned before he set me back on my feet.

"You'll get over it." He squeezed my ass, winked then swam away.

One day I would be able to refuse him. One day, he would give me a command and I would defy it. One day I would make him crawl on shards of glass.

Once we'd changed out of our wet clothes into the dry ones we'd packed in our waterproof satchels, Colette and I peered at the emerald glass bridge that stretched between the Outer Isles and the Inlands. This was the only legal point where outsiders with an invitation or toll, were able to pass through the barrier.

I exhaled deeply. "You ready?"

Colette shook back her white braids and smoothed down her lilac handkerchief skirt that she'd paired with a lace-up bodice. "Ready."

I did a quick check of my own outfit. I wore a cream sweater and brown leggings that I'd tucked into beige boots.

I adjusted the loose strands of my fishtail braid and nodded. "Let's do this."

Focused on not falling, Colette stared down at her feet as we walked across the long glass bridge. It hummed with the buzz of the barrier. My heart pounded. I could sense Exekiel in every ripple.

The closer we came to the end of the bridge, the clearer I saw the grand gothic arch entranceway complete with a wrought iron gate and gargoyles. There, the barrier was weakest, and security was strongest.

The guards beyond it formed a threatening line of bronze armor. I lifted my chin and drew in a breath.

Colette and I didn't slow down but instinctively clasped hands. We were in this together.

The large guard at the gate puffed out his chest. Unlike the others, he didn't wear a helmet. His blonde hair wafted in the breeze. His cruel blue eyes looked from me to Colette.

His face pinched. "You must be lost."

Colette bristled.

"Not at all." I threw him an up-yours smirk and drew out my invitation. "We're invited."

He barked a hoarse laugh. "*You're* invited. Not that," he waved a hand at Colette, "*thing*."

My brows shot up. "Excuse me?"

He sniffed and spat on the ground at Colette's feet. She jerked back and almost fell over. The asshole sneered as his gaze trailed down her legs.

"You can pin wings on a rat but that don't make it a Pegasus."

"Careful, soldier." Rage took root in my lungs.

I stood taller and pushed venom into my voice. I tilted my head in a way I'd seen Exekiel, Adir and all the other entitled pricks do enough times. I was a contestant on Fit for the Throne, after all; eligible to rule over the entire Isles. I was done letting these bigoted assholes treat me and everyone else like scum.

"According to the law of the Five Isles, any outlander with an invitation is welcome beyond this border. Are you above the law?" I spat. "If so, I'll be sure to inform the Primary when I see him at Solstice. I know he'll be thrilled when I question his guard's prejudice on live Orb-vision."

Every part of me hoped to avoid the First Primary of the Five Isles for as long as possible, but this shit-of-a-Fae didn't need to know that.

His jaw ticked. His pale cheeks turned ruddy. He glared at me so long, the dragon within me reared its head. It begged to be set free. I briefly worried that my eyes would shift but I didn't look away.

Finally, the fucker tossed me two tokens and nodded to the others to open the gate.

"Good luck, sea slugs," he snarled. "You'll need it."

His words sent shivers rippling through me. I half expected the other guards to jump us. Even so, I didn't show any fear and I didn't look back, as the gate creaked open and Colette and I sauntered across the barrier and into the Five Isles.

5

VARIALLA:
INFINITY CITY

If one more bright-eyed nymph with a Fae fetish gave me that fake apologetic smile, I was going to scream. We'd been traipsing the streets of Infinity City for hours. So far, every place we'd tried to check-in to, claimed they were fully booked due to the high number of people traveling in for solstice. I was pretty sure they just didn't want a couple of sirens staying at their fancy inns and B&B's.

Infinity City was a world reserved for those they called the Blessed. From their storefront windows stacked with jewels, to the types of people who strolled down the floral-scented streets. Each one wore a flowing dress or a fitted tunic and polished boots. Some had their hair styled in ridiculous updos that resembled griffins and snakes or various other creatures.

Every building was beige with gabled roofs or domes, and quaint cafes and restaurants lined the cobbled streets. Their seating areas spilled from the inside out. They were separated by delicate white fences or walls of floating vines.

Sultry music poured out from open doorways. A few people danced and laughed in the middle of the beveled brick road as Pegasus-pulled carriages wove around them. They didn't have a care in the world.

I pretended not to notice the outraged cries and death stares when Colette and I were spotted.

"Let's forget about lodgings for now." Colette marched ahead of me. "I say, we go get our dresses and then some much needed wine."

I could have happily skipped straight to the wine, but all clothes worn at solstice celebrations had to be in the traditional colors; gold and black. Deepest night and brightest day. They also had to be brand-new. Apparently, it guaranteed prosperity or some crap like that.

We walked down a path between tall redbrick buildings and stepped out into a courtyard. In its center was a giant armillary sundial like those in Greek history. It had a bronze spherical shape and an arrow through its center. Around its base, Fae, elves and witches sprawled on brown plaid blankets and enjoyed a picnic.

Here, a bronze sign swung from an iron rod that protruded from a building's wall. It read, Infinity Strip. It looked a lot like the street we'd just come down only here, most of the buildings were red and the roofs were steepled. The streets were more crowded and instead of lavish dining experiences and jewels, the establishments offered stylists, rare magic, and expensive clothes.

After five minutes on Infinity Strip, I was pretty confident that the siren-cents Loch had given us from our meagre reserves, wouldn't be enough. I would have much rather worn a dress I already owned but he was determined we didn't look weak. That the Inlanders knew they hadn't broken us.

Even if the only reason he'd been able to scrounge up the money at all was because the giants had been willing to give us a discount on the grain, they sold us.

"There." I gestured to a white brick shop with a large golden statue of a ball of yarn on its roof. Across the front, were the words: *Enchanted Designs.*

Colette shrugged. "A seamstress might cost less."

We waited for a Pegasus-drawn-carriage to pass before we crossed the graveled road and headed towards the shop. Inside, the owner—a witch with dark curls—spotted us. She rushed forwards and quickly flipped the open sign to closed. Then she locked the door.

She looked right at us. Her stare cold and lips curled in disgust. My nostrils flared.

"What the—"

"Don't." I cut Colette off before she launched into one of her tirades. "Don't give her the satisfaction."

Colette growled but together we turned from the witch, in search of another tailor.

It was a while before we found one that didn't immediately lock its doors. This one was called, *Fae'd Seams*, and was situated near a pond.

A bell chimed as we entered.

A harsh voice snapped, "Out!"

I froze. A beady-eyed man with a hooked nose actually shook his broom at us.

"I'll have no business with the likes of you, sea-slugs! Out!"

I was too stunned to respond as he practically swept us out of the shop and slammed the door.

"It's nice having you two here," a low voice said. "It gives the rest of us a break for a change."

Colette and I turned to where a centaur with suntanned skin and bright blue eyes perused a stall of horseshoes. The seller—a warlock—watched every move he made and rushed to wipe down anything he touched. As a result, the centaur touched almost everything.

Colette snarled, "How do you stand it?"

"I don't come to Infinity Strip often." He snorted and pushed aside the strands of blonde hair that snaked from beneath his bowler hat. "Evermore is the place for us."

My brows lifted. "Evermore?"

"A place for the outcasts. Land given to us by the Shadow Saint."

"What?" I almost shrieked.

"It was the Protector's duty to keep the peace." The centaur shrugged. Behind him his dark brown tail swished. "And streets stained in blood didn't suit the Blessed."

My stomach turned. "So, he gave you, Evermore."

"It's on the outskirts of the Isle of the Eternals. A place where our businesses can flourish without fear of being burned down. And where the children can play without their parents worrying, they might never make it back home."

Colette leapt up from where she'd slid down the wall. "For fates sake, lead the way!"

The centaur chuckled and picked up another horseshoe. He inspected it closely then breathed on it and wiped it on his coat. I thought the seller was going to pass out.

He audibly whimpered and when the centaur set it down, the seller whipped out his cleaning salves. He was so engrossed in his polishing that he failed to notice the centaur slip another set of horseshoes into his satchel.

The centaur winked. "This way."

The streets of Evermore heaved. Centaurs and satyrs hollered from stalls. Witches whizzed overhead on low-flying brooms. Nymphs danced for gathered crowds and goblins performed death-defying tricks. Apparently swallowing blades of fire was magical in any realm.

My mind whirled. This was nothing like the pomp of Infinity Strip or the flash of the Eternal city, where everything was for show; orchestrated for the Games and those who played them. This was pure, magnificent chaos. The number of Blessed here was considerably less too. I breathed a sigh of relief.

I hadn't expected Colette and I to be welcomed with open arms, but I had started to get worried. However, this place was something else. Something raw that spoke to the essence of my soul. A place that promised acceptance to any who asked for it.

Colette must have felt the same. Her gait relaxed and she greedily eyed the centaur who guided us.

"I wouldn't mind riding him, if you know what I mean," she murmured.

I snorted and shook my head.

"It's not bad, is it?" The centaur called over the crowd.

We passed a group of nymphs playing steel drums.

Colette squealed and gripped his muscular arm. "Not bad at all."

Though I knew her excitement was partly an excuse to touch him, the wonder in her eyes tugged at my heart. This was her home, but she was as much of a stranger to it as I was, because the Council had cast her out.

"What's your story?" I asked the centaur.

"Not as interesting as yours, Ms. Hastings."

I wasn't surprised he knew who I was.

"They call me Odus Deneli; talented musician and devilishly handsome." He tipped his hat. "I came to the Five Isles over a decade ago. When one of my songs made it across the barrier, a noblewoman invited me to play for her daughter's birthday." He shrugged. "One performance led to another and soon I got my citizen stamp."

He lifted his arm to reveal a symbol burned onto his inner bicep, close to his elbow. It was shaped like a four-petalled flower and in the center was a V; the Roman numeral for five.

According to Lucinda, Latin was once the national language of the Fae who'd spent a lot of time on Earth masquerading as Roman gods and angels. Over time the language had faded but the numeric system remained.

I looked from Odus to Colette. "That's the Citizen Stamp?"

My stomach turned. Loch had mentioned a system where the Royal Court kept tabs on the outlanders in the Isles, but I didn't know it involved branding their skin.

"The Inlanders call it a Citizen Stamp. We call it a Track and Trust." Odus' smile was grim. "If they can track us, they can trust us."

"Please tell me, you're joking."

Odus jumped as a small satyr waving what looked like rainbow-colored candy floss, ran beneath his flanks.

"Unfortunately, not," he said casually. "But it's not all bad. It only alerts them if we venture too close to the barrier. Fates forbid we should try to visit our families."

"You're not allowed to leave?"

He chuckled drily. "We can leave anytime we want. It's coming back that's the trick."

I shook my head. Outlanders weren't welcome without an invitation, but shouldn't a citizen stamp trump that?

We stopped outside a grey-walled shop with a narrow stoop and an awning with the name, *Fates Fabrics* embroidered on it.

"Let's get you them dresses." Odus trotted up the steps and pulled open the door. "Then we'll discuss everything over a nice cask of wine."

6

VARIALLA:
SHOWTIME

The field of fates was stunning. It was at least three times the size of a football field with shimmering emerald grass. The trees were tall with braided trunks and willowy black leaves. The air felt alive and pulsed with power. It was so potent I could almost taste it.

Apparently, it was where the Conduit had first appeared. For that reason, the Field was the main party location for every solstice celebration.

Slightly dazed, Colette and I met Odus at the gates. He did an appreciative once-over of the dresses he'd helped us get the other night. Then he gestured for us to follow him through the bustling crowd. Summer solstice was officially here.

Beings dressed in black and gold danced around crimson fires that burned in stone pits. Above the flames, glittering depictions of the Fates tap-danced to upbeat Celtic-style music.

Further in, gold and ivory carriages sold food from their open windows like a Five Isles' version of a food truck. A medley of spiced aromas rivalled the scents of honey melons and roasted figs. A hunched woman at a table beneath an extravagant gazebo waved her hands over a crystal ball and called to passersby.

Everything was captivating. I didn't know which way to look.

"There you are," someone shouted seconds before a winged figure pounced on Odus. Her legs wrapped around the centaur and rested on his back as she flung her arms around his shoulders. Their mouths met in a collision of hungry tongues.

"Damn it," Colette grumbled beneath her breath.

I blinked. Odus, a centaur, was kissing a Fae. Those around us glared and spat at them as they passed. The couple didn't seem to notice. I wished I hadn't. These people painted themselves as the Blessed—the Saints, and yet they were the worst of the worst.

I glared at the next assholes that looked like they might approach. They took one look at me and Colette and gave us a wide berth. I tried to feel triumphant but their obvious disgust and fear left a foul taste in my mouth.

I almost choked when the kiss broke, and I recognized the Fae. She had paper-pale skin, thick black wings, sharp cheekbones, and upturned eyes. She was a contestant from the Games. Jia something.

I didn't think any contestants supported the Outer Isles, other than me, Maximus and Lucinda.

"I know what you're thinking," she said as she uncoiled her legs from around Odus and leapt down. "What can I say? I like a big dick."

A beat of shocked silence past before I burst out laughing. Even Colette chuckled.

"I really wanted to hate you," she openly confessed. "But Odus was right. We're going to get along great."

Jia laughed. Colette and I linked arms and followed the two unlikely lovers through the crowd. The waves of animosity that rolled towards them was enough to make my skin itch.

"Doesn't that bother you?" I snapped.

Jia shrugged. "We're used to it."

She snuggled closer to Odus who had his hand rested on her shoulder.

"People believe what they're told and they've been told that our union is unholy. That love can somehow be controlled."

I snorted. If only that were true.

"If I win the throne, it will be the first thing I change. People will be allowed to love who they want to love regardless of what side of the barrier they come from." She rolled her eyes.

A large crowd gathered around a frothing purple fountain. We beelined towards it.

"Are you ready for this?" Odus called.

"What is it?" I studied the liquid and those who filled their chalices with it.

"Wine," he cried.

He snatched a golden goblet off the fountain's ledge and handed it to me. "Every solstice our delightful Fates Fountain changes its water to wine."

My eyes popped open. "You're joking!" I cackled.

His brow wrinkled. "Why's that so funny?"

"Because…" I shrugged. "Jesus."

"Who?" He and Colette asked in unison.

I shook my head. "Never mind."

They knew as little about my religion as I knew about theirs. Although it'd been hard for me to believe in anything growing up. I was too busy being passed between families and living on the streets. I'd always thought there was something out there. An energy that made the sun rise and the birds sing…but I never gave much thought to what.

"Trust me." Jia squeezed my hand. "It's divine."

I snickered at her awful and yet brilliant pun.

"Alright." I held my fishtail braid back as I leaned closer to the fountain. "Let's do this."

"On three," Odus bellowed over the raucous cheers around us. "One, two…"

We plunged our golden goblets beneath the water-turned-wine.

"To the Fates," he roared.

We drank. Crisp fruity flavor bloomed across my tongue. My eyes rolled and I swallowed a moan as I drained my cup.

Colette gripped Odus's arm. Her legs crossed as if she was fighting the urge to dry-hump him or perhaps the fountain.

"Best wine ever," she breathed.

"I'll drink to that." Leaning over, I refilled my goblet.

"Where the hell have you been?"

I swiveled. My heart soared. Lucinda and Maximus were standing behind me.

They looked incredible. Maximus wore a gold-sequined jacket over an unbuttoned black shirt, and baggy black trousers. Lucinda's dress was an elegant sweep of gold fabric that fell to her ankles with a black bow tied beneath her breasts. Her dark hair was pulled into a chignon and dotted with gold leaves.

She arched a brow. "Do you know how many messenger ravens I sent to Residence Manor before I found out you'd left?"

"It wasn't planned."

She frowned but I didn't want to get into Loch right now. I wrenched her into a hug. She threw her arms around me and squeezed.

"I must have pinged you at least a thousand times on enchant-a-gram," Maximus added as his arms enveloped the both of us.

I breathed in his fresh pine scent and smiled. The stress of the Games and whatever else lay ahead was temporarily forgotten in the cocoon of their arms. It was crazy how much I'd miss them.

"Despite all the magic in the realm, the Coral Court hasn't mastered technology working underwater," I said; my words muffled against Lucinda's shoulder.

I didn't add that Loch had confiscated my phone anyway, and basically kept me as a prisoner. His little doll.

Maximus' dreadlocks tickled my cheeks as we pulled back.

"Next time, find a way to get in touch," he huffed. Then he smiled and planted a kiss on my cheek.

"I missed you guys." I blinked back unexpected tears.

"The feelings mutual," he called and strutted off to fill his goblet in the fountain.

Before I could follow, Lucinda gripped my arm. "How have you been since…everything?"

By everything she meant since I'd tied my life to Exekiel's, found out I was part dragon and been betrayed by the one male I thought I could trust.

I snickered. "Ask me when I'm not on my third cup of Fate's wine."

Her eyes searched mine. "Have you experienced any symptoms from the tainted bond?"

"Symptoms?" It'd been two months since then. Other than crying myself to sleep a few thousand times, I hadn't noticed anything. "Will there be symptoms?"

Her mouth twisted. "Hard to say. Most people don't taint their mate bond but there are a few theories and fables about it."

"And they involve symptoms?"

She chuckled. "I'm sure you'll be fine."

The first notes of *Fates Everlasting* began to play. The crowd fell silent. It was an ethereal ballad that marked the start of the celebrations. All my senses sharpened. It was time for the contestants to come together and officially greet the people.

Streaks of magic burst across the sky. They lit up like fireworks before they rained down like confetti. Everyone cheered then swarmed towards Fates Flame. It was the largest flame in the field and burned gold around the edges of its crimson. Unlike the others that burned in stone pits, Fates Flame somehow burned on top of the grass without setting anything on fire.

Behind it, the Conduit was on a towering stone platform. Apparently, that had been its original pedestal before it had been taken underground by the Council. A shimmering beam of blue and green flecks blazed from the center of the Conduit's pool and straight towards the heavens. Inside, symbols of the Fates swirled.

Its power was a pull in my veins. A force that made my pulse race.

The crowd cheered as the six members of the Council and the current ruling Primaries, flew in on Pegasus-back. I glared up at First Primary Adir, as he waved and did a lap overhead. Finally, they stopped beside the Conduit. Their expressions seemed colder under its icy blue glow.

I didn't listen as he launched into his speech welcoming everyone to the festivities. I followed the other contestants out to the center of the gathered crowd. I glanced back at Colette and Odus who'd snagged a spot in the front. They gave me a thumbs up. I smiled then got into position. Males on one side and females on the other. It took everything I had in me not to look *his* way; but I knew he was there. I felt him and his power that echoed mine.

Max's fingers lightly brushed my hand as he passed.

When our eyes met, he mouthed the word, "Showtime."

7

VARIALLA:

THE LONGEST NIGHT

Step. pivot. step. Together. Hold hands. Twirl. Step. Repeat.

I recited the dance in my head as I moved through the routine that had been ingrained in us during initiation Trials.

The music was transcendent; a symphony of notes that called to my inner siren. I tried to lose myself in it. I tried to focus on the reverberation of the strings, the cry of the flute, and thump of the bass. However, all I was aware of was how each note brought me closer to him.

In the corner of my eye, I caught glimpses of him move. I saw the shudder of his magnificent wings scored with threads of violet. I heard the gasps of the females as he pulled them close. His aura pulsed through the space like a damn beacon. I was drawn to it like gravity at the edge of a cliff.

This was going to be harder than I thought.

The tempo rose with the pound of my heart. I twirled from one male's arms into another. Every second moved too fast. The people cheered and camera-orbs swooped overhead. It was the official start of the Games. One of us would be crowned the next Primary.

For the audience, it was all a game. For me, it marked the beginning of the end. I had no idea what that end would look like. All I knew was if Exekiel won, his barrier would never come down. The Outlands would never be free. Cherise's mother and countless others, never healed.

I spun into the bastard's arms. Our hands met and electricity speared down my spine. I drew in a breath that didn't reach my lungs, then dragged my stare up to his.

Pain lanced through my chest as if just being near him broke my heart all over again. I'd played this moment out in my head so many times but now he was here, I didn't know what to do. I couldn't think. Couldn't speak. I was paralyzed beneath his piercing stare. Held captive by the pulse of power that rolled off him and straight through me.

Fuck, he was breath-taking. Stunning in a way that made the Fates pause and the world stand still. His dark hair was disheveled. His pink eyes were bright as they devoured me. He wore a lace black shirt that elegantly exposed the hard-packed muscles beneath, and a pair of fitted black slacks tucked into hefty boots with gold buckles. On the peaks of his pointed ears, golden cuff earrings had been attached.

My toes curled. How was anyone this beautiful? Every vow I'd sworn to destroy him now felt as damned as a flame in the ocean.

His own heated stare took in my black and gold dress. At the top, it was nothing more than golden leaves fused to my bare skin. They snaked up my torso and climbed over my breasts. They then continued up around my throat, in a diamond shape that left my cleavage bare. A black bow hung between my breasts. In the shop, I'd thought it would make unwrapping them feel like a gift.

Exekiel made a low sound in the back of his throat which suggested he'd had the same thought. My heart raced. On the bottom half, the dress rippled down in a shimmering flood of gold and black that hugged my hips. It was possibly the most elegantly sexy thing I owned.

The seamstress had insisted that every solstice dress pass the Triple F test; fitted, feminine and fuckable. Judging by the hungry gleam in Exekiel's eyes, I'd passed. A muscle ticked in his square jaw. My mouth went dry.

People murmured around us and dragged me back to the present moment. *Shit.* How long had we been standing here staring at each other? Seconds? Hours?

I stood taller. Exekiel slid his arm around my waist and pulled me close. He covered one of my hands with his and I braced my other on his hard chest. His heart pounded beneath my palm. It almost matched the unsteady rhythm of my own. Then we moved. His body effortlessly guided mine to the beat.

Every eye in the audience was fixed on us. For weeks, the people had fought and rioted in our honor. Those who supported the barrier and segregation out of fear or prejudice, were against those who wanted change. Now they waited to see how Exekiel and I would fight each other.

The laws of the Games, set in place centuries ago so a ruler could be fairly chosen, demanded we be civil. However, I had nothing civil to say. As the song played, I focused on the steps and on getting this dance over with. I acted like my heart wasn't about to beat out of my chest.

"I see you've forgotten how to dance since I last saw you." The timber of his voice rumbled through me. It caressed every corner of my soul. "Not much dancing in the Coral Court?"

I stiffened. "There's not much time for dancing when you're tending to the sick and scavenging for food."

"You say that like it's my fault."

I stepped in a circle around him with one hand rested in his. "If the asshole fits."

He chuckled then spun me away from him, harder than the dance intended. I glared and righted myself before I could fall on my ass.

Too quickly, I was back in his arms. His grip on my waist was tighter now.

"I suppose you had plenty of time for dancing between banquets and blowjobs?" I spat.

His eyes widened and he let out a reluctant snort of laughter. "Not exactly."

"No?"

He twirled me away from him again. He never missed a beat. He danced like he fought and fought like he fucked. Fluid, brutal and precise. He drew me back against him. This time my back was crushed to his front. His arms locked around my waist. My breath skipped. He was too close…*too close*.

"Then what were you doing whilst the Outer Isles starved?" My voice was husky. I'd wanted it to sound as bitter as it had when this dance began.

Exekiel lowered his lips to my ear. His breath was hot on my cheek.

Shit. I couldn't take much more of this. Our bodies were pressed closer together than the other contestants. Our hips moved as one. This was dangerous. *Stupid.*

"I was protecting the realm," he murmured.

My skin grew hotter. I became achingly aware of everything. The soft feel of his shirt as it grazed my arms. The hard swell of his thighs that shifted behind me. The possessive feel of his fingers splayed across my stomach.

Fuck.

"Protecting it from what?" I panted.

"Not all wars involve battles and blood, sea-witch." His fingers flexed on my abdomen. "Some involve a well-placed siren and perfect timing."

He moved his hips. I smothered a moan. Heat coursed through my veins.

"And if I said I had no schemes, this time, would you believe me?"

"You've never given me a reason to."

He spun me around to face him. Our bodies swayed.

"You smell like him."

I narrowed my eyes. "Like who?"

He pulled me close and dipped me over his arm. Somehow my leg ended up in his hand and hiked up around his waist. This wasn't part of the dance.

Exekiel moved into me. Pleasure sparked through my blood.

He leaned in. "Like the man who tried to kill me."

Our gazes held. Each one filled with fury and desire.

"I'm also the woman who saved your life."

His fingers dug into my sides as he pulled me upright. "And now you think I owe you."

"You could say thank you."

His hand closed around my neck and he dragged his thumb along my bottom lip. I trembled. Exekiel leaned in so close, his breath met mine.

"Thank you," he whispered against my lips. My head spun. "Thank you for saving me so I can save the realm from you."

My tongue stuck to the roof of my mouth. Before I could unpeel it, another partner stepped up to join me and Exekiel spun away.

"He thinks he's so great," I raged as the solstice celebrations rallied on. "With his perfect hair, and perfect teeth and pompous Protector bullshit."

I waved my chalice and spilled Fate's Fountain wine down my arm.

"He doesn't know anything about me or my intentions for the realm!" I paced between the others who were sprawled in the grass by a crimson firepit.

I wasn't sure how long I'd been ranting about Exekiel but I didn't see myself stopping anytime soon. I couldn't help it. Whenever the conversation lulled, his name burst from my lips. Some ridiculous part of me wanted to talk about him. Wanted to relive the way his touch kindled inside me. Even now with the heat of his hatred seared into my blood, I couldn't stop.

"He knows you intend to free the Outer Isles and that's all a Fate-stain like him needs to know," Colette crowed and took a large gulp of her drink.

She and Maximus weren't sitting with the others. They rocked to the music, and occasionally wolf whistled at attractive passersby—which was everyone.

"You know your intentions and that's all that matters," Jia concluded.

She was draped on top of Odus who'd rolled his horse end onto its side. His human half leaned against a boulder, and his arm was slung over Jia's small frame. His fingers idly stroked her wings.

"You're here—chosen by the Conduit. A Blessed-Unblessed with a legitimate claim to the Eternal Throne," she went on. "The Fates couldn't make it clearer that it's time for things to change."

"And it's long overdue," Calder agreed.

He was another contestant from the Games. A wolf shifter, if I remembered correctly. His skin was that natural shade of golden brown that most people who tanned would envy. His dark goatee was trimmed and he had thick bushy brows that were currently pulled down in a frown.

"The barrier imprisons us as much as it keeps others out," he grumbled and drained the contents of his cup. "Many of us; Outlier and Inlander, are fed up with being told who we can associate with and the places we can go."

"Long live the revolution," Colette cheered.

She turned and planted a kiss on Maximus' grinning lips.

Lucinda tutted from where she leaned back on her elbows and stared up at the stars. She didn't have to say anything. Her expression said it all.

My friend still believed there was some way for Exekiel and I to work together. That the Fates had bonded us for a reason.

From what I understood, a mate bond meant we were the most compatible for each other in every way. It meant we could procreate powerful heirs. However, there were plenty of mates who were happy with nothing more than a beautiful friendship. Some even fooled around.

It was only when they let emotions get involved, when they chose each other with all their heart, that there was no turning back. It was powerful and unbreakable.

I couldn't let myself believe that Exekiel and I had reached that point. I didn't need any reason to be more in love with him than I already was.

I dropped down beside Lucinda. She folded her arm around my shoulders.

"It will be worth it in the end," I told her. "You'll see."

After I won the Games, I would build a world without borders. Where people could be who they were and not judged or ridiculed for it. Where a Fae could love a centaur, and a siren could dance with a warlock.

My gaze trailed over my friends. Jia and Odus had launched into a full-on make-out session. Her hand edged dangerously close to his mammoth erection. Calder was locked in conversation with Kylin; an elf with bright blue eyes, a shaved head, and skin that rivaled the night's pitch. Colette and Maximus continued to howl at anyone who passed and Colette taught him the lyrics for *Sonu di Carghel*; the song all sirens would sing once the Outliers were free.

This was what it was all for. The heartbreak. The struggle. The loss of love and lives. It was all in the hopes of building something greater. A future where we could live as one. I would do whatever needed to be done to bring that future to life. To keep the promise, I'd made to the living and those who had died for it.

8

EXEKIEL:
SIRENS AFTER SOLSTICE

One whiff of her scent, one stroke of her silken flesh and I'd gone from wanting to kill my little bud to wanting to fuck her. Right there on the sacred grounds beneath the holy moon of solstice. The fire in her eyes had set me aflame. Her scent, which had been sharper than usual; sweeter, had pulled on my cock. Everything about her had been more enticing; tinged with the salt of the sea and the ferocity of its tides that roared in her soul.

I wanted to be the shore she crashed against. The only beast strong enough to withstand her. Her passion. Her fury. Her desire. Again, and again.

I ground my teeth until my jaw ached. Whatever effect the sea-witch had on me, she couldn't be trusted. She'd proven that with every lie, every attempt on my life, every hidden shell, and secret meeting.

Fists clenched, I stalked towards the gates of the Field of Fates. I'd had enough celebration for one night.

With my hood drawn, I cut across the deserted streets of Infinity City. I slunk down the alleyway between Everlasters Tavern and Infinite Academy. When a quick scan of the area told me that I was alone, I splayed my wings and flew up to the domed building's roof. The vantage point from up here meant that I'd be able to see the fucker no matter which door he stumbled out of.

Crouched in the shadows, I blew warmth into my hands and waited.

My Five Isles phone vibrated. I pulled it out of my cloak pocket. A hologram bubble emerged from the glowing screen. Ilbryen's face blinked at me from within.

I tapped it. The bubble grew until it was as if the alchemist was on the roof with me.

"Ilbryen," I said by way of greeting. "What news?"

He adjusted the horn-rimmed glasses perched on the edge of his nose. He didn't need them but thought they made him appear smarter and attracted the ladies.

"I've collected some results from the poison we extracted from your system." He ran his tongue over his pierced lip. "It disturbingly contains skin and hair fragments of Varialla von Hastings and you."

My grip tightened around the phone. It made sense. In order to fabricate a poison powerful enough to affect me, it'd had to contain my essence and traces of the woman who matched it.

"That's not the worst of it."

A door slammed. I peered over the edge of the roof. A satyr shuffled out and threw a bag of trash into the skip outside the tavern.

I turned back to Ilbryen's hologram. "Don't leave me in suspense."

His expression turned grave. "The poison also has traces of the Conduit." He paused to let his words sink in. "That means members of the Royal Court are involved. This is huge."

My jaw ticked. I hadn't told Ilbryen about what I'd discovered in the decades since my barrier became less volatile.

He didn't know that during the Brutal War, the sirens hadn't attacked Shifter Springs on a murderous whim. They'd been sent there by members of the Royal Court and Council after they'd struck a deal.

The councilmen had wanted to keep their seats of power. However, dragon shifters had won a few too many Games in a row. So, the Court and Council had conspired to get rid of them. The sirens had been all too willing to be their weapon, so long as they were taken care of in return.

I'd never said any of this to Ilbryen. The less he knew, the safer he'd be.

"I'll be in touch." I moved to swipe my finger across the bubble and cut off the call.

"Exekiel." He was one of the few who referred to me by name. "Be careful."

I nodded and ended the communication.

Within the hour, the back door of Everlasters tavern was flung open. This time Knox Borbora, the Primary of the previous Games, stumbled into the alley. A nymph hung off his arm and a goblin sucked on his cock.

Behind him was Count Victus; the most influential sovereign of Elf Bay. He rode out on the back of a female centaur. One of his large hands reached around to squeeze her ample breast whilst his other rested on the hip of a witch who was straddled in his lap. She threw her head back and deeply moaned.

Coming in last was the Fate-stain I'd been waiting for. A citizen-stamped siren, Anakin Glabba, who masqueraded as a water nymph.

It wasn't long before their undergarments were off. With her skirts hitched up around her waist, the witch bounced in Count Victus' lap and unleashed explicit moans.

Knox thrust himself deeper into the goblin's mouth whilst his hand pumped between the nymph's thighs. She stood in front of him with her leg bent over his forearm and her hands braced on the wall at either side of his head. Her breast was shoved into his suckling mouth and she moaned just as enthusiastically as the witch. An intentional distraction.

The only one who didn't join in the festivities was Anakin. He never did. He simply watched as Count Victus lost himself to the throes of passion.

Balanced on the top of a trashcan, the Count plunged his tongue inside the witch who was now splayed on the centaurs back, and thrust his cock in the centaur's rear end.

He didn't notice as Anakin slunk over and sang a song of chaos in his ear.

For a second, the Count paused. His eyes glazed over. The witch and centaur exchanged a knowing look. Then the Count snapped his hips and returned to feasting between the witch's legs with even greater ferocity. On cue, the women cried out in pleasure.

Anakin nodded to Knox who grinned over the nymph's shoulder. Then the siren turned and strode away, whistling a tune.

I followed from the skies veiled in my shadows. Anakin sauntered down deserted alleys and offered solstice greetings to stragglers heading home. His job was done for the night. Now Count Victus had been left in the duplicitous hands of Pre-Primary Knox.

When the siren turned down a narrow alley between Timeless Theater and a brewery, I descended. The fucker kissed the concrete as I landed on his back. He flipped over but before he could open that mouth of his, I had the heel of my boot crushed to his windpipe and my ruby-hilted dagger, Shira, at his cock.

"Who sent you to Shifter Springs during the Brutal War?"

"What?" His pale, bony fingers clamped around my foot and he tried to pry me off.

I pressed closer. My blade cut a hole into the fabric of his pants. "Who negotiated the deal for the sirens to assassinate the dragon shifters?"

His silver eyes watered as he struggled for air. I lifted my boot just enough for him to speak.

"I don't know what you're talking about," he rasped.

I twisted the knife. "Who offered you the throne of Shifter Springs in exchange for killing the dragons?"

Venom flashed in his eyes. "Eat shit, Shadow Saint. Fuck knows how you survived that night."

I bowed my head. I was getting tired of dealing with shits like him. It was always the same. First, denial. Then anger. Then they usually caved, crapped themselves or tried to kill me. They were just the pawns; the pieces on a vast board. I wanted the fuckers who'd set the rules.

"Who made the deal?"

"Fuck y—"

I stamped on his throat. His windpipe caved beneath my boot. Blood spluttered from his mouth. I grabbed the scruff of his shirt and yanked him to his feet.

"Who?" I flung him against the wall.

Anakin wheezed and opened his mouth to sing. I surged forward with my wings splayed and shattered his jaw with my fist. His face ruptured. Blood spewed from every orifice.

He bellowed something I couldn't understand and crumpled to the ground trying to catch his teeth. A bluish tint had started to color his skin. He wouldn't survive much longer with his airway butchered.

I knelt on the concrete beside him.

"Let's try this again." Magic filled my lungs. *"Thesona."*

The Fate answered. I pressed my hand to the back of the sirens head. He flinched to get away. I held him steady. In seconds, his windpipe healed just enough for him to not die during this conversation.

"I know the sirens signed away the dragon shifters lives to secure themselves a seat on their throne. Who gave that order?"

Anakin spat blood at my face.

I lifted the hem of my shirt and wiped it clean. "I knocked your teeth out and you're pissed, so I'm going to let that slide."

A high-pitched sound whistled from his damaged throat. His chest heaved.

"You're a dead man," he croaked.

I tutted. My patience was wearing thin. I needed to know who was responsible for the death of my brothers, my kin. Who brought the realm to its knees and looked me in the eyes and called themselves friend? Who were the Fate-stained fuckers that apparently planned to do it again?

Anakin snickered and unsteadily pushed to his feet. He used the wall for leverage. His mouth was swollen, blood streamed from his nostrils and a bruise formed beneath his right eye.

"You put up your barrier to try and stop us but you just gave us more time to perfect our plan and sow our seeds of dissent." He grinned with what little teeth he had left. "You've already lost, Shadow Saint."

His laugh was a rasping wheeze that grated on my nerves. I lashed out.

In seconds, Anakin was on the ground with my foot on his chest and his tongue pinched between my forefinger and thumb.

"I had planned to do this after I killed you," I snarled. "But this way feels more satisfying."

I raised Shira above my head. Moonlight bounced off her blade. I swung it down and cleaved through Anakin's tongue. He screamed; a muffled sound drowned in blood.

9

VARIALLA:
THE GREAT DEBATE

This was it. Solstice weekend was over. The Games were about to begin. I walked across the familiar blue carpet of my room in Residence Manor and flung open the terrace doors. The morning air was cool. The sky was a crisp blue. The gardens were a rainbow of green grass and wildflowers.

Everything was as I'd left it including the sheets on my bed. The sheets where, the last time I was here, Loch had had his fingers pushed between my legs. He'd forced me to lay there as he'd brought me to the brink of an orgasm I hadn't wanted. Anger and arousal simmered inside me.

I stormed over and ripped the sheets off the bed. One day, he'd regret it. I'd make him regret everything. The more time I spent in the Isles, the more my power grew. Soon it would be strong enough to break the hold he had on me.

A fist pounded on my door. I'd barely opened my mouth to say 'come in' before it burst open. Five females surged into the room. A smile split my face.

"Eudora!" I raced around the chaise-longue and into the nymph's open arms. "Peoni, Bella, Cyrus, Fay." They each joined the circle and tightened the embrace. Their flowery scents and bell-like laughter washed over me.

"Fates, eight weeks feels like a lifetime, doesn't it?" Eudora cried as we pulled back. Her eyes were bright. The ends of her antlers shimmered with gold glitter.

As efficient as always, she strutted into the room and clapped her hands. The girls launched into action. They unfolded their racks and took out their collection of clothes. Make up was spread across my dresser and shoes were laid out in boxes.

"I hope you're well-rested." She grinned. "Getting you Game ready is going to take a while."

Thunderous applause echoed around the arena. The air crackled with a thirst for blood and victory. Flares of magic shot from the tips of fingers and ends of raised wands. Banners for each competing cast billowed in the wind.

I recognized most of the emblems. There was the symbol of the leafy tree inside a circle of vines for the elves, the horned tribal eye for the shifters, the crescent moon inside a star for the warlocks and witches and, crossing swords with wings in place of their blades for the Fae.

There was another symbol I'd occasionally seen during the Trials but hadn't known its meaning until recently. It was a gothic-style hourglass with a sun on one end and a moon on the other. Inside, instead of sand, it plumed with shadows. It was the symbol of the Fate Zorsch; Fate of Death. Father of one—Exekiel V'alin. The only Bravinore ever known to wield the Fate's shadows.

However, the last symbol was what held my attention. It was an open clamshell. In place of a pearl, there was the upright tail of a mermaid—a siren. The banner was being waved for me.

I wished I could see Colette's face right now. I'd said goodbye to her earlier, before I left for Residence Manor. Later, Eudora and Odus would escort her back to the bridge. I'd offered to take her myself this morning, but she'd wanted to see the start of the Games and spend as much time on this side of the barrier—and with Odus—as possible. I didn't blame her.

Now my eyes searched the stands. From this far, it was impossible to pick out her dark skin and white braids. But just knowing she was out there was enough.

Centaur guards were stationed at every corner of the stands. Occasionally they leapt in when fights broke out between the casts. Most of the animosity was aimed at those who waved banners for the sirens. Still my supporters stood together and chanted my name.

I let out a breath. This was surreal. I'd never understood the pandemic of football hooligans that seemed to plague the entire UK population, but now I wanted to smear paint across my face and thump my chest. I stood a little taller in my chainmail dress that came to mid-thigh. It crisscrossed at my back and was bunched in tight coils over my shoulders and around my neck. Beneath my breasts, chains swung giving glimpses of flesh and the lower half was a ruffle of metal scales. Beneath, I wore black leather leggings and boots buckled to my knees.

The crowd roared. I turned to where Vivienne stood on a raised platform with Goather and the shifter, Camal Silverhound. He'd ranked third in the Trials.

Today Goather's orange goatee was curly. His brown hair was pulled into a bun between his horns, and he wore a polka-dotted waistcoat.

"There are countless threats that the barrier protects us from," Vivienne was saying. Her white wings were folded behind her and her dark hair was pulled back in a braid. "Not just the wrath of the Outlanders but the creatures that dwell beyond the horizon."

My fists clenched. It was more of the same bullshit propaganda that had been spouted all morning. The Outlanders weren't a threat. They were victims of prejudice, narrow-minded assholes.

"Make me your Primary and I will ensure that the Shadow Saints barrier is strengthened," she bellowed.

A large group of the audience cheered.

"And what of the divide between the Outliers and the Blessed?" Goather asked.

He said it casually, like he was solely asking for the masses. I knew he craved her answer as much as I did. What would this Fae who'd had everything handed to her, her whole life, do for those who had nothing?

"I'm not ignorant to the struggles of my people. They may be Unblessed, but they are not forgotten," Vivienne said with fake sincerity. "If they support my claim as Primary, I will lower the entry toll to one that everyone can afford."

All the Outliers could afford was free. However, the crowd lapped it up and shouted their support.

"Thank you, Vivienne." Goather gestured for her and Camal to step down. "And now, to our fan-favorites!"

The crowd erupted before he'd even finished.

"Our foreign temptress from beyond the veil, Varialla von Hastings, and our number one player, Exekiel V'alin. Please make your way to the stage."

Squashing the flurry of nerves in my gut, I strode towards the dais with my head held high. I took the wooden stairs in quick strides and went to stand to the right of Goather.

Exekiel stood on the left. His scent of woodsmoke and warm apples filled my lungs. I swallowed thickly and kept my stare ahead. I refused to back down or be sidetracked by his overwhelming presence.

When the crowd finally settled, Goather brought his microphone to his lips.

"Varialla von Hastings, many believe that as an outsider, you have no right to rule," he said. "Tell us, what is it that you believe makes you fit for the Throne?"

I stepped up to the podium in front of me. There, a microphone rested.

"I understand the people's concerns. Since I was hunted and chased out of the realm at birth," I threw a sidelong glance at Exekiel, "I was forced to grow up ignorant to this world and the horrors everyone faced. But that is exactly what makes me fit for the throne." I let my words settle.

"I am not governed by old prejudice and baseless grudges. I see the good in both sides. I want what's best for everyone. A world where we stand as one. Outliers and the Blessed."

A large part of the audience cheered.

"Pretty words that mean nothing." Exekiel's low voice cut through the applause.

I glared at him. He returned it.

"If peace was that easy for the Isles, don't you think we'd have it by now?"

"Not with your fucking barrier between them," I snapped.

The audience ooo'd.

"And to keep the peace?" he snarled. "What will you do to stop the murders and riots that inevitably break out?"

"The transformation won't happen overnight." I turned to the crowd. "Once a week, Outliers will be welcomed into the Five Isles to worship at the Conduit like they used to. When they're done, they can take a parcel of its magic to help rebuild their lands."

Less of the audience cheered now. Some booed. Exekiel snorted. It echoed through his microphone and was met with raucous laughter. My fingers curled around the edge of the podium.

"And you, Shadow Saint?" Goather turned to him. "What makes you fit for the Throne?"

Exekiel stood taller. "What I offer isn't false promises of peace. Lies to placate you whilst the enemy slip in."

More of the audience roared now.

"Many think my methods are barbaric, but I've made it my life's work to protect this Realm—to bring peace to these shores—and that's what I'll continue to do."

The audience went mad. It was sickening. They practically worshipped him. One girl threw her panties and a cry of, "We love you, Shadow Saint," rang through the arena.

"However, I see how my methods have caused a rift between our people and I plan to rectify that."

I frowned. The crowd went silent.

"Make me Your Primary, and I will not take down the barrier but I will remove the need for invitation or toll."

My heart raced. Without the invitation or toll, Outliers could come and go as they pleased as long as they were checked at the border.

"However…"

My shoulders tensed.

Exekiel looked from me to the audience. "Along with the citizen stamp, any siren who enters, must wear a collar."

The ground pitched beneath me. *What did he just say?*

"These collars will be enchanted to prevent the wearer from tapping into their magic and from using their voice."

Murmurs rippled through the crowd.

Goather stumbled over his words. "Don't you think that's a bit extreme?"

"The sirens were the only ones who kept fighting when the fighting stopped. Who insisted on war and bloodshed when all everyone else wanted was peace." His voice rose with the cries of the crowd. His shadows gathered at his back.

"It is because of the sirens that thousands of us were slaughtered; the dragon race wiped out! It is because of the sirens that the shield went up in the first place. That the cost of toll increased. There is nothing too extreme."

His words were swallowed by the commotion of the people. It was hard to tell who was for and who were against his plan.

I spun towards him. "Are you really that much of a fucking monster?"

His eyes flashed. "You call me a monster. They call it freedom."

"Freedom?" I barked a bitter laugh.

Goather rushed to hold up a microphone between us. He couldn't let those ratings drop.

"Forcing people into collars, isn't freedom, asshole." I marched up to him. "It's more oppression."

"And yet, those in the Outer Isles will no longer be punished for your peoples' sins." Exekiel pressed closer. He towered over me. "Those in the Five Isles will no longer be caged behind my shield. I offer food, shelter, and access to the Conduit for everyone including the sirens."

"As long as we wear your chains," I bellowed.

"You brought this on yourselves." His eyes burned with cold fury. The kind that was born of centuries of hate and had been left to fester. "A petition has already been sent out and signed by most Outliers."

"You're lying," I snarled through gritted teeth. He had to be.

"Am I?" He sneered.

My breath sawed out of me. Somehow, we were toe-to-toe. His shadows shifted like wraiths at his back and curled around his wings.

Goather whistled. "On that heart-pounding note, let the Games begin."

10

VARIALLA:
LIGHTNING STRIKES

Camera-orbs zipped around Goather's head and panned over the audience. The satyr promptly launched into the rules of the Games. I tried to concentrate but my mind reeled.

"This season, Phase One and Two of the Royal Games will take place in the Fields of Fury," Goather boomed to wild applause. "The third and final Phase will take place here in Infinity City."

I couldn't get over what Exekiel planned to do. I knew he'd never lower the barrier but I hadn't expected enchanted collars to cage a siren's power. My grip tightened on the strap of the leather satchel slung over my shoulder. It was crammed with clothes, dried food, and other supplies. I inhaled deeply and stalked back to my podium.

Goather went on, "There will be twelve levels to get through. Some harder than others. To exit each level, you must follow the map and collect the keys." His hooves clopped as he paced before us. "However, in each level there will be one less key than the number of competitors. Fail to secure a key or rank in the bottom half, and at the end of that Phase, you will be entered into the jousting tournament."

The audience and players whooped in delight as two beings in gold-plated armor rode into the arena on the backs of Pegasus. The contestants behind me stamped their feet.

Someone in the audience screamed, "Breed me!"

Despite myself, I glanced at Exekiel. Even his lips had quirked up in the corners. My gaze stalled on his mouth, the strength in his jaw, the thick column of his throat. How could anyone that beautiful be so hideous?

His stare slid to mine, as if he'd felt me staring. I wrenched my gaze away. The riders charged towards each other with their jousting lances poised. The ends glistened black with obsidian glass. My stomach dipped. These weapons were designed to make sure no one survived a killing blow, not even a Bravinore Fae.

The riders came within an inch of each other then the Pegasus' shot into the sky. The crowd hopped in their seats. I gaped up in awe as the joust continued in the sky. The riders tore around and towards each other and narrowly avoided lethal strikes. My heart was in my throat. My anger temporarily forgotten.

Camera-orbs dipped and weaved around the riders. They recorded every angle and played on the large hologram screens positioned around the arena. At last, the riders clashed their lances together and stood up on their Pegasus' back. They bowed to riotous applause, then soared off above the clouds.

"If you fail to rank in the top three of the joust," Goather's booming voice echoed over the stands. "Then you forfeit your life to Zorsch or to serve at the palace."

A hush fell over the crowd. The air was tight with tension. That joust had been a well-choreographed performance, but the actual tournaments would be nothing like it.

Goather strutted across the stage. "Not only is this a race for the keys but a race against time. The longer you take to complete a level, the lower you rank." He leapt up onto a Pegasus-pulled chariot. "Fare thee well, enchanters. May you go with the brave and the Blessed."

The earth shook. The audience howled. I gaped dumbstruck as the sand in the arena seemed to spill into a widening gap. I lunged back but the other contestants rocked on the balls of their feet with wild anticipation in their eyes. The ground split wider. A scream tore from my throat as I fell beneath the world.

Sand cascaded after me. Cries of the other contestants rang through my ears. All I saw was a blur of light and shadow. My stomach lurched. Then I hit the ground.

I groaned. I was on my back and stared up at a brilliant turquoise sky. On the horizon, large gray clouds moved closer. They picked up speed and darkened as they approached.

My heart stammered. The clouds gathered like plumes of smoke. The air came alive with magic. I shot to my feet. Around me, contestants shrieked and did the same. These weren't ordinary clouds.

I scanned the players and found Lucinda with Maximus. I pushed towards them.

Overhead, a disembodied female voice said: **"Phase One; activated."**

A vibrant blade of blue lightning shot towards the ground and cleaved it in two.

Someone yelled, "Run!"

The heavens opened. Rain poured down like a bucket tipped over my head.

A blur of bodies barreled away from the chasing clouds. My satchel bounced on my back and my feet slipped in the dirt that was turning to sludge. I raced towards Lucinda.

She met me halfway, with Max on her heels, and panted, "Stay close."

She phished out her Five Isles phone and tapped the glass base. The holographic screen emerged. On it, was a map of what I guessed was the Fields of Fury.

Clouds that spewed lightning darted across the screen, stick figures raced down a narrow brown path which must have been us. A scarlet key blinked up ahead.

"That way!" Lucinda shouted and tucked the phone back into the belt strapped over her chest.

Together, we ducked and weaved through the crowd. Soon, the open area we'd landed in, became dense with trees. The bolts of lightning ventured closer. Each one created a crater in the earth.

Screams bounced off the trees. Terror choked my lungs. Someone had been hit. Judging by the harrowing cries, they'd been killed.

"Keep up!" Lucinda bellowed. She swept beneath a tree branch and skidded through puddles like a dancer made for this.

I hurtled after her with less grace but equal determination. Maximus did the same. I barely took note of the other contestants. They were faceless shrieks that blurred around me. My feet pounded the earth. The only way out of this was to run. No magic I knew of could stop a storm.

A heavy weight slammed into my side. A sapphire bolt struck a nearby tree. The ground where I'd just been caved in. Leaves and tree bark scattered to ash on the wind.

I gaped up at the figure who'd crashed into me; saved me. Their hand cradled the back of my head.

Holy shit. Dark pink eyes met mine. They swept over me, like they were checking for injuries then they slid back up to my face. Exekiel's jaw ticked. Just for a second, his eyes betrayed his concern. My heart thrashed against my ribs.

"I'm okay," I breathed reading the unspoken question.

His nostrils flared. His grip on the back of my head tightened until he had the ends of my braided pigtails fisted in his hand. I sucked in a breath.

"You almost died."

I licked my lips. "I'm okay." Thanks to him.

He looked at me for what felt like an eternity but it couldn't have been more than a few seconds. He clenched his jaw and lowered his forehead to mine. My heart skipped a beat. He was half on top of me. His leg overlapped with mine. His other hand was braced on my hip. My skin tingled where his fingers touched.

"Try not to get us killed on the first day, sea-witch," he snarled.

Before I could respond, he hopped to his feet and disappeared in the crowd.

Shaken, I rolled and narrowly avoided being trampled. I stood up. That was…I shook my head. I didn't have time to think about what that was. I ignored the spike of pain in my chest and how Exekiel's alluring scent clung to my skin. Fuck, I hated him. I hated what he wanted to do to my people and I hated this effect he had on me.

Gritting my teeth, I raced to catch up with Lucinda and the others who charged ahead.

Max glanced over his shoulder and sagged with relief when he spotted me.

"What happened back there?" he shouted. "You disappeared in the crowd."

"Long story."

We came to the edge of the trees. There was a tunnel across the clearing. According to the map, that was where we needed to go. It was a bottleneck. A mass crowd hurtling towards a singular narrow point.

Everyone must have had the same thought. Shifters burst into beast form and knocked others aside. Fae tried to spread their wings. We were too cramped together but one managed to break free. He soared into the clearing with a victorious whoop.

A bolt of lightning tore through his spine and impaled a leopard shifter on impact. The leopard let out a piercing whine. His feet kicked in the dirt and he uselessly struggled to break free. The bolt exploded. Flesh and fur showered over us, as potent as the rain.

I was going to be sick.

We ran. It was our only option. A few feet ahead, someone fell. In seconds their skull was trampled to dust.

Ice slid through my veins. This was a game of war and everyone was playing to survive. The blades of lightning grew faster now. More screams soaked the air.

Maximus grabbed my hand. Lucinda took hold of his. Jia and the others who had caught up, led the front.

In a chain, we ploughed through the throng. Heads down and elbows out, we rammed the others aside. Every step was a struggle. My feet stuck or slipped in the thick mud and splashed in icy puddles that soaked into my boots. Bitter wind slapped my cheeks. My clothes were drenched and heavy.

I kept one eye on the tunnel and one on the skies as lightning rained down shards of death. Bodies fell at our feet. The entrance to the tunnel grew closer. More of us crushed together to fit through.

"Almost there."

"Attention: Your time is running out." said the voice overhead. **"Your time is running out."**

I glanced back at two shifters who were still charging through the trees. Desperation was stark across their faces. They weren't going to make it. The blades of lightning grew closer together. There was barely an inch between them now. To attempt to cross the clearing meant death but to stay behind could mean the same.

"Your time is running out."

One of the shifters, a dark-skinned girl in a red headscarf, clutched a stitch in her side and screamed. She was frantic to escape but knew she was stuck. There was no way out.

The crowd surged around me. I raced into the darkness of the tunnel.

I stumbled blindly; fingers scraping along the damp stone wall. Max still held my other hand in his. We ran on, blundering over loose stones and churned earth. The dark was the deepest shade of pitch. It seemed to muffle sound as well as sight.

Then, light winked up ahead. It flickered like jeweled fireflies.

Someone shouted, "The keys!"

People crushed in at my back. Blind to everything around me, I followed the reek of sweat and the rasp of panting breaths. Five of the keys faded as we approached; one for each life that was already lost. This meant that there was still one less key than there were people in this cave.

The air became charged. It crackled with desperation and fear. Whoever failed to get a key would either die in the jousting tournament or become a servant to the Crown. Their lives would no longer be their own; titles and treasures forgotten. The joust was a way to fight back into the Games but losing this early meant it would be impossible to restore their rank to one that mattered.

Finally, the keys hovered overhead. Their light cast an amber glow across the people's faces and shadows along the wall. The scrabble of limbs that reached for them was like climbing thorough a pit of writhing snakes. I drew on my power, sang a soft note and pushed its energy into my legs. It was a short burst but enough to propel me forward. With a gasp,

I leapt up and reached out. My hand closed around an ornate iron key.

11

VARIALLA:

EVERYONE HAS A STORY

We'd been out here for weeks. In that time, I'd been chased by killer lightning bolts, almost fallen to my death from a rickety bridge made out of frayed ropes, and I'd been attacked by psychotic Sleeping Vines that really didn't like to be woken up.

We were only three levels in and I was already done with the Games. The cold was unbearable. I needed a proper meal and desperately wanted to bathe. My desire to survive was the only thing that overrode my bone-crushing exhaustion.

"Remember your why," Lucinda called from where she led the charge.

"Sod your why," I huffed beneath my breath.

It was the same thing she'd said when Maximus'
foot got caught in the bridge and he'd almost fallen
off, and, again, when we'd all been naked in a stream
rubbing salve onto our blistered bodies because we'd
been coated in the Sleeping Vines venom.

Remember your why.

Maximus chuckled from where he strolled beside
me. "She's right. If we want to get through this, we
need to have a reason other than the Conduit made
us."

I scowled at him. I wasn't sure if he was as
knackered as I was or just keeping me company back
here. Either way, I was glad.

"Of course, she's right," I grumbled.

Remembering that the Outer Isles would never
be free and that Exekiel planned to fasten collars
around my people's throats, helped me keep going
when I wanted to stop. Remembering the promise,
I'd made to Cherise, to build a better world and get
her mother to the Conduit, helped me find nutrition
in sour berries and dried bread.

"What's your why, Maximus?"

He arched a brow. "I don't want to become a
slave and I want justice for the exiled. Isn't that
enough?"

"It is but," I shrugged. "They say everyone has a
story. I wondered if there was more to yours."

He smiled. "There's always more but I don't often
tell it." He raked a hand through his dreadlocks. "My
reason is my sister."

I almost fell on my face. "What?"

"She was part witch on my mother's side and part nymph on her father's."

I gaped at him. In all the time I'd known Maximus and all the questions I'd asked; he'd never mentioned a sister.

His gaze drifted to the rose-gold streaks of sunset in the sky. "On the day of the land-shift, she'd been visiting her father in Creatures Copse."

I tensed. Goather had told me that Creatures Copse was once joined to Elf Bay but when the land-shift happened, it split in two leaving most satyrs, nymphs and centaurs stranded on the Outer Isles.

Maximus sighed. "My parents fought to get her back but by then, the realm had gone to Gorge."

Gorge; another name they used for hell.

"Communication with the Outer Isles was almost impossible, and those who braved the swim across the beast-infested waters were usually slaughtered the second they reached the shore.

"Back then, Inlanders believed that the Conduit had separated from the Outer Isles for a reason. That associating with Outliers could damn them all. As a result, people lost their livelihood, their friends, their family."

We slowed down; putting more distance between us and the others.

"Eventually the Games were developed to put the endless battles to rest. The first Primary came into power. She introduced the toll. A fair way for Outliers to cross into the Five Isles. But the cost had been ridiculous and beyond what most could afford to pay." He shook his head. "Naturally, underground communication systems and codes were put in place. Beings were then smuggled in or out of the Isles."

I listened on tenterhooks. Maximus' gaze remained fixed ahead.

"Those in the Outer Isles were dying; my sisters father included. So, when they found a way to smuggle her back to the Five Isles, everyone agreed."

"What happened?" My voice was barely a whisper.

"She made it."

I didn't feel relieved. It was obvious this wasn't the end of the story.

"It was around then, that I was born. The Primary at that time had introduced Royal invitations as well as toll. But papers were still forged for those who weren't invited. For that reason, random checks were often done to weed out any forbidden settlers.

"I was in my early teens when guards of the Royal Court came to investigate how my sister had ended up in our home when there was no record of toll being paid and she had no invitation."

I swallowed thickly.

"They took her." Maximus' voice cracked. He drew in a shaky breath. "They carted her back into the exiled quarter of Creature's Copse. Her father had already died by then but they didn't care. They left her to fend for herself in a realm that was dying and cut off.”

He pushed aside a branch and let me walk ahead of him.

“My parents fought. They sided with the Outliers and demanded change…” His throat worked over a swallow. The air hummed with his power. “Long story short, they were whipped and then beheaded for their crimes.”

Ice cold horror drenched my soul. A ringing filled my ears.

“The guards held me down and made me watch.”

What? I wasn’t sure if I’d said it aloud.

Maximus’ fists were clenched so tight they’d leeched of color.

His words swam through my mind. His sister had been taken—left alone in a world that didn’t want her. And his parents had been executed for trying to get her back. Right in front of him.

“You see why I don’t tell this story very often.”

My mouth opened and shut. This was the world we lived in. The life these Five Isles bastards fought to keep. Damn the rest, so long as they were safe.

When the Trials ended a few weeks ago, Maximus and Lucinda had invited me to stay with them. I’d assumed they meant separately. Now, I realized that Lucinda’s Coven must have become Maximus’s home.

A knot of sorrow tightened in my throat. I reached across the gap between us and squeezed his hand. Maximus didn't look at me but he squeezed back.

"Shit!" Calder's bellow cut through the words I struggled to string together. "A cyclone's coming!"

"What?" My head whipped in the direction he pointed.

Sure enough, a swirling vortex of wind and rain hurtled in our direction. Trees were torn up and tossed aside. Creatures I couldn't identify let out horrific wails. Their warped bodies were wrenched into the air. My stomach almost dropped out of my gut.

"Fuck!" Jia shouted. "Run!"

12

EXEKIEL:
CAVED IN

The succulent scent of red-horned stag filled the cave. We'd collected wood before the storm hit. Now, I skinned and cooked the meat over an open fire. Trilla hacked off smaller pieces and pickled them for us to store and eat later.

"Careful you don't cut yourself with that knife, little shadow," Kraxus V'alin grunted. He sat opposite me and used his fists to tenderize the meat.

I arched a brow. "Says the bunny."

His lips curled. "What did you say?"

"Can the two of you stop bickering for five minutes?" Vivienne snapped from where she poured over the map of the Games and planned the route, we'd take to reach the next level.

Kraxus puffed up his already large chest. "The little shadow is trying to disrespect me. Someone needs to put him in his place."

I barked a laugh. "Don't be like that, bunny boy."

The veins bulged in his tree-like neck. It was always the same with Kraxus. Like me, he was *Bravinore V'alin;* born from and of the Fates. His mother had been the Huntress Fate, *Fadea.* However, his unwitting father had been a rabbit shifter.

Kraxus didn't appreciate when I reminded him of this. He had a complex when it came to me. I wielded shadows of death. He sprouted a puffy tail. The fact that he was a seven-foot-tall behemoth of a man with a thick trimmed beard and long scraggy hair made the whole bunny transformation more hilarious.

It didn't help matters that Vivienne, who he believed was his mate, had spent the better half of a decade in my bed.

"You wouldn't be laughing if I pressed your face into this fire," he huffed.

I looked him straight in the eye and tilted my head to one side. "Try it."

Fate-stains like Kraxus were the reason I'd found my home amongst the dragons. Unlike everyone else, they hadn't tripped over themselves to sit on my dick or constantly tried to outdo me.

Vivienne let out an exasperated sigh. "I swear if you t—" Her voice cut off.

My attention snapped to the entrance of the cave. Six shivering figures stood with weapons in their hands. My gaze zeroed in on the one at the front.

Water dripped from the ends of her braided pigtails and sopping clothes to create a puddle around her feet. Her breasts, that were visible through the wet fabric of her white blouse, rose and fell as she panted. She was probably freezing yet her hazel eyes were fire bright.

An irrational need to protect her swept through me. I squashed it. Varialla was not mine to protect. She was not my anything.

I stood and wiped my blooded hands on my thighs. "Are you lost, little bud?"

Varialla's stare sharpened with hatred so potent, I could taste it. "Not at all."

"Then leave." My wings unfurled.

Her full lips pulled into a smirk. "Make me."

Atlas launched forwards and burst into his yeti form. Nikolai did the same, only he became an impossibly large lion, the color of turned sand. Behind Varialla, the shifter I recognized as Calder Dupond morphed into an enormous russet wolf.

I arched a questioning brow at Kraxus. My lips quirked up. Was he going to shift into his terrifying bunny form?

The shifter threw his middle fingers up at me then stalked towards our intruders.

"You have five seconds to get the fuck out."

Jia rounded on him with her hands on her hips and her wings splayed. "Or what?"

Kraxus grinned in a way that said he'd hoped she'd say that. The air around him built with power.

"Enough!" Lucinda's sharp voice echoed through the cave. "Let's cut the griffin-shit. We're all tired, cold," she flicked her head at the roasting meat. "Hungry."

Nikolai's yeti growled. He licked his lips.

"So how about a truce?" Her stare swept over each of us. "Tonight, we share the cave. Tomorrow, we go back to hating each other's guts. Well rested, fed and in one piece."

"The witch is right," I cut off any argument the others might have had.

Varialla von Hastings had just wandered into our den, like a lamb to slaughter.

"We need to focus on winning the Games."

Varialla glared at me. She was probably reminded of what my victory would mean for her and her people. Maybe it was a bit extreme but the sirens had no problem getting across my barrier with the help of the Royal Court. I'd needed a way to suppress their power once they made it across. The collars would do that.

"Fine!" Vivienne huffed. "But if you think you're getting a bite of our stag, think again."

Calder snickered and sauntered to the other side of the cave. "Wouldn't dream of it."

I took first watch. The others crawled into their beds of grass and leaves.

As always, Kraxus curled up behind Vivienne. I was mildly surprised when she rolled her eyes but didn't shove him away like she had the previous nights. Vivienne believed the shifter was her mate as much as he did, but she wanted nothing more than friendship. I envied her restraint.

When it came to Varialla, I'd loved her before I knew what not loving her felt like. I'd sensed her the second I'd travelled across the veil. My hunter instincts had been heightened by the Fate *Fadea*, and a part of me had known then, before I'd met her, that her heart was made for mine.

I made my way to the cave's mouth. Beyond, the night was still, save for sounds of distant birds and the plume of mist that rose from the ground and drifted between the trees. The storm had passed.

I settled on the damp earth and propped my elbows up on my knees. Footsteps approached. I turned to see Varialla. Her steps faltered when she noticed me.

"What are you doing here?"

I looked down at myself then back up. "Sitting in the dirt."

She rolled her eyes. I tracked every step she took towards me; enthralled by the graceful swing of her hips.

The initial mouth of the cave was narrow before it opened up into the larger cavern. Varialla glared down at my legs that were stretched across the opening.

"Can you move? I'm on first watch."

I returned my stare to the swirling mists. "I can keep watch on my own."

She snorted. "And I'm supposed to trust you not to slit our throats whilst we sleep?"

I shrugged. "That is tempting."

Varialla nudged my legs with her foot. "Move."

"No."

"Move!"

I sneered and parroted her words. "Make me."

I wasn't prepared for her to sit on my shins. With a triumphant grin, Varialla wriggled her hips until my legs were forced apart and she sat between them. She leaned back against the opposite wall with a smirk. Some of that smugness waivered, however, when I shifted my legs that now barred her in.

Her lips pursed and she draped her own legs over mine. My throat tightened. Her thighs were now parted and all she wore was a white shirt that fell just above her knees.

I snarled, "Are you trying to freeze to death?"

She gave me a bemused grin. "Lucinda whipped up a potion to temporarily stave off the cold whilst my warmer clothes dry. She would have made it sooner but she'd needed the fur of a fresh-kill."

She was trying to get a rise out of me by letting me know they'd gotten to our meat. But that wasn't what had my blood roaring.

"You only packed one set of warm clothes?"

Her brow arched. "Careful, Protector. You sound like you give a shit."

"It's not your life I care about."

She narrowed her eyes. "Of course not. You only care about the pure-Blessed. Everyone else can starve and die of sickness for all you care. Or better yet, they can be chipped and collared."

Varialla murmured something beneath her breath—something that involved calling me a bastard. I should have let it slide. Should have shoved her off me and not said another word. Yet I had some sick need to stoke the fire that raged inside her. I grasped her ankles and wrenched her towards me.

She gasped and braced her hands on my chest as I drew her onto my lap. Her knees pressed into my shoulders. The heat of her sweet little cunt was inches from my cock.

A growl rattled in my throat. The need to claim her pulsed in my skin. This woman was the symbol of everything I'd fought for the last two centuries. The reason all I'd had was taken and what little remained could be lost just as quickly. I should have let her go, but right then, I felt compelled by something greater.

My arm snaked around her waist and I held her against me. The little beauty quivered.

"What are you doing?" she snapped.

I grinned and let my gaze devour her. From her toes that were buried in the dirt, to where her shirt bunched up around her thighs. I tracked the slope of her hips and the swell of her perfect breasts. I noticed the pulse jump in her slender neck, the pout of her full kissable lips, until at last, our eyes met and held.

Fuck me.

It had been a mistake to get this close to her.

"If you have something to say to me, sea-witch, don't mumble." I sneered. "Say it to my face."

13

VARIALLA:
Too Close

*S*hit. What was going on? How did I get here? My heart thumped against my ribcage. The cells of my body ran into overdrive. I couldn't think. Couldn't *breathe*.

Something about being this close to Exekiel consumed me. It filled every empty crevice of my being. Electricity crackled between us and burned where his hand splayed across my back. The pressure of his fingers was rough and all too familiar. I needed to get away.

"Well?" he rasped.

Well? My mind struggled to keep up. *Well, what?*

His other hand came to rest on my thigh. My heart thumped harder. With each gentle sweep of his thumb, Exekiel awoke something inside me—

something I'd fought so hard to tie down. The hem of my shirt slid higher. His gaze zeroed in on the spot between my thighs, as if he could see straight through the fabric.

Fuck. I hated how breathless his touch made me. How resisting him took physical restraint. I dug my fingers into the ground and fisted handfuls of wet earth. Why, after everything he'd done and planned to do, *why* did I want him?

This was crazy. Wrong. I shoved his hand off my thigh.

"I said you really are the monster they said you were."

I moved to stand but he gripped my waist and held me in place. My body sparked. I was achingly aware of every part of me that touched every part of him.

His hands moved up and down my sides. I barely suppressed a shiver.

"Everyone's a little monstrous, little bud," he snarled. He subtly pushed his hips forward. I gasped. "Some people are just better at hiding it than others. Like Loch fucking Orqanz and the brat who warms his bed."

Anger blazed through me. He had no idea how wrong he was. He only saw what he wanted to see and believed what he wanted to believe. All he craved was revenge. He didn't care if it was justified or not. Exekiel wouldn't be happy until he'd delivered the same fate to the sirens that they'd delivered to the dragon shifters.

"Fuck." My eyes fluttered as I felt him harden beneath me. I clamped my lips together to stifle a moan and resisted the urge to move into him. "I can't believe I ever let myself feel anything for you."

His pink eyes flashed crimson. "Believe me, little bud, the feeling is mutual."

He yanked me against him so hard, my breasts smacked into his chin. My stomach tightened. He lifted his hips again and his length rubbed against me. My lips parted, but no sound came out.

"The last thing I want is to feel the way I do about the daughter of the demon that took everything from me," he growled. "The last thing I need is to want to do the things I want to do to you."

He glanced down at my breasts that were practically shoved into his mouth. His hands tensed on my waist and he guided me over him. I moved willingly. My toes curled. My skin flushed. How on earth had I ended up in his lap? And how did I end up grinding on him?

I gripped his shoulders as if that could put some distance between us. Like it could stop the friction that built between my legs.

"For once, we agree on something." I didn't hold back the bite in my tone. "I don't want anything to do with you, and you want nothing to do with me."

Shit. My body was on fire. I couldn't slow the rapid hammering of my heart. I gritted my teeth and forced myself to sit still.

The pads of Exekiel's fingers dug into my sides just shy of painful. He sat taller. His face was barely an inch from mine.

"Your mouth says one thing, but your eyes say another." His hand wrapped around my neck. He stroked his thumb down my jawline. "Your eyes say you want me to fuck you as badly as I want to."

Holy shit. I grabbed his wrist and tore his hand away from my neck. I couldn't do this same song and dance again. No matter what I felt for him, Exekiel was a murderous bastard and he wouldn't rest until he saw me and those I loved in chains.

"You will never touch me again."

I squirmed to get away from him and was horrifically aware when I pressed down on the bulge of his cock. Of the heat that immediately swept through my core. He wasn't even fully erect but I felt every indent of him through the fabric of his breeches. Fucking Fae asshole.

My shirt rose up around my waist. Wet earth clung to my icy skin.

"Let me go," I hissed.

His jaw clenched. "Gladly."

His fingers unhooked from me like the talons of a bird from its prey.

I shot to my feet, adjusted my shirt, and raced from the cave.

"Where are you going?" he barked.

I threw him a dark glare over my shoulder. "Don't act like you care now, Protector."

"Where?" He looked like he might follow.

My upper lip curled. "To take a fucking piss."

Before he could say another word, I stalked around the side of the cave.

I couldn't walk fast or far enough to not burn with the heat of being near him, to not feel the echo of Exekiel's touch. One brush of his fingers and I'd been right back to where I'd been all those months ago. Desperately in love with a monster. A man who would rather see me in chains than seated on his precious throne. Silenced rather than freed.

But I'd been quiet for too long about too many things in my life. First, I'd been a quiet, obedient girl desperate for someone to love me enough to want to keep me. Then I'd been the girl who silently stole away in the night and never looked back. I'd held my tongue when the money sent to my foster families for my care was spent on booze and bets. I'd said nothing when they left me to do chores whilst they took their "real children" on trips to Blackpool. I'd sobbed silently in my bed when I woke up and found that even the families who'd claimed to love me had left me in the night.

I was done being silent. Now the world would hear me roar.

14

EXEKIEL:

THE POISONED HEART

Fuck!

I PACED OUTSIDE the cave like a caged beast. The sea-witch was going to be my undoing. My muscles were tightly wound and I rolled my neck to ease some of the tension. Varialla's ocean scent tinged with strawberry still lingered in the air. I still felt the weight of her on my lap. The way she'd squirmed and grinded into me. *Holy Fates.*

I scrubbed a hand down my face and stretched out my wings. I needed to fly. Needed to fuck. Needed to burn the world down just to escape this constant ache. This maddening need to be near her; inside her. It was as if only she could fix the parts of me that she fucking broke in the first place.

I prowled long enough for her to return. When she didn't, I stilled. Head cocked, I strained to listen beneath the rising howl of the wind that now cut through the trees.

Shadows looped around my wrists. I strode towards the side of the cave where she'd ducked behind. Knee-high flowers shrouded in pale mist shuddered in the wind. They made a shrill crying sound like they were shrieking from the cold. I squatted beside them. A path of footprints led directly past. They weren't hurried or dragged which meant Varialla had left willingly.

Steadily, I crept around the back of the cave where towering trees gathered close and reached through the fog. Eyes sharp, I searched for a glimpse of her earthy brown skin, full lips and fiery eyes. I tried to detect a whiff of her on the air.

Nothing.

What are you up to, little bud?

Moving faster, I stalked around the back of the cave to the other side. She was gone.

My wings shuddered. They itched to take flight and scour every inch of this place. But the wind would only knock me off course and in this fog, I could see clearer on the ground.

Fists clenched; I followed the trail of footprints. They ended at the line of trees where the canopy overhead was thick and cut off any light from the moon.

For the sea-witch to have gone in there, she was doing something she shouldn't. Perhaps she'd found a way to communicate with her rebel lover through more secret shells. Or maybe she'd run ahead to somehow rig the Games. When it came to her, anything was possible. She'd proven that the night she'd tainted the bond between us that I'd held so fucking sacred.

I drew up the hood of my cloak and stepped between the trees. The silence was sudden. Most woods had sounds of wildlife but there was nothing alive here. No noise beside the crunch of my boots over dry leaves and brittle patches of ice that forced me to go slower than I would have liked. Even the winds howl was now a distant wail.

The dark wasn't as deep as I'd anticipated. Shafts of moonlight sliced through the canopy and my eyes adjusted quickly. I caught glimpses of the mist that swirled around my feet. Shadows of gnarled trees loomed in the distance. But there was no sign of the little sea serpent.

Someone murmured a soft curse. I spun. My strides devoured the distance between me and that fleeting sound. Light flared a few paces ahead and I jogged towards it, straight into a small clearing. There Varialla stood with her phone in hand. Her shirt was rolled up beneath her breasts. My gaze fell on her ass, and the lacy black thong that was swallowed by her plump cheeks.

Fates, save me.

I skidded to a stop. Blood rushed in my ears and shot down my shaft.

"What are you doing?"

Varialla swiveled and dropped her phone. Its torchlight bounced across her features. Her eyes were wide.

"Holy crap," she gasped and rushed to pull down her shirt. "You scared the ever-loving shit out of me."

I gritted my teeth and strode towards her. I wasn't sure if I was angrier at her for coming out here on her own, or at myself for how badly I wanted to tear off that shirt and rediscover every inch of her.

"What are you doing?" I snarled.

"Nothing."

"No one comes all the way out here to do nothing."

She bent and snatched up her phone. "I needed some space from assholes like you."

As she stalked past me, I grabbed her wrist.

"You're hiding something beneath that shirt."

"Whatever I have beneath my shirt is none of your business. I thought I made that clear."

Need rumbled in the base of my throat. I was overcome with visions of exactly what was beneath her shirt and how they felt against my tongue. The way she writhed when I stroked them, sucked them just right.

"Now feel free," she gritted out. "To fuck off."

She tried to yank her wrist from my grasp but I pulled her towards me.

"As soon as you show me what you're hiding."

Her fist swung for my cheek. I caught it before the blow landed. She wrenched free and smacked me around the ear.

I snarled, "For someone who has nothing to hide, you fight like you do."

She shuffled back. Her hands were raised in fighting stance. "I just don't want your hands on me."

I chuckled. "We both know that isn't true."

I lunged. She spun to the side. It was like a dance. I stepped one way. She stepped another. She swung. I ducked. Jab. Block. Swipe. Dodge. She was faster than when she'd first arrived in the isles. But not fast enough.

Eventually, I had her cornered between me and a tree. "Finished?"

Her hazel eyes narrowed. "I'm just getting started."

The barbaric little witch slammed her knee towards my groin. I barely dodged the attack. She ran but I caught her around the waist and yanked her against me. Her back was crushed to my front and I strapped her arms across her chest. She tried to stamp on my foot but I turned it to the side.

"Use your words, little bud."

Varialla writhed and cursed my name. I chuckled and hefted up her shirt. Her body dotted with goosebumps as the chill struck her skin.

"You fucking—"

Whatever she said was lost to me. All I saw was the mark that gleamed silver on her dark skin. It was an intricate pattern of curved lines and delicate swirls that climbed up the side of her body.

My throat bobbed.

I trailed a finger over the lines. Varialla arched into me. Her round ass pressed into my cock. I glanced down at her. Her face was creased in what looked like both pleasure and pain. I stroked the mark again. The sound she made had my balls tightening and the way she bucked...*fuck*.

"Get off me," she seethed.

I blinked to clear the fog of lust that had settled over me. Her reaction confirmed what I thought. This mark on her skin was a mark of myth. One I'd read about in books but never thought I'd see.

Varialla blinked up at me; her head tipped back.

"You know what it is," she rasped.

It wasn't a question but I said, "Yes."

My fingers idly traced her skin. It was like I couldn't stop.

Varialla shuddered. Her legs pressed together. The scent of her arousal climbed down my throat. I groaned; my cock was instantly hard.

"What-what is it?" she stammered as I continued to explore the swirling lines. "What does it mean?"

What it meant was impossible. What it meant filled me with the most dangerous thing of all. Hope.

"It is the Poisoned Heart," I murmured.

Varialla jerked when I rested my palm flat against the symbol. Her ass bumped my cock again. *Fates.* I shouldn't be holding her like this. I was supposed to keep my distance.

This female was the greatest threat to the entire realm. She had the ability to legitimately reign over the Isles and put murderers on the throne. Those who would twist the minds of millions and bend them to their will.

I shouldn't have been holding her against me. I should have been slitting her fucking throat.

She drew in a deep breath. "What is it? What is the Poisoned Heart?"

I swallowed. I still couldn't reconcile this mark on her skin.

"It's proof of how you feel about me," I said at last.

"Disgust?" she panted then winced as if the mark hurt.

According to the stories, the one who tainted their bond with a mate they truly loved would feel pain—amongst other things—whenever their mate touched the symbol.

"Hatred?" she went on when I failed to answer.

My grip tightened around her. "It means all that and more sweetheart. It means you're mine."

She glared up at me. "I'll never be yours."

My lips slanted into a smirk. "You already are."

My hand slid inside her black lace thong.

Her body went rigid. "What are you doing?" she hissed but didn't pull away.

I almost got on my knees when I felt the fine curls of hair that had started to grow back since the last time, I'd touched her.

"I'm giving you five seconds to tell me you don't want this," I growled. My cock strained against my breeches. "Or else I'm going to make you come harder than you ever have before."

Her hazel eyes flared with a blend of fury and desire.

I waited for her to stop me; for one of us to have some fucking sense. But her gaze held mine.

"Five," I held her closer. "Four..."

I worked my fingers lower until I felt the heat of her hot, wet cunt.

"Three…two…one." I dragged my finger along her slit. "Fuck."

Varialla unleashed a breathless moan and the world and all the reasons not to do this fell away.

Half feral, I parted my sweet bud's lips and dipped a finger inside her. She cried out. My balls tightened. Heat pulsed in my skin. I was already halfway to unleashing my load.

"Fuck, I've missed this cunt."

Varialla bucked as I plunged another finger inside her. She groaned and squirmed, and strained for breath.

Teeth gritted; I watched her chest heave and her eyelids flutter. I watched her face crease in tortured pleasure. She was a goddess and a demon all in one, sent to satisfy and slaughter me in the same breath.

"I—I want to touch you," she panted and tried to pull a hand free.

I held her tighter; caged her arms across her chest. If she ever got her hands on me, I would be eternally and unforgivably hers. This, the smell of her on my fingers, the feel of her against my skin was all I could endure, without putting her and her happiness above everything I was fighting for.

"We don't always get what we want," I growled and pressed down on her clit.

The beauty bucked. My vision blurred. Blinding pleasure speared through my cock. I ground into her so desperately we staggered and fell against a tree.

I released her arms and she grasped the tree trunk as I curled my other hand around her neck and tipped her head back. I held it there; her hazel eyes trained on me. I wanted to see every reaction play out on her face.

"I want to see you come, little bud."

Shadows curled around my wings and snaked across my skin. My cock was rigid—stiff and pulsing. It ached for release as my little bud fucked my hand. Her tits scraped the rough bark of the tree but she didn't care. She moaned louder and ground her hips into me until I couldn't see straight.

"Exekiel," she gasped.

I moved into her. My heart pounded. "I love when you say my name."

My cock throbbed as her tight little pussy sucked my fingers in deeper and coated the ends in the juice, I was desperate to taste. To drink until she was empty.

"Fuck, my little wet witch."

Varialla whimpered and spasmed on the edge of my hand. I devoured it all. The hitch of her breath. The sweat that soaked her skin despite the fierce cold. The way her eyes rolled. She bit her bottom lip as if that could stop the screams, I would elicit from her. The sounds that I would make sure the whole damn woods heard.

Fuck. I couldn't get enough of her. The sweet and salty scent of her skin, her plump lips and supple breasts. I couldn't escape the urges she provoked inside me. When it came to Varialla, I would always make the wrong decision because nothing ever felt this fucking right.

15

VARIALLA:
One Little Slip

If Beyoncé could see me now, she'd hang her head in shame. According to her Single Ladies lyrics, if someone wanted to be with someone, they should 'put a ring on it'. Exekiel didn't even like me. Yet, here I was, with my legs open, grinding on his fingers like he'd paid me. I'd sworn he'd never touch me again. Vowed that the last time was the last time. Now I panted his name; half wrecked from one simple stroke.

Fuck. How did we get here? How had I gone from wanting to claw his eyes out to riding his hand? My breasts stung where they were scraped against the tree bark but I didn't care. I didn't want to pull back; didn't want this to end.

Hot pangs shot through my core. My toes curled inside my mudded boots.

Exekiel bowed his head. His dark hair slanted across his brow. Our lips had come so close so many times, but he didn't kiss me. He just watched me come apart on his hand. He watched me lose my fucking mind for him.

"Are you almost there, little bud?"

I nodded, unable to form words. I was so fucking close.

"Let's try something." Exekiel brushed a finger across the Poisoned Heart. The heavens opened. The stars sang. My world ruptured. It was him. Whatever that mark was, somehow, it was him burned into my skin.

Exekiel groaned deeply as if just seeing me come, brought him to the edge. He didn't slow. He pumped his fingers harder and faster. My body shook. My mind fizzled. The world spun. I somehow came again. Harder than before.

"Shit!"

There was nothing but him. No sky, no earth, no wintry fog and pale moon. Only him. His body. His heat. And the sound of our weighted breaths.

Eventually, when my soul slid back into my skin, I blinked up at Exekiel. My neck was still caged in his grip.

His eyes searched mine. In them I saw desire, regret, longing, pain. I'd never wanted his ability to read minds more. Exekiel's stare seemed to echo everything I felt. As much I hated him, I hated this. I hated that our lives and circumstance had kept us apart before we ever had a chance to be together.

"What are you thinking?" I whispered.

I knew I wouldn't get another chance to ask, to be this close to him again. I wouldn't let myself get this close again.

Exekiel clenched his jaw. I saw the shift as plainly as day turned to night. His nostrils flared. His eyes shuttered. Then his hand tightened around my throat enough to cut off part of my air supply.

He snarled; his pink eyes now a violent red. "I'm thinking how good you'll look with my collar around your neck."

His eyes flashed crimson. Shadows surged around him. My breath caught. Before I could fully grasp what was going on I felt a tightening around my wrists. I gaped up at him as his shadows locked my arms around the tree.

"What the fuck?"

I tugged but it was useless. Their grip was unrelenting.

Exekiel smirked. "Never let your guard down, little bud."

He turned and strode away.

"Exekiel!" I shouted.

I thrashed against his shadows crippling hold. They writhed like snakes born of smoke around my skin. "Exekiel!"

He disappeared into the dark between the trees and left me; stranded and chained.

16

EXEKIEL:
LEVEL FOUR

My clothes were stiff with frost from the frozen lakes we'd swum through. My knuckles were raw from having to punch through the ice. Sleep had become a cruel joke. We only stopped when necessary. To eat or shit the shit we ate.

Now, we closed in on level four. Heads down and cloaks pulled closed, we raced through a narrow mountain pass. The air was unforgivably cold. The ground was slick with ice and patches of melted snow. Flight would have been faster but it was impossible to see through the blizzard that whirled around us.

If I attempted to fly above it, I would lose sight of the trail. It was hard enough to make out the contestants that thundered behind us beyond flashes of their power and glimpses of their shadows.

"Duck!" Kraxus shouted.

A bolt of silver power lobbied over our heads and crashed into the side of the mountain. The ground shook.

"Idiots." At this rate, they'd bring an avalanche down on our heads.

"On your left!"

I didn't know who shouted the warning but I wheeled around as a great white bear dove from the mist. It pounced on Vivienne. Its scent confirmed he was a shifter. He raised his claws and moved to strike. Vivienne knocked him back with a well-placed kick to his chest.

The bear slammed into the ice and reverted back to his human form with a whimper. Vivienne hopped to her feet. She barely missed a step as we ran.

Kraxus' eyes searched her with a panic he tried to hide. He was smart enough not to ask if she was okay. Perhaps he was her mate, after all.

We ran until we came to an impenetrable wall of solid ice coated with frost. To anyone who hadn't studied the map, it looked like we'd come too far and hit a dead end. The only way out was up. Up was exactly where we needed to go.

"Like we planned!" I shouted.

We flung ourselves at the wall. Spikes that we'd fastened to the front of our boots to use as a weapon now pierced the ice, and gave us a foothold. We linked arms and leaned back as we climbed. Nikolai and Atlas were at either end. They partly shifted and embedded their claws into the ice for extra support.

"Fates, fuck me, it's cold," I growled through clenched teeth.

The frost in the air burned my lungs. My breath fogged in front of me.

"Your lips are turning blue," Vivienne stammered. Her own teeth chattered uncontrollably.

If she were Varialla, I might have joked about it being better than my blue balls. Ever since I'd fingered my little bud against that tree the other night, I'd had a semi-permanent hard-on. One that only she could satisfy but never would. The sea-witch surely hated me after I'd left her tied to that tree. She wouldn't understand that I'd done what I had to. The sooner I got her out of the Games, the sooner the sirens lost the only chance they had of getting on that throne.

I licked my lips for added warmth. Vivienne tracked the movement. Whatever she said was drowned out by the howl of the wind but based on the hungry glint in her eyes, I could hazard a guess.

Not for the first time, I wondered why it couldn't have been her. Why hadn't I fallen in love with Vivienne when I'd still had a chance of loving someone else besides that infuriating siren?

Kraxus slipped. Pulled by his weight, we slid down a few feet, and scrambled to reposition ourselves.

"Fuck."

Other contestants were gaining on us. Their shouts came from all directions. Some had brought ropes and grappling hooks. Winter elves carved stairs out of the ice. It was a tactic that could have put them in the lead, but the steps were wet and their ascent was slow.

"Almost there!" Atlas bellowed.

We scaled fast. Despite the cold, sweat trickled down the back of my neck.

At last, we crested the mountain peak. Here we were met with an eerie silence so at odds with the storm that raged below. At least fifty giant statues carved of ice stood like sentries on the snowcapped peak. They were clad in frosted armor with blades of ice in hand.

Behind them, streaks of green and gold swirled above a large tree. It had a bulbous base and countless gnarled branches that twisted in all directions. In place of leaves, there were keys that hung from golden threads of power.

Beyond the tree was an unassuming wooden door. No walls or windows attached. That was where we needed to go to reach the next level.

"If I had to guess, I'd say these fuckers move." I gestured to the giant ice soldiers that stood at least three times my height.

Atlas nodded. "Then we move faster." The end of his sentence was more of a growl as he morphed into his yeti form.

His fur was white enough to blend in with our surroundings. The only way to discern him was by the flash of his yellow teeth and the glare of his red eyes.

On my right Nikolai shifted into his lion. The green trident of *Ulius* lit up on the back of Kraxus' hand. Trilla reached for her silver sword.

"That blade won't help you here," Vivienne murmured.

The Autumn elf swallowed. A hint of her anxiety touched the air.

I held out my hand. "Hang on tight."

Trilla's eyes shone with gratitude as she rushed into the circle of my arms.

I scanned the skies then unfurled my wings. "Let's move."

Without waiting for the others, I shot into the air. I was barely ten feet off the ground when bolts of electricity spliced through my wings. My body spasmed. I bounced across the snow as I struck the ground. Trilla rolled from my grasp.

"This is a no-fly zone," announced a disembodied voice. **"This is a no-fly zone."**

"Fuck."

I sheathed my wings in the seams of my spine and pushed to my feet. Kraxus roared with laughter. I glared at the bastard and shook clumps of snow from my hair.

Behind us, other contestants reached the mountaintop. Some battled each other whilst others charged heedlessly forwards with warrior cries.

I nodded to Trilla. "You might need that sword after all."

I drew my longsword; Andromeda, from its scabbard. "Come on."

My feet sunk in the powdered snow as I ran towards the first line of guards. The air grew colder. Snowflakes fluttered around us. A storm was coming.

"*Ulius,*" I breathed.

The Fates symbol glowed green on the palm of my hand. The nearest ice guard straightened as we approached. Its pale eyes turned a violent blue.

"Get ready!"

Kraxus raced beside me. Nikolai and Atlas' beast forms barreled ahead.

The ice guard hefted up its sword and swung it towards us. With a roar, Kraxus and I punched up. Our fists slammed into its blade. The impact knocked me back as the weapon shattered. Arms thrown over my head; I ducked then rolled to my feet.

The metallic scent of blood struck my nose as red sprayed across the sheet of white. I swiveled. Trilla had been struck down by a different soldier. Her head, severed from her body, sank beneath the snow.

Vivienne screamed.

"Run!" I bellowed.

There was nothing else we could do. Sword in hand and wreathed in shadows, I ploughed through the snow. The mountaintop was overrun as players surged towards the tree. Whorls of magic rivalled the blaze of the night sky and shouts echoed across the peak.

A song cleaved through the chaos. The lilting notes sailed over us and the world stood still. Every player stopped. A force weighed on my limbs. The more I pressed forward, the slower I moved. This was the effects of magic. This was a siren's song.

I scanned the snow. At the edge of the mountain's peak, was Varialla. Her braided pigtails whipped behind her. Her hazel eyes were bright as embers.

My shadows should have put us days ahead of her. Somehow, she'd caught up.

Varialla's haunting yet beautiful voice tugged in my chest. It didn't affect me as much as the others. It possibly had something to do with our blood bond and the fact that powerful beings took longer to succumb to a siren song.

She looked straight at me. She was too far away to make out her expression but I felt the bite of her stare. Varialla continued to sing. As she did, she ran. Orbs surged behind her and followed the blazing tracks she left in the snow.

An ice soldier barred her path. Varialla altered her song's pitch. With a wave of her hands, a slash of magic carved through the sentry. It burst into chunks of ice that melted into the snow.

Fates, fuck me.

Her mother had needed an army of sirens to command a few well-placed dragons. Varialla had only herself to manipulate the minds of almost every contestant. Some of the most powerful beings in the Realm.

Her voice didn't waiver as she ran. It glided as swiftly as she did across the snow. I wrenched on my shadows. They climbed lethargically through my skin but the second they broke the barrier, they soared.

Unburdened by the magic that pressed on my physical form, my shadows swept around me. I welcomed the rush of power then hurled them at the sea-witch.

17

VARIALLA:
SHADOWS & SONGS

A storm of black barreled towards me. My heart lurched. I dropped to my knees in a cloud of powdered snow and crawled. Breathlessly, I hummed, so the effects of my song lingered.

Exekiel's shadows swept low. I rolled from their path and straight into the swing of an ice soldier's blade.

Fuck!

With a cry, I threw up a blast of magic from the palm of my hands. It brought me one millisecond. I used it to roll again, then quickly resumed humming. Loch recently taught me that once the spell was cast, the magic remained in the sound of my voice regardless of what I said.

Another ice soldier swiped at me. This one had a fucking axe. I leapt to my feet and sang in what I think was an e-sharp. I had no idea how I knew that. The ice soldier jerked then shattered.

Shit. My chest felt tight. I was power shaped into a person. A crackle of burning energy fueled by adrenaline. But my muscles shook under the strain of the power I exerted. I couldn't keep this up.

Once again, I was off. I weaved through the players that barely moved. They tried to speak, but in the time, it took them to open their mouths, I was gone. This wasn't what I'd meant to happen. I'd just wanted time to slow down enough for me to catch up. Now it was like the whole world had almost come to a complete stop.

Pain pounded in the back of my skull. My song started to slip. I clung to it. I couldn't stop now. I needed to get closer to those keys.

Exekiel's shadows swarmed after me. That asshole was determined to see me lose. He wanted my people to remain oppressed. He wanted to make me a prisoner of the Crown. Or worse an inmate in Blacktomb Bay, alongside my mother, if she was still alive. Exekiel had already stolen my childhood, my family, my home. He would not take my freedom.

The tree was in my sights; a few paces away. I focused all my attention on dodging the ice soldiers as they swung at me. I ran as fast as I could. The thick snow made it almost impossible. The icy wet seeped into my bones.

Almost there.

Shadows clamped around my middle and wrapped around my throat. My voice was cut off with a whimper and a wretch. I went down.

The command of my song shattered. The players burst into action. It was a mad rush to reach the keys. Roaring, they stampeded to where I fought darkness on the ground. I hoped Lucinda and the others were among them. I had no idea what Exekiel had done with my friends.

Desperate, I tugged on the binds around me. The strength of Exekiel's power was equal to mine. It took some push and pull but I should get through it. It was how I'd broken through the shackles before. However, this was something else. The bastard had thrown all he had into restraining me.

My gaze tracked Exekiel as he charged across the snow. He was in the lead. His eyes were a blazing red. They settled on me and he didn't look away as he swung, dodged and parried the blows of the ice soldiers. He barely looked or paused as he took them down; one after the other.

My stomach tensed. He couldn't win.

A cry broke out of me. I could hardly breathe around the chokehold his shadows had me in. The more I struggled, the tighter they squeezed. It felt like my bones were about to snap.

I managed to stagger to my feet. My vision swayed. I swallowed lungsful of air and forced my heart to beat slower. I closed my eyes and blocked out the chaos that raged across the blood-splattered snow.

He couldn't win.

Fists clenched, I yanked on every shred of magic in my soul until a shimmer bloomed to light in my hands. I pressed my palm to his shadows. They dispersed like oil in water. I gasped as I stumbled free.

A handful of players, Exekiel included, had already made it to the tree and begun their ascent. I raced towards them.

I vaulted up the trees bulbous trunk and swung from branch to branch. Loch was a psychotic shithead, but he'd trained me well.

The keys were high up. They dangled from golden threads of magic. I blew sweat from my eyes and kept climbing. Other contestants shoved me aside. One in particular hounded my back.

Exekiel prowled towards me like a panther. He moved as easily as he would on land. When he was close enough, he reached up and gripped my ankle. I shrieked and grabbed onto the nearest branch. I kicked back with the heel of my boot and got him square in the face. This only seemed to piss him off more than he already was.

A growl like thunder rumbled from his throat. I kicked again and again. Finally, Exekiel lost his grip. I scrabbled forwards like the devil himself was after me. Then again, the son of Death was a close second.

My palm split on a thorn I hadn't noticed. I hissed and forced my legs to keep moving. Exhaustion weighed me down. My head continued to pound and every muscle trembled.

Finally, I flung myself up and snatched an emerald key from the branch above my head. Exekiel grabbed his own key at the same time.

Our eyes locked. I made sure he saw every ounce of hatred in mine.

He was already ahead of me in the ranks. Number one to my number ten spot. A spot I'd only gotten because of the people's votes and the fact that Cherise had died for me. That I'd killed her. A life taken too soon because of the monsters he served. Yet he was still doing everything he could to stop me.

"Well done," he snarled. His voice was as vicious as I felt. "You've just reminded everyone why they shouldn't trust a siren."

18

VARIALLA:
Come Clean

Applause was the first thing I registered, followed by the shift of sand instead of snow beneath my feet. I blinked up at a midday sun that blazed in a cloudless, turquoise sky. I'd stepped through the door behind the tree and was back in the arena. Back in the Eternal City.

The stadium was packed. Like the day we left, the audience waved banners and shot up sparks of magic in a rainbow of colors. My mind reeled. It was like no time had passed but it had been weeks.

All around me, the other contestants stumbled in, as if from out of nowhere, as they stepped through the door. There were less of us now than there'd been at the start of the Games but too many to count at a glance.

On a wooden stage in the center of the arena, Goather trotted from one side to the other. Today, he wore a tweed jacket and a comically large bowtie. His orange goatee was braided and his hair was slicked between his horns.

He announced each contestant as they arrived and added any saucy tidbit or highlight from the Games. Mine had had something to do with Exekiel but I hadn't been listening.

On a separate circular stage, was the Conduit, backed by the Council. Its power pulsed like a beating heart that reverberated through the sand. Even in daylight, the silver symbols of the Fates that glowed within its misty blue-green channel, were hard to miss.

The crowd roared as the last contestant came to stand beside us in the sand.

"Congratulations, contestants," Goather called. "You have successfully completed Phase One of the Games and have acquired the four keys needed to advance to the next level."

A large group of Pegasus charged out onto the field and raced around us. They were various colors, from silver and gold to pinks and greens.

"Over the next two days, those of you who ranked the lowest, will compete in a jousting tournament along with those who were disqualified."

Goather gestured to the stands. There the contestants who'd been removed from the Games because they were either injured, failed to get a key or didn't reach the next level in time, were seated in the front row.

They each wore some form of battle armor, marked with the symbol of their cast. My heart lurched when I spotted Calder. He hadn't made it. I bet Exekiel and his team had had something to do with it.

The Pegasus stopped prancing and herded us towards a glass dome. Its walls were so thin and clear I hadn't noticed it at first. I scanned the other players reactions. No one seemed concerned. Although that wasn't saying much.

"There will also be a great feast in your honor," Goather went on.

I caught sight of Kylin's dark skin and shaved head. I squeezed through the other contestants to reach her.

Goather bellowed, "But before we get to all that…"

The audience chorused with him, "It's time to come clean!"

Icy water rained down from the domed ceiling. I shrieked. Kylin caught me as I stumbled back.

She raised her eyebrows. "If you're done screeching like a banshee, we need to undress."

"What?" I spluttered as the sweet-scented water spilled over us.

Beside me, contestants began to shirk off their armor and soiled clothes. Half were already butt-naked.

What the heck was going on?

"Take it off! Take it off!" The audience chanted.

"Believe it or not this is as much a part of the Games as the rest."

I scoffed. Kylin peeled off her top and exposed her perky breasts.

"How is me getting my tits out supposed to help me win the Games?"

She chuckled. "A leader must be confident in all situations. They must be willing to humble themselves for their people." Kylin kicked off her leggings next. "Most importantly, we must show we have nothing to hide. That we aren't smuggling anything out of the Games."

"Time to come clean," I sighed.

The audience's chant suddenly made sense.

Kylin nodded. "Exactly."

I groaned. Giant hologram screens blazed from strategically placed camera-orbs and showed almost every angle of every contestant. I'd never been shy about my body, but I didn't particularly love the idea of having it broadcasted live on orb-vision for thousands of gawping spectators. However, if this was what it took, to gain the people's trust then so be it.

As soon as I pulled my shirt over my head, I realized my mistake. Excited murmurs rippled through the crowd and contestants. I'd forgotten that my body was a canvas of secrets.

Someone whispered, "Is that a Poisoned Heart?"

Another gasped, "Fates gorge, it is."

The voices rose higher.

Every eye was on me. Even Kylin gawked at the swirling lines of the Poisoned Heart and the symbol of the Five Isles inked onto my skin since birth. There was no way to explain either of them without inviting more questions.

I glanced to one of the giant screens which had zoomed in on every curled loop of the Poisoned Heart. Panic rose in my chest. I didn't fully understand the implications of the symbol but they seemed to and it wasn't good.

"A mark forged from true love between mates that will never be," Goather's voice echoed across the arena. "I daresay this is confirmation. Our fan favorites are mated!" He had to shout to be heard over the commotion. "However, it seems our foreign temptress has tainted that bond. That is how dedicated she is to taking down his barrier and uniting the Nine Isles!"

The crowd erupted. Some cheered. Others booed.

"How romantic," one contestant gushed

"It's selfish," another spat loudly as she glared daggers at me.

Like the audience, the players were divided on this and they had no qualms about letting me know. No matter which way I turned, people shot me looks of awe, sorrow or disgust.

A guy to my right, gave me a comforting pat on the shoulder. "That's very noble of you to sacrifice a love like that."

I stepped away from the naked elf and shook my head. For the first time, I felt like a reality TV star. Everyone seemed to have an opinion on my personal life and I was apparently supposed to take it. I was pretty sure that by the time I left the arena, something about the mark would be trending on enchant-a-gram.

"Of course, this does bring up the question of whether or not our foreign temptress will be fit to rule when the time comes."

I frowned. What did that mean?

"We all know the expression, 'madly in love', was born from those driven mad when they tainted a true love bond." His grin was serpentine.

The hair rose on the back of my neck.

"Will Miss von Hastings, be able to sever her connection to the Shadow Saint before the Poisoned Heart severs her connection to reality?"

His words blew through me. I rocked back.

"What?" I gaped at Kylin. "I'm going to lose my mind?"

She grimaced. "Apparently, the mark will grow until it reaches your heart. By then, the pain will be so excruciating, it will drive you mad."

My blood ran cold.

"There are ways to undo it," she quickly added, although she didn't sound convinced. "I'll explain when we get out of here."

Numbly, I finished undressing and let the icy water splash over me. It soaked into my mudded hair and slid between my breasts. I groaned and let myself melt into the moment. Kylin said there was a way to undo the Poisoned Heart and I was willing to do anything.

"No stress, no mess," I whispered to myself as I teased the ends of my braids.

I couldn't remember the last time we'd found a stream or pond to bathe in. I accepted the bar of soap Kylin handed me and began scrubbing at dirt that was caked into every crease of my skin.

An awareness tingled inside me. A tendril of heat crept up my spine. I froze. Someone was watching me. Their gaze was like a physical caress across my body. I released a breath and tried to tame the rapid spike of my heartrate. I didn't know how I knew it was him. Didn't know how I felt him inside me, but when I glanced over my shoulder, there he was. Beautiful, scarred, tanned and naked.

Water spilled over Exekiel's stacked abs and chiseled jaw. It took all my restraint not to look down at what I knew hung between his legs.

Every eye was on him. As always, his eyes were on me. My breath stalled. My tongue flicked over my lips.

Exekiel's burning pink stare trailed down my body; over my breasts, my hips...They darkened when they reached the apex of my thighs. My toes curled in the rough sand. My whole being went hot. I was already naked but beneath his stare, I felt exposed.

Hot desire pulsed in my blood. *Shit*. How did he have this effect on me every time? Exekiel was on the other side of the dome and yet everyone between us seemed to vanish.

Look away, I chanted in my mind. I couldn't even blink.

Exekiel dragged his thumb across his bottom lip. My gaze locked on that movement. On the way his teeth flashed and his tongue slid over the slightly pointed edges.

My nipples tightened to painful points. I prayed anyone who noticed would blame the cold bite of the water. But I no longer felt the cold. Heat snaked through me and an ache brewed in the base of my belly.

After exploring every inch of me, Exekiel's stare trailed back up to my face. The fire of his gaze slammed into me. I bit my lip and sucked down a deep breath. The connection between us grew taut. Strained and ready to snap.

Somehow, I knew he was remembering as vividly as I was the feel of his fingers inside me. The way he'd restrained me against that tree and drove me to the edge of oblivion. I remembered all the times he'd kissed me, pinned me down beneath his hard, punishing, cock.

Someone gasped. Someone else shrieked. The audience whooped. Finally, I tore my gaze away from his.

"Well, well," Goather drawled into his microphone, "Whoever thought we'd see the Shadow Saint at full mast."

Immediately my gaze dipped to Exekiel's thick cock. It was standing at attention. My stare shot back to his. His lips curved into the hint of a smile. His shadows coiled around his waist. They shifted and pulsed in a way that just made him more tempting. Made me want to tear through his shadows and explore everything underneath.

For fucks sake.

I stepped back and uselessly tried to shrink into the crowd as every head swiveled from him to me.

Goather cackled. "You two are a reality show's dream."

19

VARIALLA:
THE JOUST IS UP

The last few hours had been a blur of Poisoned Hearts, Fae cocks and Game gossip. I'd barely had chance to catch my breath. As soon as I'd entered my room, the nymphs had pounced. Whilst I'd been bathed and dressed for today's jousting tournament, they'd explained more about the Poisoned Heart.

Apparently, there were three ways to undo it before it infected my heart and my mind. I either had to get over Exekiel, return our bond to the weird romance it had been, or completely sever our connection. The only way to do that, was if the love I felt morphed to pure hate. If I was being honest, not one of those seemed possible but I was determined to try.

For now, I shoved all thoughts about it to the back of my mind. Today was about supporting Calder in his return to the Games.

"By the Fates," Cyrus breathed.

Her eyes were wide with wonder as she took in the sprawling sky-field of the jousting tournament. The stands that usually surrounded the sand in the arena, now floated high above it. Today they encircled a ring of soaring Pegasus with riders on their backs.

"This is incredible."

Cyrus had watched the tournaments for centuries on orb-vision but never live. Close enough to smell the blood. The clouds within reach. Apparently, nymphs weren't allowed to attend these types of events, which was exactly why I'd invited them.

"This is a bad idea," Eudora murmured for the hundredth time.

I waved her off. "When you have something important to say, you have to make some noise." I levelled her with a look. "And we have a lot to say."

Today we were taking a stand. We were letting the Realm know that Outliers would no longer let others' perceptions or labels define them or the things they could do.

"Exactly," Cyrus enthused. "We're like the Outliers who recently stormed the great library and demanded access to the knowledge that has been denied them."

"Try not to sound so thrilled," Eudora drawled as she stepped around a spilled drink and discarded plate of noodles. "All that's done is lead to riots, vandalism and violence. Exactly what the barrier was trying to prevent."

My brows shot up. "At the cost of your rights. Your freedom. You were never given a choice. You were assigned a role and expected to follow it."

"A small sacrifice for peace." Eudora looked across the sky-field. Her golden-glittered antlers caught the light.

I scoffed. "It's not peace if it's forced. It's a bomb waiting to go off."

"And you're about to detonate it," she mused.

I snickered and splayed my fingers. "Boom!"

The stands heaved. The press of sweaty bodies felt like a bad orgy. At least, I'd chosen a pair of cut-off shorts and halter-top for the occasion. Since they didn't have denim here, the shorts were a mix of lace and a cotton-type fabric I couldn't identify. But they were cool enough for this midday heat.

Balanced in the back of a gold chariot, Goather hollered, "*De Cinque Istrovos*, are you ready?"

The audience cheered. For the first time, I joined in. The energy was electric. Down below, an orchestra of goblins played instruments that sounded like trumpets and saxophones and had a killer base.

I shimmied my hips to the music and laughed with Cyrus and the others.

It wasn't long before I detected low murmurs that followed us as we maneuvered towards the front rows.

"I told you this was a bad idea," Eudora hissed, but her steps didn't falter and she kept her head held high.

"Ignore them," I said.

The growled insults grew louder. I clenched my fists and exhaled deeply. This was what we wanted; to get people talking. To get them to acknowledge that change was coming whether they liked it or not.

We'd almost reached the second row where Lucinda had left space for us when a large shifter with hulking muscles and fanged teeth blocked our path.

"This section is invitation only, nymphs," he snarled.

I stood taller. "I invited them."

The shifter threw me a scathing look. "A half-creed's invitation doesn't count. You're only here because your whore of a mother spread her legs for someone who mattered," he spat.

I bristled. Those behind him laughed.

He stepped closer. His height was staggering. I didn't back away and, to their credit, neither did the nymphs.

"You might as well forfeit now, siren. I would never kneel to a beggar bitch like you."

The asshole puckered his lips and spat in my face.

I kicked before I could think. My foot slammed into his knee and there was a vicious pop as his leg snapped inwards and his kneecap swung sideways. He howled. His body hit the ground with a thud.

A steady beat of anger pulsed inside me. I wiped the pricks spit off my face with the back of my hand, then grasped his limp brown hair in my fist. I yanked his head back and forced him to meet my stare. His face was creased in pain. My inner siren ached to sing a song of suffering.

"Never say never, darling." I smiled, then shoved him back.

He fell; unable to stay upright on his busted leg. I beckoned the girls to follow with a flick of my head.

One by one, we stepped over the whimpering git. Except Cyrus. She chose to walk on him. He barked in pain. The nymph blew him a kiss, before she settled in the seat beside Eudora.

Behind us, there was the shuffle of the shifter's friends as they jumped up. They cursed and helped him off the ground. His sobs echoed as he was led from the arena. I didn't look back. My eye was on the prize. On a future where shit like this didn't happen.

Maximus' shoulders shook with laughter. "That was brilliant."

I grinned and caught the eye of a stunning dark-skinned witch a few seats down. Her eyes were stark grey and catlike with extremely long lashes. Her features were sharp and lips bowed. She wore a sapphire blue cape with a collar of thorns around her shoulders, and a quintessential witch's hat that drooped at the top. Blue and black flowers climbed up one side.

"That's Azalea Frost, High Priestess of the Red Maiden Coven," Maximus whispered when he noticed where my gaze had gone.

That was Lucinda's coven. I supposed it was his as well.

The beautiful Priestess smiled in a way that was somehow cunning and kind at the same time. I bowed my head, then turned my attention to the tournament.

Goather had unrolled a scroll and was reading out the names of those competing. My throat tightened when he called Calder. The shifter sat astride a Pegasus, decked in silver scale-mail armor with spiked shoulder plates.

Apparently, whilst Exekiel had hunted me through the forest, Vivienne and the others had attacked my friends in their sleep. They were knocked unconscious. When they came to, they were deep in the woods. Like me, they had been tied to a tree, only, their binds had been with rope.

They'd managed to make it to the mountain peak before the level ended, but by the time they made it, there wasn't enough keys. Calder had stepped aside and let Kylin take his. Now here he was, competing in the tournament to fight his way back into the Games.

Goather rolled up the scroll. "Now that we've named the losers. Let's look to the winners!"

The audience whooped.

"First, we must congratulate our Protector of the Realm. The Shadow Saint and esteemed bachelor,

Exekiel V'alin, is currently ranked at number one in the Games."

The crowd went wild. I resisted the urge to look Exekiel's way but saw him in the corner of my eye. He was in the front row. He leaned in and whispered something to Vivienne.

I tensed. Jealousy I didn't want to acknowledge pulled tight in my chest. I couldn't believe we'd eye-fucked each other in the arena earlier. I was clearly a glutton for punishment.

Vivienne smiled up at him. When he returned it, my nostrils flared. Not because I was jealous…I wasn't. I couldn't be. There were a thousand reasons why Exekiel and I couldn't be together. The most important being that we hated each other.

I exhaled through my nose. I needed to get a grip. I was supposed to be getting over him before the mark of the Poisoned Heart spread and I literally lost my mind. Now was not the time to be pining over the homicidal Fae-bastard.

I yanked my attention back to Goather who continued to list off the top ten.

Lucinda ranked at number eight. I whooped and made everyone do the wave. Apparently, it was just a human thing. They looked at me like I was the most peculiar thing they'd ever seen but eventually obliged.

"Finally, at number ten, we have Varialla von Hastings," Goather boomed.

Those around me shrieked so loud, I couldn't hear the response of the rest of the audience. I laughed when Eudora scooped up my hand and waved it in the air. No matter what she said, the nymph was enjoying herself.

"Those of you who have ranked above ten, don't really matter so I won't bother reading your names," Goather said flippantly.

The audience hooted. The contestants who hadn't been called shifted uncomfortably. Maximus included.

"However, your rankings have been posted on Fit for the Throne's, Enchant-a-gram profile."

Immediately players pulled out their phones. Countless holographic screens popped up in the audience.

Maximus scowled at his own screen. "Number twenty-three."

I tried not to wince. Number twenty-three was good considering there were fifty-six of us left, but it wouldn't get him on the Council or save him from a life of enslavement. That was a rule I was going to look into changing if I became Primary. Although, I wasn't sure how much of the Games I could change without impacting the way the Conduit fed the land.

The Games had been created almost six centuries ago. It was believed the originators had used an ancient and sacred pact through the Conduit that had led to a binding deal with the Fates themselves.

Goather galloped his Pegasus to the edge of the sky-field and bellowed, "Now, my darling deviants, we joust!"

There were no words to describe the hair-raising, death-defying spectacle that was the jousting tournament.

Decked in armor, the players brandished their lances and slammed into each other with no thought for self-preservation. The aim wasn't to kill their opponent but to knock them from their Pegasus. However, unless they had some way of saving themselves, the player would plummet to their death.

The Pegasus charged through the air. Their feet kicked as if they were on land. Sunlight glinted off the tips of raised lances. The clash of weapon against armor was deafening.

I whooped when Calder soared past us on a white-grey Pegasus. He was talented. He pivoted the lance easily and struck at those who lunged for him.

So far, he'd unseated a Fae-male who'd use their wings to make it safely to the sand. And a witch who'd slowed her descent by bellowing an incantation.

With every second that passed, I slid closer to the edge of my seat.

"Behind you," I screeched.

Lucinda cackled. "Calm down."

I couldn't help it. I'd never really been one for sports but this was something I could sink my teeth into. A shimmering white Pegasus with a shifter on its back dove towards Calder.

He couldn't have heard my warning, but, as if he sensed it, he looked up. The shifter was right on top of him. Calder drove his lance up and straight through the rider's foot.

The shifter bellowed. His arms pin-wheeled as he fell from his Pegasus and careened towards the ground.

My hands balled into fists. Some of the audience screamed. Others cheered. They were high on bloodlust.

Shift. I thought. *Shift, you bastard.*

But what good would shifting do unless his inner beast had wings?

He roared at the sky and waved his arms. I told myself to look away but my eyes stayed glued to his flailing form as he tumbled down. In the second row, it was easy for me to follow him until he slammed into the earth. At the same time, my eyes slammed shut. It was too late to unsee what I'd seen. The blood that stained the sand as his body imploded on impact.

On it went until, at last, only three contestants remained. Calder among them. These top three would be allowed back into the Games. It was at a significantly lower rank. But they had a chance to redeem themselves and that was what mattered.

Despite the dead and wounded, the audience howled for the victors.

"This calls for a celebration!" Lucinda announced.

Maximus rubbed his hands together. "Bring on the *crudel* shots and chaos."

20

EXEKIEL:

SONU DI CARGHEL

I pushed open the ornate iron door of Fates Cathedral and stepped inside. The white marble floor shimmered like polished bone. Overhead, the bells tolled in the bell tower.

Virgin Mothers trailed past in their scarlet robes. Heads bowed and hoods drawn. They left offerings and lit candles on the steps of the stone alters that held replicas of the Conduit. Then continued on their way.

I strode down the Archway of Angels. It was crafted from silver vines and held imposing statues of the Fates.

My eyes immediately went to the hulking black stone statue of Zorsch. When I was younger, I'd spent hours here. I told my father about my life and of how I would make him proud and earn my place beside him in Fatevale. I'd once thought my father could hear me. Now I didn't think he cared enough to listen.

"May you go with the Brave and the Blessed, brother."

The familiar voice sent warmth through me at the same time it chilled my blood.

I turned. "Satrialla."

She pursed her full lips—one of the few things I could see of her beneath her crimson hood and shapeless robe. "Mother now. You forget. Forget."

"Right."

She hadn't been Satrialla since the night the sirens' tyranny arrived at our door and slaughtered her mate; Drax, and their two-year old son. Drax had been my brother in every sense but blood.

I took a tentative step towards her. "Are you well?"

"Well, well. Always well." Satrialla giggled and linked her arm in mine.

Physical contact between a Mother and a worshipper was technically forbidden. However, her title was in name only. It had been a kindness of the women here to help a grieving widow who had lost her family and in turn, lost her mind.

I covered her hand with mine and we strolled silently through the lavish passageways and out into the gardens. There was something about the night air that occasionally soothed her haunted mind.

"Tonight, you see your love?" she asked as she walked along the pebbled paths and trailed her fingers over purple frivela flowers.

I followed. "If you mean you, then yes."

She cackled wildly and covered her face in her hands. "Not me, I mean. Silly brother."

The sound of her laughter, however chaotic, spoke to a part of my soul.

Satrialla was all I had left from the life I'd lived before the barrier. Before the sirens had swept in and razed everything to the ground on the order of the fucking Royal Court.

Satrialla tucked what I knew was a strand of brown hair behind her ear "The girl who, on your face, makes a smile."

I sighed. Despite everything, Satrialla was still a hopeless romantic. "She's a contestant in the Games so I'm sure I will."

Her eyes lifted from the flowers to meet mine. They were full of wonder and pain.

"How delightful, delightful." She shook her head. "To see your love. There. She is there." Satrialla waved her arms and spun in circles. "She is here. There. Here. Alive."

She stopped turning and shook her head again. I took a step towards her.

"Satrialla, look at me."

She continued to shake her head. Tears began to fall. My chest seized. I knew she was thinking of Drax; her mate, my brother.

"Your love is not gone." Her eyes were unfocused. "Never. No more."

I reached out to rest my hand on her shoulder. She reeled back.

"Your love is not gone!" Now she screamed and tears streaked down her cheeks.

She shook her head and began to slap herself repeatedly across the face. I grabbed her wrists and tried to restrain her as she thrashed in my grip and screamed.

"They took everything! They took everything!"

She flung her head back and slammed it into my chest over and over as if she was trying to dislodge the memories.

I caged her in my arms. Her knees buckled and she continued to scream. Now there were no words just heart rendering cries.

"You're okay," I repeated as I rocked her.

She continued to thrash; continued to scream.

"I'm here. You're okay."

I looked up and saw Mothers gathered in the doorway. Their heads were bowed. There was nothing they could do. We were all used to this now.

I gritted my teeth and held Satrialla close. Useless tears burned behind my eyes. I blinked them back and pulled her closer.

"I'm here."

I drained the last of my *Volgiskey* and set the tumbler down beside the aged scroll rolled out on my desk. For decades, this blank parchment had mocked me with the secrets it held. That was about to change.

For the first time since I'd swiped it from a messenger's satchel over three decades ago, I didn't feel the pressure of the wards around it. Reek had done it. It had cost the goblin his life but the brilliant bastard had finally found a way to break the enchanted seal.

If I was right, this parchment would lead me to the fuckers responsible for the murder of my family and the downfall of the realm. Not those who were pawns in the Court's pocket or who had been corrupted by the sirens. But those who had set the sirens on them.

I had uncovered a few of the bastards myself over the years. I'd made quick work of their deaths. Deaths that couldn't be explained, or that were summed up as a freak accident or a rare case of food poisoning. However, their deaths hadn't stopped the operation. They hadn't even slowed it down.

For each one I took out, two more took their place. That was when it became clear just how high-up this deception spread. It wouldn't help to take out a few key players. I had to strike at the heart. Fortunately, I'd positioned myself within the belly of the beast.

The blood I'd squeezed from Anakin's severed tongue sloshed in the vial I pulled from my drawer. I placed it beside the others. There were more than I could count.

In order to break through an enchanted seal, we'd needed more than a skilled goblin. We'd needed the blood of the cast that had sealed it. Reek and I had had no idea who that was, and no way of finding out.

As a result, over the decades, we'd collected blood from each cast and gender throughout the nine isles. That had included every kind of shifter, every half-creed, and the various intelligent beings of Creatures Copse. It had also included Varialla's blood. I'd had to collect it from her back the day she was whipped during the third Trial.

The amount of blood needed from each being was no small measure. Yet the real challenge had been in taking fragments of the Conduit.

Despite my clearance in certain restricted areas, I was rarely left unguarded, when in the Council. Alexov liked to keep an eye on me. I suspected he knew I'd never rest until my brother's killers had joined him in the afterlife.

I poured every drop of blood from the vials into the stone bowl on my desk. Then I sprinkled in the crystallized fragments of the Conduit, the crushed feather of a Pegasus and a few drops of exposium tonic. The mixture gurgled and popped.

Lastly, I slashed a dagger across my palm. My blood spilled from the wound and into the bowl.

My bedchamber filled with the sharp leafy stench of magic. Cracks splintered down the side of the bowl. It struggled to contain the amount of power it held.

Before it could explode, I picked up my broad-headed paintbrush. I ran it through the mix and painted over the parchment. It sizzled and its edges curled. The bitter tang of magic intensified and stung the back of my throat.

The stains of blood smeared across the parchment darkened then reshaped into letters and lines. I continued to paint. With each stroke more of the parchment was revealed.

It was a blueprint of some kind. The drawing looked like a giant horn with rounded edges that gave it the appearance of a flower. Behind the horn were three rows of seats attached by long tubes. What looked like a large glass tube was off to one side. A cable connected it to the horn and a small canister marked X.

I continued to stroke the coated brush over the sheet. Notes were scrawled beside the canister. Ingredients that matched the ones in the poison.

A sense of unease burrowed into my bones.

Arrows appeared next. They indicated that a siren was to stand inside the glass tube. Other sirens were supposed to sit on the chairs and let the one in the case siphon their power to amplify their voice through the device.

There was something else about pitch and mist emission.

Fuck.

It was a weapon. A form of mind control enhanced by the mist of the poison that would seep into the people's skin and alter the very make up of their being. Not only that, it would create a sickness that the people would turn to the Council to cure. And they would, for they had the antidote. They'd created the poison.

My nails dug into my desk. I resisted the urge to burn the fucking scroll. The dragon-shifters were just the beginning.

These Fate-stained fuckers planned to tune the device to transmit the sirens voice in a pitch that not even a Fae's hearing could detect. It was the perfect way to brainwash an entire kingdom.

There was a title across the top: *Sonu di Carghel,* and signatures along the bottom of the page. Names and initials of those who'd signed off on this. Alexov, Adir, Knox…With each one, my anger rose. Some I'd already taken care of, but there were countless others. At least, fifty.

One name stood out in particular; Wade Rorqueth. He'd been a soldier of the siren army and one of my closest friends. Then he'd gone and betrayed us all on the order of his queen; the Siren Savage. I'd thanked him by putting my fist through his skull.

21

VARIALLA:
THE SECRET'S OUT

The carriage bumped us along the beveled brick road. I wriggled back in the velvety seat to keep from falling off.

"All I'm saying is a true friend would have stripped with me."

"And who would have held all your shit?" Lucinda cried from where she sat opposite me. "Maximus was too busy hitting on the Fae behind the bar. Odus and Jia had been tapdancing on the table. And Calder and the nymphs were helping you undress."

I cackled. Celebrating Calder's win last night had gotten well and truly out of hand—in the best way. Back in the UK, I'd been lucky to get tipsy.

Apparently, that was because I'd needed *crudel* and all other manor of magical liquor this realm held.

To top it off, Lucinda had concocted a potion that dealt with hangovers. Aside from a minor headache when I woke up this morning, I felt fresh as a daisy.

"Just be glad I didn't run off with your clothes and leave you to streak home," Lucinda huffed.

I gasped. "You wouldn't."

Her lips pursed into a smile. "The thought crossed my mind."

Maximus snorted. "She was halfway out the door with your clothes when I stopped her and made her come back."

I spluttered. "Lucinda!"

The witch laughed.

Jia said nothing. She stared blandly out the window and fidgeted in her seat.

I nudged her with my shoulder. "Everything alright?

Jia blinked. "Yes." Her lips bunched. "I'm a little nervous they won't let Odus in."

"You're a contestant on Fit for the Throne and your invitation granted you a plus one of your choosing." I looped my fingers through hers and squeezed. "Odus is who you choose. They can't turn him away."

She chewed on her bottom lip. "You're right. It would just be nice to be able to attend these things together without worrying." She shrugged. "I know we pretend not to care but it gets intense sometimes."

I grimaced. Intense was putting it mildly. Last night, I'd thought a group of Inlanders were going to attack Odus when he'd kissed Jia. Thankfully, Calder's wolf form and Lucinda's reputation as a gifted blood-witch seemed to deter them.

I'd always known Lucinda was a blood-witch but hadn't given it much thought until the night she'd helped me use my own blood to save Exekiel. Now, the more stories I heard about the things she'd done, the more in awe and terrified I was.

Our carriage pulled up outside Infinity Hall. Thankful that my shimmering blue dress had slits up to my hips, I easily stepped down from the carriage and out into the cool night's air.

Jia exhaled deeply. "Here goes."

I linked my arm in hers. We followed the crowd down the footpath lined with guards and made our way to the great double doors. Odus was going to meet us there.

"I know what you did," a cold whisper slithered across the back of my neck.

I spun and was suddenly glad this dress was a halter. It had offered a slight barrier between the breath and my skin. Searing green eyes glinted at me. Shafts of lantern light carved across a pale face and moon white hair. Everything inside me recoiled.

"Vladimir."

The councilman sneered. As always, his gaze trailed hungrily over me. But not the hunger of one who wanted my warm flesh pressed against him. No. Vladimir was more likely to celebrate my death by fucking my corpse.

"I wonder if we might, have a word, in private?" he gestured to an area of grass beside the footpath.

"We may not."

I turned to walk away. He grabbed my hand. I yanked it away.

"Believe me, what I'm about to say, you don't want said in public." He looked up to where camera-orbs drifted. There was a vicious glint in his eye. A knowing that said he truly felt he knew something. "One minute of your time."

I glanced again at the area he'd indicated. It was well-lit and the footpath was heavily guarded.

I sighed and turned to the others. "I'll see you in there."

They each shot me a wary glance then nodded and continued towards the banquet hall.

I folded my arms as I turned back to the elf. "You have one minute."

He gestured for me to go ahead of him. As I did, he rested his hand on the small of my back. The feel of his cold fingers on my skin sent shivers up my spine.

Note to self: No more backless dresses.

As we stepped past the guards and stopped beside the building, he purred, "I know you bound the Shadow Saint's life to yours."

I jolted, unable to hide my reaction.

"The night of the final ball, Exekiel was found at death's door with an inexplicable scar over his heart that should have killed him." His brows lifted. "But our fearless Saint is still very much alive."

Vladimir crowded closer and forced me to step back until my spine met the building's wall.

"Judging by the size of your poisoned heart, I'd say you got it at the same time." His lecherous gaze raked over me like claws.

He stepped closer than he needed to; his body barely a breath from mine. I shoved him back but he caught my wrists and pinned them to the wall.

"You didn't want them to find out, did you?" he hissed. "Didn't want your people to know that you betrayed them by saving their enemy. So, you bound him to silence and tainted your bond."

I held his murderous stare with one of my own.

He bowed his head, like he might kiss me. "Am I wrong?"

At least three camera-orbs glided overhead. I glanced at them. Vladimir's grin sharpened, knowingly. This was a set up. He'd cornered me here in the hopes that I'd either confess my sins and turn the Outer Isles against me, or that he'd sew enough seeds of doubt, it wouldn't matter.

I pushed forward, even as his hands held my wrists to the stone. "Is this the part where I'm supposed to beg? Maybe strike up a deal in exchange for you keeping my secret?"

Surprise flickered in his eyes. Whatever he'd expected me to say, that wasn't it.

For so long, I'd wanted to tell Colette and the others the truth about what happened that night, but Loch had compelled me to do otherwise.

Coming clean on National Orb-vision wouldn't have been my first choice but maybe it was my only chance. I wanted the Outer Isles to follow me and I wanted it to be based on the truth. There were too many liars in this Court already.

"You're right," I said loud and clear. "I saved the Shadow Saint with a blood bond."

Vladimir's smile was smug. The truth was out. As bitter as it tasted in my mouth, I was relieved. The guilt had been eating me up from the inside.

The asshole leaned closer until his body was flushed with mine. I jerked my hips to throw him off but he groaned, like he enjoyed it.

He brought his lips to my ear but didn't whisper when he said, "There it is; proof that you're a traitor and nothing you say can be trusted."

I bucked my hips again. Again, he made that low appreciative sound. He kept his feet planted and his hold on my wrists was firm.

"It's in your blood, siren." Rage rumbled through his words. He pulled back slightly and elevated his voice. His hands slid down my forearms. "You betrayed the Five Isles by working with our enemy behind our backs. You betrayed Exekiel when you violated your bond. And now you've betrayed your own people to save him."

I twisted and as I did, I slammed my elbow down on his wrist. His hold on me broke. He hissed in pain. I swiveled, strapped his arm behind him and slammed his face against the wall.

"I don't remember asking for your opinion."

The only opinion that mattered was one I might not get for a long time. What would Collette and the others think when they saw this footage? The sirens I'd killed had been their friends, but at the time, I hadn't thought about that. I'd just wanted to save Exekiel and destroy Loch. I didn't regret what I'd done but Vladimir did have a point. Somehow, in some way, I'd betrayed everyone. Maybe I was the villain after all.

22

VARIALLA:
HOW THE TABLES TURNED

I was led to the head table in the banquet hall. It was ornately decorated with white linen, purple lace and extravagant centerpieces. The iron chairs had high backs and some were cut to accommodate the wings of a Fae. Those around the table were Pre-Primaries, members of the Royal Court and the top-ranking contestants.

My already crap mood soured when I found my gold filigree place setting between Primary Adir and Exekiel V'alin. Talk about a shit sandwich.

I reluctantly slid into the seat and rested my hands on my lap to avoid touching either of them. My spine was stick straight. I sighed. It was going to be a long night.

"Ms. Von Hastings." The Primary's deep cold voice slid over me.

"Primary."

Nymph and goblin servers moved around us. They dished out our first course of soup and what looked like blue croutons.

"Congratulations on making it through Phase One of the Royal Games," he drawled. "I had hoped you wouldn't make it this far."

I snorted. At least he was honest.

"I'd hoped you drown in a pool of your own vomit. Looks like we're both disappointed."

My arm brushed Exekiel's as I reached for my silver goblet. Heat flushed my skin. I felt his stare flick to mine. From the corner of my eye, I saw the curve of his mouth. He knew what that simple touch had done to me.

"Everything alright?" he asked.

"Terrific." I took a large gulp of my drink.

Exekiel reached forwards for the water pitcher. His intoxicating scent of woodsmoke and warm apples washed over me. My eyes briefly fluttered closed and I breathed him in.

It was easier to resist Exekiel when he wasn't sitting right next to me. Easier to pretend that I hadn't replayed that moment of us in the woods and touched myself at least a thousand times thinking of him.

A rasping growl shuddered in his throat. Like he knew what I was thinking.

His pink eyes met mine. My upper lip curled between my teeth.

"Perhaps you would like another round." He held my gaze as he refilled his chalice and set the pitcher down.

Shit! I'd been so turned on; I'd let my mind shield drop. The Fae bastard had wandered right in.

I sniffed. "I don't know what you're talking about."

Exekiel grinned. He sat back in his seat and tilted his head towards me.

"You're going to have to get better at masking your scent from me, little bud," he whispered against the shell of my ear. I trembled. "Unless you want me to lay you down on this table and feast on you instead of the food."

Shit, the visual of him splaying me out on this table with my tits heaving, and my legs over his shoulders had my panties soaked.

I couldn't help it when I breathlessly said, "Promise?"

Exekiel's jaw tensed.

I licked my lips and turned my head ever so slightly towards his. Now we shared the same air. Our noses almost touched.

"Or would you prefer if I got on my knees for you beneath this table?"

When Exekiel's eyes met mine, there was a storm inside them. My breath hitched. His hand curled around my thigh then slid beneath the slit in my dress.

I didn't breathe.

He held my gaze as he stroked his pinky across my clit. I jerked so suddenly my knee slammed into the table. Heads turned towards us. I tried to laugh it off but it was breathless and high-pitched. Exekiel continued to fondle me beneath the table.

"I would happily have you on your knees, little bud," he murmured, soft enough that only I could hear. "I would guide your wet mouth along my cock and hold your head steady whilst I poured myself down your throat."

Sparks of desire fractured through my system. I pressed my legs together but that only trapped his fingers between them.

Exekiel groaned. His finger slid beneath my thong and met bare flesh. Holy shit. What was wrong with us? What was wrong with me? How many times did I have to reject this man before I actually meant it?

Exekiel teased my hole that spasmed around the tip of his finger.

"Shit," he whispered.

He seemed more turned on than I was. Which wasn't a surprise. I knew all too well how voracious the Shadow Saints sexual appetite was. I'd experienced him at his height of lust. It was so exquisite it had shuddered through my cells for days.

He worked one finger inside me. A moan was choked in my throat. It took everything I had not to roll my hips. Not to close my eyes and give in to the rush that pulsed between my legs.

Fuck. He pumped his finger faster and faster. I gripped the edge of the table. I was going to come, right here in the middle of a banquet with the man who'd chained me to a rack right beside me.

I pressed my lips together. My body shook. Exekiel slid in another finger. My head tipped back.

He stopped. I abruptly snapped back to my senses and pretended to work out knots in my neck. Then I grabbed my wine and took a deep gulp.

Exekiel resumed his motion. I almost choked. My skin thrummed. His fingers were soaked with my precum as he dipped them in and out of me.

I glanced at him through my lashes. He casually watched me and sipped from his chalice.

A moan escaped me. I quickly shoved a piece of bread into my mouth. I was so wet. So hot for him. His fingers pulsed deeper, harder. His pinky continued to assault my clit.

Fuck. *Fuck!* I was going to come.

I grabbed Exekiel's wrist to stop him. I couldn't do this; not here. Not now. Instead of pushing him away, I held him against me.

He unleashed a low groan. My nipples peaked at the sound. I rocked into him. I didn't care who saw. Again, he stopped. I almost growled in frustration.

I glared at him. Exekiel grinned and subtly shook his head.

He brought his mouth to my ear and whispered, "Show me that you can be a good girl and don't make a sound."

His words only made me need him more. If anyone looked at us now, I didn't know what they'd think.

I gripped the table tighter and nodded. He was only going to do this if we were discrete. If *I* was discrete.

When Exekiel started up again, the vicious pounding of his fingers sent me to Nirvana. Heat blazed through my skin. I couldn't sit still. But fuck, I had to. My hands slipped from the table and I grasped the chair. My nails dug into the soft velvet of the seat.

There was no way around it. My release swelled and twisted inside me. It urged its way higher and burned hotter. Until, at last, it broke free.

Sweat trickled between my breasts. My entire body quivered. With painstaking slowness, Exekiel withdrew his fingers. I watched as he brought those fingers to his mouth and sucked them clean. I almost came again.

In desperate need of a distraction so I didn't mount this man right here, I drained the rest of my drink in one gulp and accepted when a nymph came to refill it.

I didn't look at Exekiel. I didn't trust what I'd do if I did. I turned my attention to where Evangeline was discussing unrest in the mainland.

"You have to see it from both sides," she argued with Camal and a few Court members near her. "They're not responsible for the war and yet they're being punished for it."

"Punished?" a rake of a woman with pinched features shrieked. "They have all they could want in Evermore. I am sympathetic to their plight but by insisting that they stay in our lodgings and dine at our cafés, they're causing unnecessary turmoil."

Grateful for the distraction, I opened my mouth to retort.

Evangeline snapped, "The problem isn't two centaurs wanting to enjoy a meal in Infinity City. It is the small-minded, Fate-stained bastards who insist on chucking them out."

Adir laughed. It was clearly forced. "You'll have to forgive my mate. She's always been an idealistic dreamer."

"You were too, once!" The death glare she threw him was chilling.

I knew the Primary's weren't madly in love and had consorts in their own casts. Now I wondered if they even liked each other. Maybe they were the type of mates who could enjoy physical satisfaction without affection.

"You say that like being a dreamer is a bad thing, Primary," Lucinda stated from where she sat beside Second Primary, Evangeline.

He rolled his eyes. "Of Course, a Red Maiden Witch would say that. The lot of you believe this war can be won with declarations of love." He waved a lofty hand in mine and Exekiel's direction. I tried not to squirm. "Two mates divided to become two mates united, or some drivel like that."

He scoffed and those around him chuckled. I shifted in my seat and took another hefty slurp of my wine. When was the second course coming out?

"Don't suppose there's any hope of that happening?" Evangeline looked between us with a whisper of hope in her eyes.

"None," Exekiel growled.

The bite in his tone stung more than it should have.

"Especially not if the other contestants get their way and remove Exekiel from the competition," Camal chuckled but there was no laughter behind his eyes.

Exekiel arched a brow in a way that made him more irresistible than he already was.

Dear God, get me out of here.

He raised his cup and sneered. "They can try."

Tension crackled across the table. It was no secret that the other players were gunning for Exekiel's first place rank. In the Games, it was either win, die or serve. And with Exekiel at the helm, winning was almost an impossibility. A select few would be fortunate enough to get Council member positions but with Exekiel out of the picture, the playing field would be more even. Plus, it would put Camal in the lead.

The shifter sneered right back. His teeth seemed sharper, like he'd let some of his inner beast shine through.

Violent hacking coughs stole my attention. Every head swiveled to where a pale man with a whiskery beard and a balding head hunched over. He struggled to catch his breath. I hadn't been properly introduced but his picture was recently posted on Enchant-a-Gram. He was Fororsh; the lead crafter of the Collar.

Those around him thumped his back but then their eyes widened. Their faces turned purple and they too started coughing.

The craftsman's skin started to purple and foam frothed from his lips.

My heart raced.

"Poison!" someone gasped, then louder shouted, "poison!"

I gaped as more people at the head table started to choke and convulse. What the heck? I looked to Lucinda who thankfully seemed fine and as shell-shocked as I was.

"What the hell is going—" Adir was cut off by a sudden cough that had blood spurting from his mouth.

His eyes widened in horror. I didn't like the bastard but I matched his stricken stare. What was going on? Courtiers burst into action. They grasped him around the middle to try and force him to throw up.

Exekiel lurched back. His chair crashed to the floor. His wings extended and he turned his gleaming eyes on me.

I recognized the scent at the same time he must have. The bitter tang of the poison that was used on him the night Loch and the others had attacked. The night I'd bound our lives and tainted our bond. Only this scent was sharper—the toxin purer.

Exekiel looked like he was about to rip my spine out through my throat when the great doors flew open. Loch charged in with a horde of Outliers at his back. Centaurs, nymphs, werewolves, goblins and mostly sirens. Colette, Orla and Nile were with them.

My stomach turned.

Loch didn't break stride as he hurtled towards the head table, took a flying leap and landed on top of the plates and glasses that shattered beneath his boots. All around us, guests shrieked. Some ran for cover, whilst others reached for their weapons and power.

Evangeline shot to her feet.

Loch lifted a hand. "Please, don't get up." His crooked grin turned to me. "Hello, Princess."

My mind reeled. "What the fuck are you doing?"

Loch dragged a finger along his chin. "Making an entrance."

23

EXEKIEL:
NOT AGAIN

Not again.

The words repeated in my mind like a mantra; a prayer. This scene was too familiar. It cut too close to my fucking core.

The song the sirens sang now echoed the song they'd sung then. When they'd broken into my home and butchered my family. Like then, fear I didn't care to acknowledge held my heart in a vice but anger was quick to follow. Blinding white rage that had my shadows rising.

Not again.

The siren song rose. Each note carved open old wounds. Across the table, Dimitrius; a Fae member of the Council, coughed so violently, I heard the snap of his ribs. He collapsed, shaking, and foamed at the mouth. It was a different death this time, but the result was the same. The sirens had come and death followed.

"Surrender and all of this goes away, Protector!" Loch Orqanz roared.

The Rebel Leader strode the length of the table where countless lay dead. He kicked aside plates and sent goblets clattering. I watched each step of his murderous feet.

"Let us strap one of those pretty collars around your neck; strip your power, and I'll give you the antidote. All of this this suffering will end."

I vaulted up on the table. The impact reverberated through my thighs. I stalked towards the fucker. My shadows rose and coiled around my wrists. The symbols of the Fates lit up on my skin.

"There's your first mistake. You think I would bow to your whims to save the world." Ice hot hatred slid through my veins. "The trouble is, I would rather burn it to the ground than see it in your hands."

His eyes flickered.

I chuckled darkly. "That's right. There are no heroes here."

He skipped back with a sneer. "Do your worst!"

The ground shook. A booming roar bounced off the walls. My head snapped in the direction of the doors as a hulking giant charged in.

Fates, fuck me.

He was from the Hokuraz clan. The less humanoid of the cast. He was as tall as he was wide and more than tripled my height. His bare chest was thick with hair, his beard long and he had skin like burnished copper. His bulbous nose protruded over thin lips. Eyes small like black beads. On his lower half, he wore a tattered loincloth that strained over the swell of his enormous thighs. And two sharp horns curved from his distended brow.

Screams split the air. Glasses smashed and tables toppled.

Royal Court centaurs swarmed in on the giant's heels and tried to herd him back; their spears raised. But the beast moved surprisingly fast for his mammoth size.

The ground shuddered beneath the pound of his feet.

Behind him, the Council and Court members were ushered from the hall; to safety. No one seemed to notice the grin that curved Alexov's thin lips as he looked back at the scene stained in blood. As he looked to Loch and nodded.

White noise filled my ears. I was faced with my brothers' killer but the one who had orchestrated it was getting away.

"Alexov!" I bellowed at the top of my lungs.

I leapt from the table and rushed after him. This ended now.

I unleashed my shadows. They spilled across the room. I called on the Fates. *Ulius* was first to rise. A vibrant green trident amidst a whorl of black. My shadows twisted and took on its shape then skewered rebels on its end.

Qhithalas responded next. A blue crescent moon blazed within the black. Mimicking its shape, my shadows curved like a scythe and cut down our attackers. In a crowd, I withheld their ability to kill on touch but I didn't hold back their force.

"Alexov!"

I thundered through the mass and charged towards the great doors as they groaned closed.

Guards gathered in my path. To anyone watching it would look like they were trying to fend off the giant. However, there was something in their uniformed movement and the wary gazes they cast my way, that said they were intentionally trying to bar my path.

Whether they were as corrupt as the Court or just following orders, they weren't going to let me through those doors.

I tunneled deeper into my power. Piercing, harrowed cries rang out as my shadows claimed the world. One by one the fuckers fell. They tried to run, but no one could outrun me.

The screams matched those of the night the sirens had invaded my home. The sobs echoed the sounds of Satrialla. My rage burned with the same fire.

In the back of my mind, I heard Satrialla yell, "Enough!" just like she had that night when my fists had repeatedly struck the corpse of my nephew's killer. But it wasn't enough. Nothing would ever be enough.

24

VARIALLA:
PRETTY LITTLE PUPPET

The world was falling apart and I couldn't grasp the pieces. Exekiel had become a creature of night and sorrow. His shadows were an extension of his wrath and pain. Somehow, I felt it. The devastation of his loss. I wanted to take it away. I wanted to erase all of it.

Around me nobles, Court members and contestants lay dead. Poisoned by my people. We were supposed to be waiting until I won the Games and was in a position to make a change. We were supposed to be doing this right.

That was the only thing I'd been able to trust from Loch's mouth. That he would use me to get on the throne so that I could make a change. I wasn't naïve. I knew the bastard planned to enact his revenge once he claimed a seat of power but I'd had no intention of letting him through the doors. But this, wasn't what we'd planned. It wasn't uniting the isles; it was tearing them apart.

Exekiel's shadows billowed like sails of acrid smoke. They slammed into sirens, werewolves and nymphs with enough force to break their bones and send them careening into the walls.

Exekiel's eyes were dark pools of black. His stance was rigid and jaw clenched. He couldn't tell who was enemy or ally but he didn't seem to care. No Outlier was safe, not even those who bore the royal crest.

I dove across the table. The linen cloth was soaked with spilled soup and vomit. My skirts bunched up around my waist. Wet sludge coated the backs of my legs.

My feet hit the ground. I moved towards Exekiel, determined to somehow stop him. Someone grabbed my arm and I was wrenched back.

"No hello kiss?"

The floor vanished beneath my feet as I was dragged onto the table. Loch leapt down in front of me. He forced my legs apart and stepped between them.

I lurched back as he bowed his head to kiss me.

"Are you kidding?"

Loch made a sound between a growl and a sigh. He grasped my ass and yanked me against him. I slipped closer to the edge of the table; into the hard swell of his cock.

"And here I was thinking you'd missed me."

His hand closed around the back of my neck. He crushed my mouth to his with bruising force. His pelvis rocked into mine. My heart slammed into my ribcage. Loch urged his cold tongue between my lips as he pushed harder between my legs.

I tried to pull back but his hold on my head was like a steel vice. I whimpered into his mouth. Rage tore through my skin.

With a frustrated cry, I bit into his tongue until I tasted blood.

Loch reeled back. His eyes were wide with shock and fury. He spat blood from his mouth to the tiles. The back of his hand collided with my cheek. Water sprang to my eyes. My ears rang and my face stung.

He grasped my jaw and squeezed until my teeth cut into the flesh of my cheeks. The metallic taste of my own blood filled my mouth.

Desperate, I dredged up every scrap of my power. As soon as I felt it rise and sizzle at my fingertips, Loch siphoned it into himself. His ice blue eyes glowed. He laughed, cold and cruel.

"Aren't you sick of this dance?"

Releasing my face, Loch roughly grasped my thighs and wrenched them apart before he pushed himself between them once again.

"Stop fighting me!" His spit sprayed across my cheeks.

He pulled my legs up around him. My chest heaved. My mind raced. Blindly, my fingers searched the table. They closed around a steak knife. I raised it but Loch grabbed my wrist and held it in place.

"Stop!"

I didn't. I tried to drive the blade through his forehead but our strength was evenly matched. I felt the slow stir of his power claiming mine. I felt him slip inside me like oil and seize control.

His grip was painfully tight on my hip. The other threatened to snap every bone in my wrist.

"When will you get it, princess?" He leaned in and ran his tongue across my lips. "You're mine to do with as I please." He moved into me. Harder this time. Desire, I didn't want to feel, swept through me. "I own you."

The knife still trembled in my grip. Restrained by his hold on my wrist and the crux of this fucking bind. He was a monster; a maniac and he used me like his puppet.

"Get the fuck off me," I panted but my fight was fading. It was being replaced by a desperate need for him. His will was overriding my own. I blinked through the haze he tried to cloak me in. My soul thrashed inside my skin.

Loch grinned like he'd already won. It was inevitable. The bond demanded I give myself to him.

I groaned. He couldn't do this. He couldn't command me. One thing I'd learned growing up was that a person only had as much power over you as you gave them. I wouldn't let him take mine.

"Give up, Princess." Loch continued to grind into me as he laid me down on the table. Heated sparks shot through my skin. "I'm going to fuck you right here on the remains of our enemies."

He hitched up my dress and dug his nails into the backs of my thighs as he spread them wider.

"I'm going to make your mate watch me defile you," he pushed his hand between my legs and stroked a finger down my damp panties, in the exact spot Exekiel's hand had just been, "over and over again."

I moaned. His fingers hooked around my underwear and he tugged them down.

"But first I'm going to suck on this pussy until you're weeping down my throat."

I panted, "Can't wait."

I raised the knife he'd obviously forgotten I held, and slashed it across his face.

Blood sprayed over my chest, my face, my tongue. I bolted upright and shoved Loch aside.

"Varialla!" he barked. His hand was pressed over his blooded face.

He lunged for me. I dove off the table and charged into the web of shadows.

Exekiel was unhinged. His eyes were all-black including the whites around them. He stood still; a statue of destruction. There was no wild wrath or bellows of fury. Just cold and vicious brutality as his shadows slammed into my people; my friends, and coiled around the giant.

Most people's efforts were now focused on the creature, though some battled between each other. Inlander against Outlander. In one night, Loch had managed to unravel the threads of unity that I'd fought so hard to weave together.

Both sides were as fierce as the other. They wielded their powers as one would steel. Shifters shed their human skin and revealed the beast within. They charged at the giant with their teeth gnashing, claws extended. Fae soared into the air and wove clunking iron chains around the giant's neck.

Somewhere I heard Lucinda shout, "Stop. You're hurting him."

Was this one of her friends? One of the giants who had shown her kindness when the girls in her own coven had denied her; wrapped up their petty jealousy.

The Autumn elves called to the wood and hefted up the weighted tables. They flung them at a group of sirens. Their song was silenced and those who had been ensnared by it slumped to the ground; their noses bloody.

I took off towards Exekiel. Power plumed in my limbs and my inner dragon roared.

"Odus!"

My heart lurched. I spun and caught sight of Odus. His eyes were wide with wonder and his smile was bright as he raced towards another centaur. It was a hulking brute who shared his shaggy blonde hair and deep brown coat. His brother, if I had to guess. At the very least, he was family.

Odus bellowed a name. The centaur turned and then both were thrown sideways by Exekiel's power. The brother disappeared into the chaos but I watched in muted horror as Odus shot through the air and was speared by an ice-sculpture of a jouster in motion.

Jia screamed. I think I did too. The ice lance carved through Odus' chest and left him twitching on the end. My knees buckled.

"Odus!" Jia's cries left me reeling; broken.

Not Odus. He was good and kind and allowed to be here. He didn't deserve this. None of us deserved this. And right now, I didn't know which bastard was more to blame. Exekiel or Loch. Both were so blinded by rage and grief they couldn't see past it. Both were so desperate to save what was theirs that they damned everything and everyone else.

"If bitches like you stayed where you belonged, none of this would be happening. Fucking Outlier whore!"

I swiveled in search of the voices. My stomach pitched when I spotted a group of Fae surrounding Eudora. Bile rose in my throat. How could things be this bad?

My friend held up her hands and stepped back. She tried to argue that she'd been loyal, but the fuckers didn't care. Three of the Fae shared a sneer, then they pounced.

"Eudora!" Power imbued my shout.

One of the Fae stumbled. Another doubled over covering his ears, but another struck Eudora across the face.

She cried out and went down as he and three others dove on top of her. My heart slammed into my ribs.

"Eudora!"

Again, a few of the Fae faltered, but I couldn't see what those on the ground were doing to her.

I raced towards them, gathering spheres of power in my hands.

The ground tilted then tore open. The world spun and I tumbled through the gap.

My stomach dipped. Once again, I was descending into the bleak shadows of the Games.

Not now! I struggled against the pull of magic; fought my way to my friend's side, but it was useless.

No!

A robotic voice announced: **"Phase Two: Activated."**

25

EXEKIEL:
CLEVER WITCH

The world was my canvas. A tableau of black and white except for the crimson glow that outlined those around me. A Fae with a raised fist. A satyr that charged forward with his head bowed and horns angled. A shifter that was in mid-transformation. Within the veil of my shadows, I saw it all in frozen images that danced staccato across my mind.

When I tumbled back into the abyss of the Games, it was not with rage but with acceptance. I already knew this wasn't a battle I could charge in and fight with fists and vows of vengeance. The names on that parchment, had only been a fraction of those who'd been seduced by the Court or had their minds corrupted by sirens.

Tonight, I'd let myself forget that this wasn't a tavern brawl but a war. It would take planning and strategy. I would need every weapon in my arsenal to take them down. No matter what, I would destroy them. I would tear down their tower brick by brick.

The fuckers at the top, I'd leave 'til last. I'd let them stew in their fear as they felt me moving closer. Until the day I finally delivered them to Zorsch in small bloody pieces.

Around me, players wept whilst others roared their agony to Fatevale. I knew the taste of their grief well.

I shoved to my feet and almost tripped over the satchel I'd had when I was pulled from the Games. It rested on the ground beside me. I scooped it up, flung it over my shoulder, and stalked across the mudded ground.

"Exekiel?" Vivienne called after me.

I glanced at her; a quick scan to make sure she was alright. Nothing more than a slash on her lip and a bruised eye.

I turned and took off.

"Exekiel!" she shouted.

I didn't stop. Didn't look back. I had a witch to catch.

Lucinda Ironclaw had been on my radar ever since she'd carved a crack in my barrier and formed a friendship with a female giant. They'd both been young at the time. The friendship was harmless so, as I often did, I looked the other way. But I'd kept my eye on the witch. She was powerful and not afraid to break the rules.

Now that little rebellious streak might work in my favor. Tonight, she'd called that giant by name and where everyone had been running from it, she'd been running to it.

"*Fadea.*"

The symbol of the Huntress Fate lit up on my forearm and sharpened my sense of smell and sight. I inhaled. It didn't take long to detect the familiar trace of cranberry and myrrh on the air. The witch was close.

I checked my phone and scrolled through the video log until I found the footage I was looking for. It was taken the night Lucinda had helped Varialla use blood magic to save my life.

The Red Maiden Coven were vocal about their beliefs that Varialla and I were destined to work together and end the war. So, the witch's willingness to help Varialla wasn't unusual. The fact that she'd been in the gardens at all, supposedly on her own, was what had stood out to me.

Naturally, I did some digging and what I found was enough to have the witch begging to do whatever I asked.

I ducked beneath branches and used my blades to slash through vines. The witch's scent drew closer. Veiled in shadows, I raced through the dark and after her.

Eventually, I caught a glimpse of her through the trees. She seemed to have been separated from her allies which worked in my favor. The witch ran alongside a wolf-shifter but not Calder. This wolf barely spared her a glance. It seemed more like they'd just ended up on the same path.

I stole towards her. The witch tensed, as if she sensed me coming. Her head snapped in my direction a second before I slammed a hand over her mouth and wrenched her back between the trees. She thrashed. I strapped my arm around her waist and ran. The world blurred as we streaked passed.

She didn't stop fighting and I didn't slow down until we arrived at an orb-pod. I shoved her inside the dome and bolted the metal door behind me.

Lucinda reeled around; her ice-grey eyes shone. Her lip bled. I knew she'd intentionally bitten it. Now the scent of her blood magic filled the space.

"I know your secret."

Her nostrils flared. The air was still coated with the iron of her power but she didn't unleash it.

"What secret?"

"The one that's been feeding you information since the Trials." I shrugged off my tailcoat and flung it over the back of the lone chair in the space.

Lucinda's eyes narrowed. "I don't know what you're talking about."

"Perhaps this will jog your memory."

I swiped my finger across the translucent screen of my phone. A hologram of the footage emerged. I stretched my fingers over it and the scene grew until it filled half the room.

There, in an abandoned passageway in an old quarter of the palace, Lucinda was half perched on a windowsill. She had one hand braced on the glass. Her skirts were trussed up around her waist and a female's head was buried beneath them.

The witch palmed her breast in her other hand. Deep, breathless moans filled the pod as the other female devoured her. Out of respect, I looked away and watched Lucinda instead.

Her dark skin paled. Right now, her lovers face was hidden between her thighs but the dress she wore was unmistakable. And thanks to the orb operator who had watched the footage several times, I knew that it went on to confirm her identity. To show them discuss how she would try to get as much information on the Games as she had during the Trials.

I raked two fingers down through the air. The volume lowered. I let the video continue. I let her see just how much damning evidence I had on her. How it was in her best interest to see things my way.

"I'm sure you already know the consequence of a member of the Royal Court being involved with a contestant of the Games."

Lucinda's throat bobbed with her swallow. Her gaze was glued to the hologram. She hadn't just gone and had an affair with any member of the Court but with Evangeline Degalos; Second Primary and mate to Adir Degalos.

It was no secret that both Primary's had a partner from their own cast, but these partners were of noble blood and had been approved and vetted by the Council. Lucinda was not. Lucinda was a risk to the Court, and therefore Evangeline had kept her a secret. A secret that could get them both killed.

The only reason Adir had been allowed to pursue Varialla was because the Court had believed he could coerce her into some sort of alliance and convince her to turn on her people.

Lucinda's fists clenched at her sides. Her eyes shifted as if she suspected she could find some way out of this.

I leaned against the wall and crossed my ankles. "Considering your close friendship with the sea-witch, I'm sure the Court would believe me when I say she also benefited from your connection with the Second Primary."

Lucinda licked her lips. Her eyes flicked to the shadows that swirled behind me like a cape caught in a breeze.

"Her right to the throne would be revoked. She'd be considered as much of an Outlier as the rest of them."

Panic flashed in the witch's eyes. Just the reaction I was going for.

At last, she snarled, "Since you haven't turned us in, I assume you want something."

Somehow, she seemed to look down on me though my height dwarfed hers.

I smirked. "Clever witch."

26

VARIALLA:
LET ME OUT

My fists pounded on the metal door. My mind spun. One minute, I'd been falling back into the Games. The next, I was here. In a metal dome; a camera pod, if I remembered correctly. It was where I was supposed to share my thoughts with the audience and receive supplies from supporters, if they'd sent any.

Surely, not now. Whilst the world outside burned.

"Let me out!" I shouted.

I jiggled the door handle but it didn't budge. The metal clanged beneath my fists when I struck it again.

"Hello?"

I had to get out there. Had to get the hell out of these Games and back to the banquet hall. I had to get to Eudora.

My legs almost gave out. I wasn't sure but I'd thought I'd heard her scream as I was dragged back into the Fields of Fury.

I tried the door handle again. There had to be a way out. I swiveled and scanned the small space. There was nothing more than a clear plastic chair, a small glass table and a row of camera-orbs that blinked red on the opposite wall. In the center of the table was a black metal box with my name on it.

Curiosity couldn't erase the fear that churned in my chest.

Fuck. I hoped Odus was okay. I had to believe that he was. The lance had gone through him but maybe it hadn't hit anything vital. He'd still been alive when I'd seen him—his body twitching. I sucked down a breath.

There were countless healers in that place. They could patch him up before he bled out. But would they? Would they help an Outlier? Even one who technically had the right to be on their shores? After tonight, I wasn't sure.

The only thing I could still say for certain was that I had to get on that throne. I wouldn't roll over and let myself or my people be stripped of their power and leashed like fucking dogs. I wouldn't let these senseless battles keep playing out.

Nor would I let the Crown be usurped by Loch. I didn't know what he had planned, but I couldn't let him drag this Realm to ruin, and its people into a war, most of them didn't want.

Less than a year ago, I hadn't had much more than the clothes on my back to care about. It had been a sad and lonely existence. I always swore that if I found a shred of joy, I would make the most of it. Anything that brought me happiness, no matter how small, deserved to be appreciated.

Now, I had a family, a kingdom, an entire realm that depended on me. I wouldn't see them fall into the claws of monsters.

"For fucks sake, open this door!" I slammed my palm against it.

"Hello, Varialla."

I spun around. There was no one there but the camera-orb in front of me now blinked green.

I stalked towards the chair. "You have to open the door."

"How are you finding the Games so far?" said the same robotic female voice.

It was like I hadn't spoken.

My jaw clenched. "This is no game. Now let me out."

I stormed back towards the door and yanked on the handle. It merely rattled in my grip. The door remained closed.

"Are you aware that many of the other players fear you after you manipulated them in Phase One?

I paced the pod. My heels clicked against the black metal tiles.

My heart was back in the palace with Eudora, Colette, Odus and the others. But my head had to remain in the Games. It was clear I wasn't getting out of here unless I played along.

"No." I breathed evenly. "I wasn't aware of that."

"How does that make you feel?"

I turned to the camera. The blinking green light on the orbs seemed to track every flicker of my lashes. In that moment, I felt like I wanted to punch the bloody thing in its rounded lens. I swallowed my rising anger.

I had to choose my words carefully. I hated to admit it but Exekiel had had a point. A siren's power was already feared and I'd only added to that.

Thanks to my bond with Loch, I knew what it felt like to be controlled and commanded against your will. And that was what I'd done to the other players.

"I don't blame them." I finally said. My foot tapped impatiently on the floor. "To be honest, I'd just wanted time to slow down so that I could catch up. Instead, the players had slowed down and time remained the same."

"When you realized this, you kept going." The disembodied voice stated. **"You used your gifts to get ahead in the Games and claim a key. How can the people trust you to not do the same to them? To not brainwash the entire realm?"**

My fingers curled around the back of the chair. "I would never abuse my power like that."

"You already did."

"To buy myself a bit of time."

"To put yourself in the lead."

For fucks sake. Since when did robots take sides?

"Do you deny it?"

I scowled at the camera. I knew this show thrived on drama but why did I always seem to be at the center of it? And now was not the time.

"Isn't my voice my power?" I snapped. "How is me using it to win the level any different to a shifter using their inner beast? Or a Fae using compulsion, for that matter?"

"Those abilities do not affect everyone, only themselves and those who get in their way."

I clenched my fists. "Then maybe everyone should stay out of my way."

It might have been the wrong thing to say. If this was Hollywood, I'd be a PR nightmare. But I was so done with placating these assholes. Of shrinking my power and strength to make them feel larger.

Maybe now, Primary Adir would think twice before he tried to torture me. Exekiel wouldn't be so keen to strap a collar around my neck. Maybe Alexov wouldn't root in my brain despite my agonized screams, and Loch wouldn't be so quick to put his hands on me.

Maybe it was time they all learnt to back the fuck off. These bastards had been controlling and manipulating me since I got here. I was done being forced into their mold.

The voice said nothing. I scrubbed a hand down my face. Every second I spent here, the Games continued without me. The players drew closer to the next level, to the keys, to the throne.

I smoothed a hand down the ends of my French braid and looked directly at the camera in front of me and on those who watched on the other side.

"Look, I've been an outcast my entire life. I didn't fit in in the human realm and I was hated here before I even arrived. Despite my recent slip, I would never intentionally take anyone's freedom because I know what it's like to feel trapped. I would never deprive someone of food, because I know what it's like to go hungry. I would never make anyone feel as insignificant as I was made to feel my whole life." I stood taller. "However, I won't apologize for finally finding my inner strength and using it in the hopes of defending those who can't currently defend themselves. Now let me out of this room, so I can win the Games."

The answering silence seemed endless. It was only punctuated by the pound of blood in my ears.

"Well done, Varialla." There was a hint of pride in the robotic voice when it finally spoke. **"The viewers response to this has been positive."**

A key appeared on the table. It must have been to unlock the box. I dove on it and shoved the key into the lock. At this point, I didn't care what was inside. I just wanted to get this over with so I could leave. The box clicked open. I lifted the weighted lid.

Inside was a vine of hydra-weed. My heart leapt. One bite of that and my thirst would be quenched for almost a day. Beside it, was a vial of deep red water. I uncorked the lid and sniffed.

Pippy-root tea. Why on Earth had they sent me a contraceptive? Attached to the lid with a piece of brown string was a note.

I unfolded it and read:

Just in case you and the Shadow Saint can't stop yourselves the next time he has you pinned against a tree.

My cheeks burned and I hastily tossed the note back into the box. Ever since my Poisoned Heart had been discovered, that footage of me and Exekiel in the woods was rooted out. Now, it was broadcasted on repeat. The last thing I needed right now was the memory of Exekiel and his fingers inside me. I let out a breath.

"Are you alright, Varialla?"

"Of course," I grumbled and pulled out a small glass box next.

Inside were gold leaves rimmed in blue. I peered closer. I recognized them from a potion's book I'd recently read. Oblivium; a plant with the power to put others to sleep—maybe for a lifetime. I tucked it and the weed into the satchel slung over my shoulder.

"Thank you," I said to the cameras then got to my feet.

"Don't forget your tea." The voice called. I could have sworn there was laughter in the tone.

What kind of robot was this? **"We all know you'll need it."**

I sauntered towards the door. "When it comes to the Shadow Saint, all I need is for him to lose the Games."

"What you need is for him to bend—" I stepped outside and slammed the door.

I was no longer convinced that that voice was a robot. Probably some gossip girl wannabe using a voice distortion device.

I pulled out my phone. The hologram map emerged. I had to find the others. They were already on their way to the next level.

A gust of wind swirled around me. I shivered. *Shit.* I hadn't planned to be wearing this dress when I returned to the Games. The shimmering blue chiffon offered no warmth and the color made blending in virtually impossible. At least, the slits cut up to my hips made running easy. However, the same couldn't be said for my strappy gold sandals. They wouldn't last a day.

27

VARIALLA:
SINK FAST

When I finally found the others, I wasn't the only one they'd lost during the commotion. Apparently, Lucinda was missing as well. I swallowed the knot of unease in my gut and kept running. I'd caught up. She would too.

The trees became less dense the further we ran. Soon the ground changed from mud to rock. Loose pebbles stabbed into the soles of my sandals and the straps threatened to snap. I didn't slow down. Fueled with a fresh determination, I raced on but constantly glanced back for Lucinda.

Goather had warned us that the Games got more deadly with each Phase due to other players trying to take out the competition. Lucinda was ranked at number eight, and those in the top ten were the biggest targets.

"I'm sure she's right behind us," Maximus puffed as he jogged beside me.

It was hard to tell if he was trying to convince me or himself.

I nodded. "Maybe she also got taken to a camera pod."

"Exactly."

We gave each other half smiles. I was pretty sure neither of us would relax until Lucinda was with us.

"The Shadow Saint can't win," Jia said gruffly. Her eyes were bloodshot. "He can't win."

She ran a few steps ahead of me. When her knees trembled. I gripped her arm to steady her. A tear slipped off the end of her nose. My heart cracked.

"Jia." I kept my tone firm.

We couldn't fall apart. Not now. Not yet.

"He can't win!" she shouted and pulled out of my grip. She roughly scrubbed away the tears that tracked down her cheeks. "You saw his shadows tonight. No matter what he claims, he's not on the Outliers side."

Tonight, Exekiel's shadows hadn't cared—*he* hadn't cared—if the Outlier bore a citizen stamp or if, like Odus and Eudora, they had been invited to the banquet by an inlander. All he'd seen was what they were and his shadows had restrained them one way or another. They'd skewered them on ice sculptures and shattered their bones.

"You're right." I flipped open my satchel. "Which is why I have a plan." I pushed my hand inside the side pocket and pulled out the small box of Oblivium.

I frowned when my fingers brushed the smooth glass vial of Pippy-root. I'd deliberately left it on the table. What was wrong with that robot?

Jia blinked at me then looked at what I held.

"That's Oblivium." Something other than grief shone in her eyes.

"It's a way to get our enemies out of the Games."

Oblivium had the ability to put someone in an eternal sleep. If I got the dose right, I could take Exekiel and his allies out for the duration of the Games.

Someone screamed. I skidded to a halt and gaped at the players ahead of us. They were sinking. At least five contestants were sinking beneath the ground. The harder they fought to get free, the faster they sank.

"Quicksand," Jia gasped.

My heart beat in my throat. I'd seen a few shows where people grabbed onto branches or low hanging vines to heave themselves out of quicksand. But there was nothing around this pit.

An ivory arch that led to level six glimmered on the other side. It was where we needed to go. How were we supposed to get there?

I swept my gaze across the barren land. Between the rocks that rose like waves, there were slabs of wood stacked together.

"We must have to use the wood to get across," I whispered and ran towards a pile.

Kylin followed. "They should give us a few seconds to leap across before they sink instead of us."

"A few seconds is better than nothing." I sounded more confident than I felt as I wiped my palms on the tattered gown.

The other players must have had the same idea. They each took off and snatched up as much wood as they could carry. I did the same.

I raced towards the sand. The wood was snatched from my hands by an invisible force.

"What the fuck?"

I reeled around to see that the same had happened to the others. Every contestant frowned and we each rushed to retrieve the wood.

I grabbed one then scooped up another. A force slammed into me and I was flung backwards. My head cracked against the rocks. Pain spliced through my skull. The slabs were once again torn from my grip and restacked. Splinters shredded my palms.

"We can only take one," I murmured.

My thoughts were numb with terror as I staggered to my feet.

We could only take one piece of wood each to make it across the sprawling stretch of quicksand that was eager to devour us. That meant, that even with the five of us working together, we had about a minute, to get to the archway that gleamed on the other side.

"Maybe I could manipulate the wind to carry us part of the way," Kylin suggested.

Although, the air was still.

Jia's wings ruffled at her back. "I can carry one of you with me."

Her stare hit mine. If anyone was getting across this sand besides her, she was going to make sure it was me.

Someone shrieked, "Get off!"

I spun to see two players fighting in the middle of the sand. One girl—a shifter, I think—tried to lunge onto the slab of wood she'd set down in front of her, but another girl held onto her blouse and tried to throw her off. I recognized the rake of a girl with rosy skin and dark curls. Salanda Bunch. The bitch who'd been one of Lola Black's accomplices the night they'd tried to kill me by throwing me off a cliff.

Salanda gripped the shifters shoulders and with a blood-curdling cry shoved the girl into the sand.

The shifter screamed. Her body half transformed into a bear. With a roar, her paw swiped for Salanda. Only halfway into her shift, she cried out and immediately rippled back to her human form.

Shit. Was the sand a no magic zone?

My question was answered when a Fae freed his wings and attempted to fly over the pit. He struck a shimmer of light and was knocked down beneath the surface.

My stomach lurched. Players screamed. Others cheered. No magic. No flight.

The shifter scrabbled to get back onto the wood Salanda now occupied, but it was too late. The sand had a hold of her and the more she thrashed, the tighter it held. Inch by inch she was pulled beneath.

"Ovette!" A male elf bawled from the shore.

Ovette, the shifter, never stopped screaming. She cursed Salanda's name until the sand filled her mouth and her words became choked.

Fuck.

Other contestants barely seemed to notice. They surged forwards and leapt from one wooden slab to another. Salanda wasn't the only one who was using the opportunity to cull the competition. Countless players charged after each other rather than aiming for the shore on the other side. Then again, maybe they were doing it so they could steal the other players wood and guarantee they had enough to make it all the way across.

"I see him," a familiar voice bellowed.

I turned to where Camal Silverhound and at least ten others had turned away from the sand. Their postures were stiff like they were braced for a fight.

A powerful figure emerged from the trees and swept across the rocky ground. His shadows trailed behind him like a wave of night. Even from a distance, lit only by the moon, Exekiel looked unforgivably stunning. His dark hair was disheveled. His piercing eyes were sharp and a bright, blazing pink. He must have had a change of clothes in his sack because he now wore fitted black leathers. My chest tightened.

Behind him, Vivienne and the others followed. None of them slowed as they approached Camal and his allies. If anything, they ran faster.

Exekiel didn't miss a step. His leathers clung to his honed physique and he whipped daggers from their sheaths faster than I could blink. One by one, they met their mark. The kneecap of a shifter. The wielding hand of a warlock. Every injury was precise; intent to wound but not kill.

I couldn't look away. He was captivating. An avenging god set to destroy the world. On his heels, the others fought just as fiercely.

"What are you doing?" Jia shrieked.

I whipped around and saw that she, Calder, and Kylin had moved to the edge of the quicksand.

Other players were racing past them. If we stayed much longer, our ranks would plummet. I glanced back at the fight. Exekiel had Camal's wolf form in a headlock. It was pretty obvious who was going to win this fight. I scanned the space behind him.

Still no Lucinda.

Maximus met my gaze. He pressed his lips together. I knew we were thinking the same thing. She should be here by now.

"We have to go!" Calder shouted but his stare also swept the land; searching. He grimaced and hefted up his slab of wood. "We have to go. Now."

28

VARIALLA:
QUICK SINKING

My gut was in knots as I balanced on the precipice of the quicksand pit. My palms were clammy. My throat was bone dry. The sand was about half the size of a football field and we were going to attempt to cross it with nothing but five fragile pieces of wood.

Kylin shouted, "I'll take the lead."

Before any of us could say anything, she placed her wood about an arm's length away on the sand and we were off.

Jia jumped on after Kylin and placed her wood further in front. As she and Kylin leapt onto it, the rest of us followed with Calder's larger frame at the rear.

Sweat peppered my brow. My breaths sawed out of me. My legs shook as I rushed forward and bent to lay my own slab of wood down.

"I'm going to push it even further ahead." I shouted. "We'll have to really jump."

It was a risk. The sand was almost as unsteady as water but as thick as tar. If I pushed it too hard, the wood would drift away. But if I didn't shove it hard enough, it would stay too close. We needed to cover more ground if we hoped to make it across. Fear had my heart its clutch.

Jump or drown. Those were our options.

I swallowed the dread that climbed up my throat, nudged the wood a few feet away then leapt. My gut tightened. My body was suspended above a pit of death. Then my toes hit the wood. I wobbled precariously on the edge. Maximus gasped and jumped after me.

He caught my arm before I toppled over.

"Don't you dare," he murmured. "Of all of us, you must survive."

Apparently, they didn't believe the Outliers would follow anyone else. It had to be me on the throne; someone who belonged to both sides.

My smile was shaky. I reached out and took the wood he held beneath his arm. As the others rushed to join us, I turned to set it down. My pulse pounded in my ears. My fingers were ice cold. We were about halfway across the field but were already down to our last two pieces of wood.

Sand seeped over the edge of the slab we were on. It brushed the tips of my toes.

"Shit," Kylin rocked back, trying to get out of range.

The wood bobbed fiercely beneath us and sank faster. Ignoring the cries of the other players as someone didn't make it, I knelt and placed the new slab in front of this one and shoved it forwards.

I didn't wait before I leapt. The others were quick to follow. Calder passed his own piece of wood forwards.

This was it. Our last sheet of wood. We were more than halfway now but the distance was still too far to jump. We wouldn't make it. Not unless we took somebody else's wood and left them to die in our place. The thought left a bitter taste in my mouth. They wouldn't hesitate if the roles were reversed but it didn't feel right.

Either way, it wasn't an option. There was no one around. Only a handful of contestants remained which meant we were dangerously close to finishing this level last and taking a nosedive in the ranks. Or worse, not making it across at all.

"Get ready!" I called.

I set the final piece of wood down, pushed it harder than I had before and jumped.

I almost didn't make it. The distance felt enormous. I had to splay my legs as wide as I could. My toes skimmed the edge and I stumbled forward; my arms out at the sides to keep my balance.

The wood bounced as the others landed behind me. Bile that rose in my throat. We were out of options and nowhere near close enough.

My gaze swept over my friends. Fear shone in their eyes. The same fear that made my heart pound against my ribs.

The worst thing was that if Lucinda was here, we might have made it. The distance was huge but one more plank of wood could have been the difference between whether we sank or soared.

"There!" Jia rushed forwards and knelt down.

Wood. My heart leapt.

Whoever had been on it was long gone. It was half submerged beneath the sand but it was better than nothing. It drifted not too far away.

Jia reached for it. My breath froze in my lungs. Her fingers brushed its edge but the touch pushed it further away. *Shit.* The wood we were on was sinking fast. Calder growled. Being the heaviest, the plank of wood had tilted slightly and the sand was already creeping around the soles of his feet.

Shit. Shit. Shit. I had to think. There had to be something we could do.

Jia bowed her head. "I always told Odus I would find a way to save his people."

She glanced at me. Her smile was sad.

"We will," I promised.

My thoughts raced. There had to be some way out of this. We couldn't just be dragged into the depths below. Our best chance was to jump. From this distance, I wasn't sure any of us would make it, but it was better than just standing here.

Jia stood and offered a weak smile. "The best thing I can do for his people is save you."

I realized too late what she meant when she stepped back and threw herself into the sand. A scream broke from my lips.

"Jump on me!" she bellowed. "Quickly!"

The sand had already started to mold around her body.

"Jia!" I screamed.

"Now!" she shouted.

There was no fear in her voice, only pure determination.

"I didn't do this to let us all die!"

Fuck. She was right. The last thing I wanted to do was to leap on my friend and use her as a stepping stone to safety whilst she drowned, but it was already in motion. Now she either died for something or for nothing.

I leapt. Jia was further away than the previous planks of wood and I did my best to contain my weight as I landed on her stomach.

She grunted.

"Jia, please." I sobbed. "Don't do this!"

But it was done. The sand was already claiming her and as the others piled on, she sank faster.

She lifted her arm. I grasped her hand.

"Go and change the world," she whispered.

I shook my head and clung tight to her hand.

Kylin murmured, "May you go with the brave and the blessed, sister."

She lunged the final distance and just made it to the shore. She swiveled back. Her dark form shadowed by the archway that now shone brighter behind her.

"Level Five will be deactivated in 20, 19..." called the disembodied voice I'd come to loathe.

The archway shuddered and started to shrink. My gut punched. Were they serious?

"The Fates will honor you," Calder called then somersaulted into the air and finally hit solid ground.

I didn't have space inside me to feel relieved. All I felt was bone deep dread. We couldn't leave Jia here.

"16, 15"

"I will ensure a monument is built in your likeness," Maximus promised.

He bent, brushed his lips across her knuckles then jumped with the grace of a dancer. I didn't breathe until his toes skimmed the bank. Calder and Kylin heaved him forwards to safety.

"11, 10..."

It was my turn.

My gaze collided with Jia's. I didn't know what to say and didn't have the time to say it. I swallowed around the lump in my throat and squeezed her hand.

"Thank you," I whispered. "Odus' people will be freed."

It wasn't much in the grand scheme of things but what else could I say in ten seconds?

I pressed my lips together, steeled my resolve then finally, I leapt. For one terrifying moment, I was airborne above the rolling sludge then my feet struck land. My toes teetered on the edge of the bank. My arms pinwheeled. Maximus grabbed my hands and pulled me further ashore.

Immediately, I spun back to where Jia was almost completely submerged. Icy fear stuck its claws into my chest and pierced my heart. I couldn't breathe. Couldn't move. I was frozen, wide-eyed and screaming internally. Jia was the one sinking but I felt like I was drowning.

"6, 5…"

She waved the hand that was still extended as the sand rose up and slid around her head.

"Forever reign, our Queen," she bellowed.

The sand rolled over her face. It covered her mouth and filled her nose, then pulled her under entirely.

"4, 3…"

"Jia!" I almost climbed in after her, as if I could somehow pull her out. "Jia!"

Strong arms strapped around my waist and dragged me away as I screamed at the sky. The ground shook. The light of the archway flickered as my power rallied. It surged towards nothing and everything.

Those who were still out on the sand yelped and wobbled as a gale of my anguish threatened to send them flying. I couldn't stop. I couldn't suppress the cry of my soul.

Friendship, love—I'd lived my life without either and I knew what precious gifts they were. Gifts that could cause the greatest pain but also the greatest joy. I didn't take it for granted. I treasured every friend I'd made since coming to the Five Isle's but I was burying too many of them. And the X that marked the spot, was the scar across my heart.

Warmth fell over me. The light of the archway grew so bright I had to close my eyes. The feel of the arms faded. Then I fell.

29

EXEKIEL:
MAZE-MERIZING

There had never been a silence more complete than this. One minute I'd been falling through an archway amidst howling winds and cries of grief. Now I was face down in the dirt.

Grass tickled my nostrils. Something hard and metal dug into my forehead. I reached for it and my hand closed around a glowing blue key.

With a groan, I rolled onto my back and tucked the key into my satchel. Level five was over. Where had the Games belched me out this time?

I sat up; my elbow propped on one knee and my head cradled in my hand. I'd used a lot of power tonight. It had started to take its toll.

On either side of me, hedge walls rose up high enough to rival the night sky. Beneath me the ground was grainy concrete. Ahead and behind there stretched a seemingly endless path. I was in a maze.

Fantastic.

I got to my feet, dusted my hands off and relished the release of my wings. They'd been tucked in for too long. Now they sprawled behind me and I rolled my shoulders.

I didn't need to attempt to fly to know that this was a no-fly zone. I felt the same static energy in the air that had lingered over the pit of quicksand. This meant the only way out was to walk.

With my hand rested on the pommel of the sword at my side—Goldie, I called her, on account of her golden blade—I moved down the eerily quiet path. There wasn't a whisper of wind nor caw of a bird. It was like the entire realm held its breath. I dug into my satchel and pulled out my phone.

The map of the maze emerged from the paper-thin screen to reveal an exact replica of the green hedge walls, and winding beige paths that overlapped and intersected. Some were blocked by dead-ends, others doubled back on themselves. At the base of the map, in golden letters, were the words: Level Six.

Stick figures moved along the paths. One for each player. Their colors indicated their rank. Red was the most common color for those who ranked outside the top ten. The nine yellows were those who ranked from two to ten. Then there was one green; the highest ranked player. Assuming my rank hadn't changed, every contestant in this fucking maze knew exactly where I was.

A group of red figures converged near the center. I didn't know how they'd found each other so fast. Although the red players had been placed closer together. Now the group moved with deliberate intent towards a yellow.

They charged from both ends of the path and pounced. The yellow stick figure fought wildly but it wasn't long before they winked out and vanished from the map. On the other side of the maze another figure changed from red to yellow.

My jaw clenched. Immediately my thoughts went to Vivienne, Nikolai and even that bastard, Kraxus. There was no way of knowing who had just been taken out of the Games but most in the top ten were my allies and those who weren't, belonged to Camal or her. The one girl who seemed to possess my mind.

The last time I'd seen Varialla she'd been dangerously bobbing across the sand. But I knew she'd made it. I wouldn't be here if she hadn't. I hated the level of comfort that thought gave me. The sea-witch's wellbeing shouldn't have mattered to me more than its relation to my own, but the sheer relief I felt was born from knowing she was safe.

I kept one eye on the map and one eye on the path as I trekked ahead. There was no indication of where the keys might be to end this level, but a black arrow blinked at a point that read: Level 7.

It looked far, which meant that the maze had been designed to test us. Surviving it would be the challenge. I pulled out my waterskin which was barely half full and took a deep pull. I'd have to ration the rest until I found some kind of spring to replenish. My food reserves were better. A good portion of fruit, food packets and pickled meat. It would have to do.

I didn't know how long I walked but I stopped when a red figure on the map disappeared and reappeared on the path next to mine. I crept closer to the wall on my left and peered through. All I saw were densely packed leaves and scuttling insects. Bulbador bugs and Caliug worms—both poisonous.

I glanced back at the map. Again, the red figure vanished and reemerged. They were now on the path to my right. It must have been a warlock. Unlike witches, extremely powerful warlocks had the ability to create portals. Temporary doorways that led from one place to another. The distance was never far and the accuracy was never precise. Whoever this warlock was, they seemed to be looking for me.

I slid my phone into my pocket. The last thing I needed was to face off with some desperate player who thought they could take me on. It would be embarrassing for them; a waste of time and energy for me. I wanted to reserve my strength for when it mattered. There was no telling how long I'd be stuck in this place.

Swallowing a curse, I unsheathed Delilah, my short sword. Cloaked in shadows, I raced forward and surged into the warlock's path.

"Shit!" He gasped.

His magic flared in his fingers and illuminated the dark. I dropped low and slashed Delilah across his Achilles tendon. Blood sprayed onto my skin as the back of his ankle opened. The warlock screamed. His knees struck the ground. The coppery scent of his blood filled the space between us.

I kicked him onto his back. He yelped. Egron Makaw—one of Camal's confidants.

"Word of advice," I squatted and cut through the supplies belt at his waist. "If you're planning a surprise attack, make sure your opponent doesn't have a map with you on it."

I took his water and food packets for myself. He wouldn't need them now. The Healers would be along to extract him. I uncorked my own waterskin and took a swig.

"May the Fates favor you in the joust." I patted him on the cheek then stood up and strode away.

I'd been in this fate-forsaken labyrinth for the better part of five days. So far, I'd encountered no beast or threat other than nature itself. Harsh winds that blew through the arid night and sucked all air from my lungs. Bug bites that caused vomiting and fly stings that led to a painful and itchy rash.

My feet were blistered and swollen inside boots that were wet with my blood and sweat. Still there was no sign, no indication, where the keys to the next level might be.

The solitude was the worst. Alone was how I'd come into this world and I hadn't cared for it. I'd been placed at the base of a cocoban tree with a message imprinted on my soul: Prove myself worthy to return to Fatevale. Prove myself a Saint.

For most of my formative years that was what I'd done. Proved myself strong, fast and cunning. Powerful enough to survive on my own in the wild.

It was only when I'd met Drax and the others that I finally felt like I could stop. They hadn't cared about my abilities. As a dragon shifter, Drax had harbored the deadliest creature known to man within his skin. Aquarius and Wade were sirens whose voices could kill with a word.

With them, all the differences and abilities that had made me revered or feared for most of my life, hadn't mattered. We'd just been four friends, four brothers. Until we weren't.

That brotherhood ended when Wade killed my nephew; Drax and Satrialla's son on the order of his queen; the Siren Savage. He'd shouted as my fist had caved in his skull that he'd done it so that Drax wouldn't have to. I hadn't understood what he meant until Drax charged in with a crazed look in his eye.

He'd gone for Satrialla first. His claws had slashed across her face and torso before I'd gotten to him. I'd bellowed in his face but he hadn't heard me. Or he had, but couldn't respond.

His eyes had been glazed and his wrath knew no limit. His mind was not his own but under the command of a siren. That was when Loch Orqanz had walked into my home with a shit-eating grin on his face.

A branch snapped. My head jerked up. I gathered power around my fists and raced towards the sound that had come from the end of the path. I swept around the corner and my face collided with a fist.

30

VARIALLA:
What Hides Beneath

A hand caught my wrist before I could pull back and swing again. My knuckles stung from the first strike.

"You," a deep voice growled.

I blinked up at the familiar imposing figure that towered over me. My heart did a backflip.

Exekiel wrenched me towards him. "I should have known."

Seriously? Of all the fuckers I could have found in this place, I found him?

I tried to pull free but his grip was unforgiving. He didn't seem anywhere near as exhausted as I was after endless days of traipsing through this place.

For the first few nights, I'd barely moved. Grief had kept me rooted to the spot. If I hadn't had my hydra-weed, I would have died of thirst. Jia was gone but I told myself that Eudora and Odus were still alive. I couldn't let myself believe otherwise.

Eventually, my need to survive, and keep my promise to those who had died or suffered to get me here, had forced me to my feet. Now every step I took was for them.

"Shadow Saint," I drawled. "The Fates must be fucking with me."

He sneered; a flash of pearly whites that had my heartbeat quickening. His dark hair was longer than usual and messy in the same way it was after sex. A five o'clock shadow framed his sculpted jaw and enhanced his sensual mouth. He'd changed out of his leathers and back into his suit from the banquet. His cream shirt buttons were undone and gave me an unobstructed view of the hard sun-bronzed planes of his body.

I swallowed. The levels of sexy this man possessed bordered on ridiculous. It was too bad he was as homicidal as he was attractive.

"Stick around. I think you'll find the Fates don't care enough to fuck with you." His voice was raspy; dry.

I lifted a brow. "Aren't you technically one of them?"

He threw me a bland stare, then strode past.

I didn't know why I followed. Maybe because I didn't have a clue where I was going. The last time I'd looked at my phone it had flashed with a temperature warning that said: **Too Hot to Function.**

It had sounded more like a compliment than a notice. If I hadn't been so royally screwed, I might have laughed.

Or maybe I followed him because I was tired of being alone.

"Isn't it all Bravinore's life goal to return to Fatevale?"

"For some." He glanced down at his phone which had been tucked into the pocket of his trousers.

"Not you?"

His jaw ticked. "How is it you can talk so much?" He licked his cracking lips. "How much water do you have?"

I scowled. "My supporters sent me hydra-weed."

He practically salivated at the mention of the plant. He spun to face me.

"And food?"

My eyes narrowed. I reached for the dagger I'd strapped to my thigh. I wouldn't put it past this bastard to try and rob me.

He snarled, "Unless you're about to offer me your cunt as a meal, take your hand out of your dress."

My fingers halted, inches from my blade.

"What did you say?" I gasped.

I was turned on and pissed off at the same time.

His eyes darkened. "Unless you're about to offer me y—"

"I got it!" I held up a hand to cut him off, and tried to shake off the effect of his words. "Do you ever think about anything else?"

His lips twitched. "I asked you about food, little bud. You're the one who stuck your hand inside your dress."

I flushed. Exekiel took a step closer. He smelt like woodsmoke, warm apples and something purely primal that I couldn't get enough of. Everything was undercut with a hint of days old sweat. Instead of being repulsed like a sane person, I wanted to taste it. To lick it from the thick column of his throat.

"How much food do you have?"

I stared up at him defiantly. "Why?"

A muscle ticked in his jaw. His stern gaze trailed over me. I stood taller. Of course, he looked like a frigging model aside from a few slits on his chapped lips, whereas I felt like shit and was sure I looked even worse.

My skin was ashy. My bare feet were blistered. As expected, my strappy sandals had snapped the second I was dumped here. I still wore the stained and tattered dress from the banquet because I hadn't had chance to pack spare clothes before we were wrenched back into the Games. Although, right now, I'd prefer to be naked. This place was like a sauna in Hell.

The humidity had reverted my hair back to its natural afro curls which I'd styled using a scrap of fabric I'd torn off my dress and wrapped in a bow around my head. Now the turquoise-tipped curls tumbled free at the top like a pineapple. Every strand was covered in dirt, leaves and flecks of quicksand.

Exekiel's gaze settled back on mine. It burned with an intensity that pushed into my lungs.

"Not much," I begrudgingly admitted. "A fruit bar and some nuts."

For some reason, he grinned. Blood seeped from where the movement caused his lip to split.

"A truce then."

I frowned.

"I'm low on water," he turned and started walking.

"So, we're allies?" I scoffed but rushed to keep up.

If he was offering some of those sweet berries I smelt on his breath, I was all in.

"For now." He jerked his head at me. "Hand over the hydra."

I stuck my hand in my satchel and pulled out the vine that quenched my thirst with a single bite.

"What do I get?"

Exekiel snickered. He tucked his hand into his sack and pulled out a chunk of pickled meat. My stomach rumbled in anticipation.

I handed him the weed. "Pleasure doing business with you."

It was nice to have company. Even if he didn't say much, just brooded and stomped ahead. There was something about Exekiel that always made me comfortable. The second he walked into any room; crowded or empty, I felt less alone.

Eventually, I yawned. He glanced back at me.

"Do all humans yawn like they're trying to wake the dead?"

I glared at him. "That's how you're supposed to do it." I stretched. "It's how you enjoy the yawn."

His eyes widened and he laughed. It was a delicious and rare sound. "Enjoy the yawn?"

A lock of hair slanted across his brow. I had the urge to brush it aside and let my fingers linger on his cheek. I'd missed him, as much as I wanted to pretend I hadn't.

The ground shook. I yelped as I was thrown back and careened into the wall. I grasped at the sharp twigs for balance but reeled back when something wet slid across my knuckles.

The earth rocked again. I was flung the other way. Exekiel caught me and took the brunt of the fall as we went down and rolled.

"What the heck was that?" I panted from where I sprawled on top of him.

He grasped my shoulders and pushed up to his feet, taking me with him.

"You don't want to know."

The ground shuddered again. Fissures broke through the concrete. I braced my arms out for balance and met Exekiel's sharp stare.

"I think I do."

His eyes searched the ground. It was like he expected something to emerge.

"Get ready to run."

"Wha—"

The ground split. It was cleaved in two as the largest, most terrifying wormlike creature shot from beneath the earth. Its long, wrinkled body filled the entire path. Time stood still. My heart stopped.

The worm-thing reared up. Its mammoth head swung from side to side and blotted out the sun. Its face was a crumpled mess of yellow slit eyes and a too-large mouth of jagged fangs that went all the way around.

Its bulbous head turned downwards. It made a horrifying hissing sound that snaked down my spine, when it found Exekiel and I gaping up at it.

The sound seemed to strike something in Exekiel.

He grabbed my hand and bellowed, "Run!"

31

EXEKIEL:
Ride Or Die

Varialla kept up easily. As we ran, she threw looks over her shoulder.

"What is that thing?" she hollered.

Hot wind buffeted us back. I lowered my head to crush through it.

"A wyrd-worm!"

A fucking wyrd-worm!

We swerved around a corner. For one blissful second death wasn't at our backs. Then the earth shook and the creature burst out in front of us.

Fuck. We skidded to a halt and swept back the way we came. Concrete ruptured around us as the beast tore through the ground like a sword through flesh. Its mouth was the size of a carriage. Large enough to consume me in one bite though my wings might give it some trouble.

I'd seen fuckers like this before. They were part of what I fought beyond the barrier. This was the largest I'd come across. They didn't die easily. Usually, I had the ability to fly out of range And regroup. Today, that wasn't an option.

"I'm guessing we're it's next meal," Varialla shouted as we careened down another path then another.

Wyrd-worms were large and it took them time to maneuver their body's and turn corners. Not long but enough to get us a few paces ahead.

"Funnily enough, they don't eat meat." I pulled my phone from my pocket. "They're just murderous little bastards."

Varialla pulled out her dagger and hacked at the hedge on our right. I joined her. With my sword, Goldie, in hand, I slashed the rest of the way. Varialla jumped ahead and I climbed through after.

She panted, "I wouldn't call that thing little."

There was another rumble beneath the ground, right under our feet. We started running as the earth cracked. The beast surged upwards.

Varialla couldn't run as fast as I could as Fae. She squeaked as I swung her over my shoulder and ran at full speed. But instead of away from the beast, I spun and ran towards it.

"What are you doing?" she screamed.

"Improvising!"

I hurtled beneath the wyrd-worm as it arced over us. My plan was to get behind it before it realized and decided to flatten us.

It thrashed wildly overhead and screeched as it tried to sniff us out. The good thing about wyrd-worms was that they were almost completely blind and their noses were small slits.

I made it three-quarters of the way under its swollen form before Varialla tensed.

"Do you see that?" she gasped.

I followed the point of her finger. There, dangling from a chain tied around the beast were three keys. The very thing we needed to advance to the next level.

"Shit."

The wyrd-worm let out a piercing cry. I leapt aside and barely dodged a glob of spit as it angled its dripping maw downwards. We'd been found. Its body twisted as it tried to curl in on itself—on us.

I slid my hand up Varialla's leg and beneath the tattered hem of her dress. She gasped in a way that made me want to find out what sounds she'd make if I pushed my hand higher. But now wasn't the time for that. There would never be a time for that. I unsheathed the dagger strapped to her thigh and held it out.

"Take it!"

The wyrd-worm bawled above us. Its body undulated. I had to duck to avoid being pummeled.

Varialla looked at the weapon. "Can this hurt it?" She sounded skeptical.

"Not much, but enough to buy us a few seconds."

She shifted on my shoulder. Beneath the howls of the creature, I heard her call, "We need to get on its back."

I groaned but she was right.

"Get behind it."

"What do you think I'm trying to do?"

I sucked down a labored breath, then once again, tapped into my Fae speed and ran.

Whatever she huffed in response was drowned out by the thunder of the wyrd-worm coming down. Flabs of rubbery flesh folded around us. I weaved between its hanging skin. Varialla swiped with the dagger. The wyrd-worm hissed and arched out of range of her blows, just long enough for me to skid beneath its form and out the other side.

She slid from my shoulder as I caught my breath against the wall. Using this amount of energy on an empty stomach hadn't been my best idea.

Varialla eyed the beast now with more curiosity than fear.

Her lips pursed. "Any idea how we get onto its back?"

The earth jumped as the wyrd-worm slammed into it and tried to shake us loose. It hadn't realized we'd escaped, but it would soon enough.

"I can think of one way." With painstaking slowness, I unfurled my wings. My entire body protested. Exhausted didn't begin to describe the heaviness I felt in my bones.

"This is a no-fly zone," Varialla reminded me. But I didn't need to fly high or for long.

I beckoned her closer with a flick of my head. "Come here."

The veins in her slender neck jumped. I couldn't help the smirk that curved my lips. I still affected her. Maybe as much as she affected me.

Reluctantly, she stepped into the curl of my arms. She fit against me so perfectly, it was almost distracting.

"Hold on." I bent my knees then shot into the air.

My wings beat; once, twice. Then a familiar force slammed me back down.

Only this time, I was prepared. I flipped until I was directly over the wyrd-worm. I drew Shira from her sheath and slammed the dagger into the worms back. It screeched and reared up. My jaw clenched as I struggled to hold Varialla in one arm and hold onto the blade with the other.

She flung her arms around my neck and locked her legs around my waist.

"Here," she called and pressed her own dagger into my other hand.

I released her and slammed the second blade into the worm. It thrashed beneath us and bucked in a desperate attempt to throw us off.

"Hang on," I breathed into her ear. Her hair tickled my cheek.

She nodded against my shoulder.

Instinctively, I retracted my wings to stop the wind from getting under them and ripping us off. Varialla wriggled closer. Her legs fastened tighter around me. My inhale was sharp. Fates, even in the midst of running for our lives, my body responded to the feel of her beneath me. Noted how perfectly I fit between her legs.

The wyrd-worm hissed and ploughed beneath the earth. Varialla covered our heads with her arms as debris rained over us. Stone cut into my trousers and carved slashes across my skin.

The worm resurfaced just as quickly. Its huge body took the brunt of the force. We came up in another part of the maze. Here the shrubs had violet berries, but it was impossible to tell how far we'd traveled.

When I was sure we weren't about to fly off, I used my grip on the daggers to pull myself up so Varialla was straddled across my lap. She stayed there a while with her head rested on my shoulder. Both of us were breathless. Our chests met on every inhale.

Finally, she lifted her head. Our eyes locked for the briefest second then she glanced behind her.

"I'll get the keys," she shouted over the beast's cries.

"How exactly do you plan to do that?"

She smirked at me in a way that made my balls tighten. Without a word, she leaned all the way back until she was flat against the worm.

Blood pulsed in my cock as I peered down at her. Her legs were still strapped around my waist. I sucked in a breath. What the fuck was she doing?

I'd positioned us as close to the chain as I could in the short time I'd had but it was still a few arms lengths away. Varialla shuffled backwards and stretched her arms above her head. I couldn't help noticing how that pushed out her firm breasts. Blindly, she groped for the chain.

"A little higher," I instructed.

She wriggled more. I clamped my elbows down on her thighs to hold her steady.

"Don't let me fall."

"Don't get us killed."

She glared at me then arched her back. I blinked. *For all that is hated and holy.* What was she trying to do to me? The urge to run my nose across her stomach and bury my mouth between her thighs was driving me to the brink.

Her fingers skimmed the chain. Bracing my weight on the blades, I nudged her forward with my hips. She gasped as I pressed into her. My muscles tightened, but the slight movement was enough for her fingers to latch around the chain.

She smiled then slid her legs from around me. My body went still.

"What are you doing?"

"Getting the keys."

She didn't let me argue, not that she would have listened if I did. With gritted teeth, Varialla clung to the chain, pulled away from me and crawled along the wyrd-worms back.

I was as tight as a bowstring as I watched her heave herself forward. The chain cut into her palms. The iron scent of her blood reached my nose. She continued. In this moment, she was fearless, or at least, brave enough to conquer it.

The keys dangled down the side of the beast. My gaze tracked every move Varialla made as she pulled one hand from the chain and reached for them. My heart didn't beat. The wyrd-worm squirmed and snarled. Too often, she was thrown upwards. It would be all too easy for her fingers to slip from that chain.

As exhausted as I was, my shadows curled from my skin like faint wisps of smoke. The seconds seemed to bleed into hours. I didn't move. Didn't blink. My gaze was solely fixed on her.

"Got 'em!"

Tension drained from my body as Varialla shimmied back along the chain—back to me. She eventually hooked her legs around my waist. When they were secure, she released the chain, pulled herself up and settled back on top of me. My grip tightened on the blades I held still wedged in the creature's back.

I couldn't ignore the thrum of rightness that pulsed in my skin, and the ease that slid through my veins. This was where she belonged. In my arms.

"Piece of cake," she breathed.

Sweat coated her warm almond-colored skin and her palms dripped blood.

"No cake I want," I grunted.

Varialla laughed and rested her head on my shoulder. Her nose buried into the nape of my neck. Her arms draped around me.

With one dagger fisted in my hand, I curled my arm around her waist and held her close. She smelt like sea salt and strawberries. I licked my lips like I could taste her.

"We should ride this thing until we get close to the exit," I called over the wind's howl.

From this vantage point, I got the occasional glimpse above the hedge walls and the Fields of Fury that stretched outside of the maze. The creature had covered more ground in a single moment than we could in hours.

"Where are we now?"

"Get my phone!" I shouted into her ear. "It's in my front pocket."

Varialla shifted and pushed her hand between us. Her fingers fumbled and finally slid into my pocket. I jerked when they brushed my cock. She tensed then changed direction.

"I think I feel it," she gasped.

My eyes closed. Her fingers were relentless and brushed my dick more times than I could count. By the Fates, was she doing it on purpose?

"That's not my phone," I snarled.

I couldn't keep the hungry growl out of my voice. One touch and, even here with our lives in the balance, I wanted her wet and dripping around my cock—mewing my fucking name.

Varialla hissed something I couldn't hear then her fingers bit into my shoulders and she elevated her hips. *Fates save me.* Her breasts brushed my chin. It took everything I had not to tear down the scraps of her dress and suck her pert nipples into my mouth.

I exhaled through my nose, released her waist and tightened my grip on the dagger pommels.

Varialla's fingers continued to roam. To stroke. To tease. Blood roared in my veins.

"For fuck's sake, sea-witch."

"I got it." She finally pulled out my phone and settled back into my lap.

She swiped her thumb across it and the map emerged.

With her bottom lip curled between her teeth, she studied it. "If we continue on this path, we should reach the exit by nightfall."

I nodded. "When we get close enough, we jump."

32

EXEKIEL:

REVELATIONS

Varialla straddled across my lap for an indefinite amount of time was a torture I never considered. Once we'd adjusted to the rhythm of the wyrd-worm, it made sense for us to match it to keep from falling off. Our bodies moved as one, up and down. Every so often, her fingers flexed into my back and stroked the seam of my wings.

My teeth grinded together. I needed her to sit still. I was achingly aware of every graze; every sigh. Of the way her full breasts brushed my chest. Of how the curls that had slipped free from her headscarf tickled my cheek. I was too aware of her and of the way she made me feel. Like an ember, that if lit, would burn down the entire realm.

"How much longer?" I nudged her with my shoulder.

The steady rhythm of Varialla's breath shifted. She stirred awake and pulled back just enough to meet my eye. I wished she hadn't. Her bright hazel eyes bored into me. Her full lips were so fucking close.

She unleashed a soft, adorable yawn, then peered at the phone she'd had nestled between her breasts. "Not much longer."

I barely resisted the urge to stroke my thumb down her cheek; to meet her lips with mine.

"Good."

She seemed to hesitate before she finally said, "Back in the banquet, you looked like you were trying to go after Alexov." Lines crinkled between her brows. "What was that about?"

I paused. "You expect me to believe you don't know?"

"If I did, I wouldn't ask."

I narrowed my eyes as I stared into hers. I doubted she knew about the weapon. By the way she'd spoken on that podium, it was obvious she believed the griffin-shit she was spewing about uniting the isles. However, it was impossible to believe that she didn't know about the deal the sirens had struck with the Royal Court in exchange for Shifter Springs. Loch Orqanz must have told her every barbaric detail as she lay in his arms.

I bared my teeth. "Maybe you should ask your betrothed."

"That bastard is not my betrothed and I'm asking you."

Anger flickered in her eyes. They searched mine as if she might find the truth in them. As if she was still being kept in the dark and was trying to fight her way out.

"The way the Rebel Leader tells it, you're practically mated." I couldn't hide the shadows that wreathed my wrists at the thought of her and Loch Orqanz.

"That asshole said a lot of things that aren't true."

I couldn't pretend I wasn't relieved at her little outburst. The thought of that fucker's hands—of anyone's hands—touching what was mine, made my blood simmer.

"Now," she levelled me with a glare. "Tell me why you were going after the Council leader."

The last thing I wanted to do was revisit this with the daughter of the bitch responsible and the one female who could do so much worse, on my lap.

"The attack on the dragon shifters wasn't random." I watched her; every flicker of her lashes and crease of her brow.

"What do you mean?"

"The sirens made a deal with the Royal Court."

"What?"

"At the time, dragon shifters ruled Shifter Springs. They maintained their titles of Kings and Queens even after the Game's treaty was signed and the other Isle leaders agreed to go by Count or

Countess. They were proud and powerful creatures and made a habit of winning the Games."

Varialla nodded. "I read about the previous Games. Season one was live and everyone was welcome to attend. Then they introduced toll and the Outliers couldn't afford to attend. That's when the camera-orbs were introduced. A Bravinore witch won one season and dragon shifters won the others."

I dipped my head. "They were well on their way to win again when the Court struck a bargain with your people." I couldn't keep the bite out of my voice. "If the sirens got rid of the dragon shifters, then they could have their throne."

Varialla gave me a look between a smile and a frown like she couldn't decide if I was joking.

"Are you serious?" she finally asked.

"Yes."

"You expect me to believe that the sirens and Royal Court were in cahoots?"

I snarled. "I don't give a shit what you believe. You asked. I answered."

She shook her head. "The sirens would never work with the people who condemned them. They would never attack an entire cast just to take their throne."

A tendril of raw anger curled in my throat. "Why does this surprise you? I told you they were power hungry monsters."

"No! They were just hungry. They believed they were forming an alliance but instead were betrayed by my mother's lover and had to fight to defend themselves."

My laugh was cold. "Is that what they've told you? Open your eyes, little bud. You're surrounded by monsters."

Her nails cut into my shoulders. "That I already know. But this is bullshit." She scoffed. "You would say and do anything to get me to turn on my people; to mess with my head."

"I would but this isn't one of them."

Her nostrils flared. Uncertainty shimmered in her eyes. She hadn't known. I'd been torturing the truth out of bastards for centuries. I knew when a man was lying; the telltale signs to look out for. Varialla's reaction was genuine.

"I don't believe you," she said, at last.

I sneered. "Of course not. You're so willing to be their perfect little puppet you tied the strings yourself and can't even see that they're wrapped around your fucking neck."

Rage flashed in her eyes. A sharpness that made the hazel brighter and threatened to melt the flesh from my bones.

Fuck. That look made me want to be inside her and throttle her at the same time.

"Says the bastard who wants to put me in a collar," she spat. "If anything you said were true then why aren't they on the throne? Why are my people still starving, dying?"

"Because of me."

She jerked back.

"Because the only way to stop the Fate-stained fuckers had been to put up a barrier that kept them out."

She looked back and forth between my eyes. I didn't know what she saw there but her upper lip curled and anger flickered in her gaze.

"That's the first honest thing you've said." She snarled, "You are the reason my people suffer."

"And the reason mine don't."

I didn't care what Varialla did or did not believe. There were deaths that needed to be answered for and future lives that needed to be spared the same fate. It was a shame that all Outliers had had to suffer for the sins of a few, but I would gladly take their hatred than see the realm under the thumb of those twisted fucks.

Fire flashed in Varialla's eyes. It was one that promised to burn everything to the ground. I met it head on; dared her to unleash it.

The air crackled between us. It was like the first spark of electricity before lightning struck. Her breath brushed my lips. Beneath her, my cock throbbed. Varialla's stare dropped to my mouth. My grip tightened around the hilt of my blades.

This was a mistake. That conversation just proved that we could never be. One of us would always have to lose so the other could win.

I cleared my throat and looked over her shoulder. Away from the eyes that threatened to undo me.

"Get ready to jump."

The wyrd-worm barreled closer to where the edge of the maze loomed. It was a gap in the hedges that led out to a sprawling forest.

"Now!" I shouted.

I wrenched the blades free of the wyrd-worms back. Beige blood bubbled up from the gashes. I swiveled to face its rear end and slid down its wrinkled hide. Braced in my lap, Varialla used her feet to hold us steady and steer us when we started to lean too far to one side.

We hit the tip of the worms tail then careened through the air. There were a handful of seconds when we were suspended then we tumbled towards the ground.

I should have dropped her—should have let her break her legs and forced her from the Games but I didn't let her go. I pulled Varialla closer and inhaled the sweet yet salty scent of her skin as we descended.

When we were close enough, my wings unfurled. I barely stifled a groan. Every cell in my skin ached. There was only so much power one could exert before it physically and mentally drained them, and I was close to my limit.

It wasn't a graceful landing. I partly glided and was partly thrown by the wind. At last, we hit earth. Its powder crumbled between my fingers and I smelt the fresh scent of grass.

The maze's exit was a few feet away. Varialla lunged off of me and we ran. Behind us, the wyrd-worm pursued. Its mammoth form rattled the ground and its head slammed into the earth. We didn't slow. Not until we cleared the exit and descended deep into level seven territory.

I peered at the map that hovered above my phone. There were no indicators for caves or lakes or anything else we might use to survive the night; only winding paths and endless trees.

Varialla stalked ahead of me. She shivered as the temperature dropped to a dangerous low. If we continued on much longer, we both risked frostbite.

I let out a breath that clouded in front of me. "We have to find shelter."

She didn't respond but knew I was right. We'd freeze to death out here.

I dug in my satchel and pulled out my cloak.

"Here," I flung the fabric at her.

Her nostrils flared and she glared at me.

"Pout all you want, little bud, but put the fucking cloak on."

"Don't tell me what to do," she snapped.

Her teeth chattered but the stubborn little thing just stood there.

"Put the cloak on, Varialla." I took a step towards her. "I won't let you be the reason we die tonight."

Her body visibly shook. She scowled but pulled the cloak around herself. It swallowed her small frame. I strode ahead.

A large boulder loomed in the distance and I veered towards it. It was about a foot taller than I was and almost as wide. Not as secure as a cave but better than nothing. I stalked behind it and instantly felt the force of the wind fade.

"We'll sleep here." I knelt and began digging into the earth that cracked with ice.

Varialla knelt to join me. I couldn't help inhaling her ocean scent.

"You sure this isn't some sick way to get me to dig my own grave?"

I let out a reluctant puff of laughter. "If we pack the dirt around ourselves and huddle together, we should make it through the night."

I didn't miss the way her fingers faltered.

I cocked my head to one side as I turned her way. "Think you can handle that sea-witch?"

She arched a brow. "Handle what?"

"A night wrapped in my arms."

Her throat worked over a swallow but she settled me with a glare.

"I can handle anything you throw at me Fae-boy."

33

VARIALLA:
HOT & BOTHERED

I was in trouble. The kind I couldn't run away from unless I wanted to freeze to death. Although I was seriously starting to consider it. Anything had to be better than being the little spoon in this twisted enemy's embrace.

Exekiel's body folded around mine like it was made to be there. His arm was draped over my waist and his wings curled around the both of us. They were warm, soft and so infuriatingly familiar. I knew the veins of sapphire that tracked through them, like I knew the tips of my fingers that had trailed across them so many times.

I sighed heavily. I didn't know how long I'd been lying here with the side of my face pressed into the ground but I didn't see myself falling asleep anytime soon. I wriggled slightly to put some space between me and the heat of Exekiel's body. It was ironic that I felt so safe in his arms when all they offered was danger.

He grunted, "Keep still."

I froze. I hadn't known he was awake. Now, his warm breath fanned across the tip of my ear.

He pulled me closer; closing the gap I'd just put between us. Was it because he was cold or because he wanted me against him?

I shook my head. It didn't matter. It couldn't matter.

"Are you going to fidget all night?" He grumbled.

"If it annoys you."

His hand flattened across my stomach. My breath crystallized in my lungs.

"Everything about you annoys me," he snarled.

My pulse skipped. The gravel of his voice, the indents of his fingers splayed across my abdomen—it was too much. He was too close.

"Believe me, if I could get away from you without freezing, I would." I rolled onto my back. I needed to escape the feel of him pressed up behind me.

Exekiel propped himself up on his elbow. His brilliant pink eyes gleamed down at me. My heart beats tripped over themselves.

"There is another way we could stay warm." His voice drizzled over me like warm honey.

I sucked in a breath. Icy wind swirled around us but I was on fire.

"Do you really think you have a chance of getting into my pants right now?"

"What?" His frown was so genuine, I immediately shut my mouth.

His own curved into a smirk.

"What exactly do you think I'm suggesting, little bud?"

My cheeks burned. Apparently, I'd been the only one with my head in the gutter.

He chuckled and bowed his head until his brow rested on mine. My heart galloped in my chest like it was searching for a way out—a way to escape the bastard who could claim it so easily.

"That would be fun," he purred.

His breath was hot against my lips. My eyes fluttered closed but I forced them back open. I wouldn't let myself be reeled in by his proximity. His hand still rested on my stomach but now he slid it around my waist. My entire body tingled.

"But I was thinking more along the lines of dragon fire."

My stare snapped to his.

"You haven't tapped into that side of you since..." His voice trailed off but I knew the night he was referring to. "Why? Why did you let me fly you when you have your own wings?"

This bastard was too perceptive for his own good, and not nearly as arrogant as I'd once thought. I'd hoped he'd assume I'd let him take the lead because he was a big strong man and I was a defenseless little woman. But Exekiel never saw me as defenseless; not even when the entire Royal Court had. He saw strength in me from the beginning; long before I saw it in myself.

I hesitated. It would be so nice to unburden myself with the truth. To tell him that Loch had betrayed me and that he held my dragon abilities in his hand. But there was a list of people I would trust that secret with before I trusted the Shadow Saint.

Exekiel already thought I was a villainous tyrant. If he knew part of me was controlled by one, I had no idea what he'd do. He couldn't kill me but there were fates worse than death. As Protector of the Realm, he was skilled at every one of them.

He could injure me enough to force me from the Games for good. He could let the entire realm know that my mind was not completely my own. That I couldn't even guarantee unity within my own Court.

"It only seems to come out when my emotions are heightened," I finally said. "Like the night I almost lost—" I cut myself off.

What the fuck? Why did I always seem to get verbal diarrhea around him?

His gaze collided with mine. My chest tightened.

"The night you almost lost me." His voice was low. Something unguarded flickered in his eyes. There and then gone.

I looked away before I nodded.

I'd been so desperate to save him I'd tapped into some vault of power and tied my life to his—my enemy. And I'd betrayed my own people to do it.

His fingers squeezed my waist. "Do you regret it?"

"Can you just go to sleep?"

He grinned then his devilish stare dropped to my mouth. I couldn't contain the flutter in my chest. After all this time and everything we'd been through, I still wanted him.

How? How could I love and despise this man at the same time? He'd taken everything from me. He'd chased me from my home and left me stranded in a world I didn't belong. He'd imprisoned my mother and left hundreds of thousands of people to rot beyond a barrier he built.

His hand moved on my waist. I sucked in a breath as his fingers stroked the Poisoned Heart.

His voice was rough when he said, "Nothing's triggered it since then?"

I barely whispered, "Nothing's come close."

His eyes darkened. I held my breath and silently cursed my honesty.

The heat of his stare was consuming. It was like he'd stripped away what was left of me and saw into the depths of my soul. Into the core of who I was. But he didn't recoil like so many before him had. He leaned in.

Fuck. I wanted to kiss him. I wanted to feel his lips on mine; to taste his tongue as it slid over my own. But we'd been here before and it hadn't ended well. I was fighting to free my people and he was fighting to chain them.

Exekiel lowered his head. Every cell in my body burned for him to close the gap; to brand my mouth with his. But I clung to the one brain cell I had that was still thinking clearly.

I rested my hand on his chest. "Good night, Shadow Saint."

Before I could change my mind, I rolled onto my side and closed my eyes.

A few months ago, I'd found out that speed-walking was an Olympic sport. I'd laughed so hard Tequila Sunrise had squirted out of my nose. Now, however, it made perfect sense. I was apparently going for gold.

My feet ached and my lungs burned. With every hour we didn't stop, I was increasingly thankful for the months I'd spent training and building up my stamina. Before, just running for the tram had left me breathless.

I glanced at Exekiel. There was a sheen of sweat on his brow but he showed no signs of slowing down. He'd been on a mission since we woke up not long after sunrise. We'd originally intended to separate as soon as we'd made it out of the maze, but earlier, we agreed that our food and water alliance meant we were better off together. At least until we found our original teammates.

In the daylight, our surroundings were breathtaking. An endless expanse of green hills, reaching trees of varying heights, and steep craggy cliffs. A cool breeze blew but nowhere near as chilling as it had been at night and the sky was crisp and cloudless.

"The food won't last us past tonight. We'll have to hunt," Exekiel announced. He looked back at me. "Think you can keep up."

I opened my mouth to retort but forgot what I was going to say when he dropped his weapons belt to the ground and pulled off his shirt.

My brain short-circuited. My eyes were glued to the ripple of his muscles. Each one looked like it was carved by a divine hand. Thin strands of dark hair trailed down from his bellybutton and into his breeches. His chest was smooth; his skin a golden brown from the sun.

I had to swallow to keep from drooling. *Holy hotness.* I was shamelessly ogling this man—this Fae—with his wings splayed and shimmering black in the sun.

Oblivious to my leering, Exekiel shoved his shirt into his sack, scooped up his belt, then grunted, "Let's go."

He took off. His steps were silent as he cut between the trees. I rushed to keep up, careful to stay downwind and avoid loose pebbles or fallen twigs.

Occasionally he paused, listened, then was on the move again. The three interconnected squares symbol of the Huntress fate, *Fadea*, was illuminated on the back of his hand. The marks of the other fates shone across his back.

After an unknown amount of time, it became clear that there was less wildlife here than there had been in other levels of the Game. Ordinarily, that thought would have been comforting. Now it meant there was a good chance we'd starve.

"Wait!" I straightened. "Do you hear that?"

Exekiel frowned, "Hear what?"

I tipped my head and could just make out a hissing sound beneath the caw of birds and rustling leaves.

"That!" I squealed.

Exekiel continued to stare at me with a brow raised. He couldn't hear it. His jaw ticked. Was it possible that my combined gifts as a siren and dragon shifter made my sense of hearing sharper than a Bravinore Fae's?

"Hear what?" He snapped.

He must have had the same thought.

"Water," I said unable to keep the smile off my face.

I didn't wait to see if he followed. I ran through the trees and chased that beautiful rushing sound of water rippling over rocks.

It wasn't long before Exekiel must have heard it too. He made a low sound and charged past me.

I couldn't help laughing as we hurtled down the side of the grassy cliff like children let out of school early. My feet slipped. I held my arms out at the sides to stay upright. Exekiel fell and slid part of the way down.

There, shimmering at the cliff's base was a beautiful river that ran between the sprawling mossy earth.

I whooped as I plunged into it. Icy water enveloped me. I let it spill over my lips and pour into my mouth. Every sip was a revival. My power percolated beneath my skin. It wasn't the same as being submerged in seawater but it was a glorious second.

My neck tingled. When I pressed my hand to it, gills had appeared. Usually Loch had to conjure the gills on my neck and the filament in my nose. Now I've done it myself. My siren gifts were getting stronger. I was getting stronger.

When I finally resurfaced, Exekiel was a few feet away. His gaze was fixed on the water and he held a large stick in his hand that he must have used his dagger to sharpen.

I glanced at the riverbank. My heart leapt. His clothes—breeches and all—were discarded beside a pile of floundering fish.

"You're naked," I said lamely.

"That is how bathing works." He didn't lift his eyes from his task.

The water came up to his hips but I could see the divots in his back that led down to his strong, firm ass. My toes curled in the pebbled ground.

"You look like you're fishing."

"Can't I do both?"

He stabbed the water with his stick. I drank in the way the muscles of his back bulged and shifted. He was so sexy, it was unreal.

Exekiel lifted the stick and revealed two fish twitching on the end. He smirked at me over his shoulder but the expression fell away. His stare darkened and he slowly turned to face me.

Confused, I looked down at myself. My dress had already been in tatters but now the river water had made it see-through. Even if it hadn't, the outline of my body, especially my peaked nipples, was painfully obvious. The flare of his nostrils said he could smell just how badly I wanted him.

For what felt like an eternity, neither of us moved. We didn't blink, didn't breathe.

The wind shifted and with it came his intoxicating scent. My toes curled in the wet earth. He smelt like sweat, vines and sin, and he was dripping in testosterone. Fuck.

"Stop." His tone was brusque.

I blinked and dragged my stare up to his. "What?"

"You don't get to look at me like that," he snarled.

I scoffed, "Like what?"

His gaze was unwavering. "Like you want me inside you."

My mouth opened and shut. I became a living flame. Every part of me was suddenly hot and trembling.

I snorted. "Believe me, I don't."

"Good, because that will never happen again, little bud." Exekiel treaded through the river towards me. The water bobbed at his hips so dangerously close to revealing what I knew swung beneath the surface. "Because you ruined us."

His words were as sharp as a knife. I almost pressed a hand to my chest to check if I was bleeding. He was right. I had ruined us and it had been the right thing to do. He would never see things my way and I sure as shit would never agree with his.

He stalked past me. I looked away as the curve of his toned backside crested above the water. The sooner we completed this level and found other players to ally ourselves with, the better.

34

VARIALLA:
SOMETHING FISHY'S GOING ON

Etiquette training went out the window when that first bite of fish flaked off in my mouth. My eyes closed. For a brief moment, I was transported from the Games and into a world of fine foods and explosive spices.

"This is incredible," I moaned as fish oil slicked my fingers.

Exekiel's mouth quirked up in the corner. "It gets the job done."

"Don't be modest," I scoffed. All the awkwardness from earlier was forgotten as I shoveled in another mouthful. "It doesn't suit you."

Exekiel grinned. He expertly flipped the fish and sprinkled on more of the herbs he'd gone into the trees to find.

"You like cooking." It wasn't a question. It was obvious from the gleam in his eye and the calm that settled over him.

"I did. Once upon a time."

I studied him a while. "Is this what you would have done if things were…different? Would you have been a chef?"

He dragged a hand across the back of his neck as if debating whether or not he should answer.

"My brothers and I had planned to cater at balls, host banquets and one day open our own restaurant," he said, at last. "Aquarius was surprisingly gifted with liquors. Wade had a flare for music. Drax had a way with people and I was good with food."

My chest warmed. I always said I didn't want to know more about him. This was why. The more I knew, the more I liked.

"What happened? You became the realms hero and they couldn't go on without you?"

The second his face changed I knew. I wished I could take the words back.

"I don't have brothers anymore."

The fish stuck in my throat. I downed a large mouthful of water from the waterskin we'd refilled in the river.

"Because of the war?"

Exekiel grunted a sound of agreement.

Because of my mother. I swallowed the bitter ache that rose in my chest. When I'd first heard about the attack on the dragon shifters, the sirens had made it sound heroic and daring. Everyone except Cherise. She hadn't seemed to agree. Now that I'd felt the cold grip of Loch's control, I wasn't sure I agreed either.

I'd told myself that my mother and her army had done what they had to, to keep our people safe. That it had come down to their life or the dragon shifters. But what if what Exekiel said was true? What if the sirens had made a deal with the devil to get a seat on one of his thrones?

"Treasure the memories." I blinked back tears as Eudora and Odus filled my mind. I believed they were still alive. They had to be. But sometimes fear crept in. I inhaled deeply. "Memories are better than nothing, believe me."

I had exactly three memories that I treasured. Three moments in my life before I came to the Isles that I would carry with me forever. Though all except one had been tainted. The day I thought I'd found a home before the family fled. The first day I went to the beach before the sharks came. And the day Gavin Cook found me on the streets, gave me a job at the Crowne and Lion, and let me sleep in a cot in the back office.

I missed him the most. I wondered if he was looking for me. If he'd plastered my face across social media or if he just assumed I was another sad story. Another girl who got mixed up with the wrong sort of people.

Firelight reflected in Exekiel's pale pink eyes as he rotated the fish.

"What would you have been?" he murmured as if he sensed I needed the subject change as much as him.

I snickered. "I had a lot of dreams. That's all you can do when you feel like a prisoner of circumstance. Dream of the day you're free."

He brought the fish on a stick to his lips and took a bite then leaned back on his elbows.

"And what would have set you free, Varialla?"

My breath caught. It always did when he said my name.

"Dancing," I finally said.

There was something about getting into my body and out of my head that always felt freeing.

He nodded slowly. "To be as graceful and fluid as the sea."

My gaze lifted to his. I never thought of it that way but the words resonated so deeply in my soul, I looked away.

"Something like that." I sucked the last of the fish from my fingers then tipped my head up and pointed to the stars. "Another time I'd wanted to be an astronomer or pilot." I sighed. "I was always fascinated with the sky and the secrets it held."

"You dreamt of flying."

Shit. I'd dreamt of flying…like a dragon. Even when I hadn't known this world or these people, a part of them had called to me. Tears stung my eyes and I quickly blinked them away.

I forced a shrug. "It was ridiculous, of course. I've never even been on a plane. The first time I flew was…was with you."

There was a beat of silence before Exekiel said, "And did you discover the secrets of the sky?"

I shook my head. "I found much more than that."

I'd found him. He turned his head to look at me as if he knew exactly what I wasn't saying.

The next day passed a lot like the one before. With the map of the Five Isles in my hand, we followed the trail to Level Eight which was in an area marked the Fall of Fates. It was disturbing that Level Seven's challenge hadn't revealed itself yet. It meant it could lurk around any corner.

We walked along the riverbank. It took longer than cutting through the trees but it guaranteed us access to food and fresh water.

As we travelled, Exekiel told me stories about growing up with Drax, Wade and Aquarius. Apparently the four of them had gotten themselves into a few situations they'd had to charm or cheat their way out of.

He'd been nine when Drax's family had taken him in. They hadn't been the first to find the "Boy in the Woods", marked by the Fate of Death and with little control over his shadows, but they had been the first to not turn him away.

"Alright, Drax was a dragon shifter. What about Wade and Aquarius?"

Exekiel's steps faltered, just slightly, before he said, "Sirens." He strode ahead of me and didn't look back. "They were sirens."

My stomach turned. Suddenly I remembered Orla's story about the soldier of the Siren Army that had killed his nephew. That soldier had apparently been his friend.

Exekiel once told me that some of the sirens at the base of the barrier had been his closest friends. He claimed there were two sides to every story and that I didn't know the half of it. I was quickly learning how true that was.

Something moved in the distance. I froze. Exekiel must have seen it too. His wings expanded and his eyes glowed.

"Something's out there." I whispered.

He dipped his head and unsheathed his dagger with the ruby-encrusted hilt. I palmed my own blade. Together, we crept through the overgrown grass. My eyes stayed locked on the distance.

The sun had set. With it, came the cold and a relentless fog. Tonight, something prowled within it.

With each passing second, the fog grew thicker. The hairs on the back of my neck stood on end.

"This fog isn't a coincidence," Exekiel murmured. "It's Level Seven."

35

VARIALLA:

CATCH ME, IF YOU CAN

I gripped my blade tighter as the wall of fog surrounded us. I could barely see beyond the end of my nose.

Something in the smog shifted. It was closer this time. I spun; eyes narrowed.

"There!" I shouted as a figure darted past.

Moonlight bounced off its skin. My blood ran cold. It wasn't skin. This thing was a creature made of mist. Humanoid except its head was large and oval and its limbs were long and spindly. Its eyes were misshapen holes in its head and its mouth was a gaping hole of jagged fangs. Mist rippled from it like threads of smoke.

"Don't let it touch you," Exekiel growled.

I summoned magic into the palm of my hands. Its heat was comforting.

"How do we defeat something we can't touch?"

His fingers closed around mine.

"We run."

We did. I could barely see a thing in front of me as we blundered through the trees. The creatures' rasping growls thundered after us. More of them peeled away from the fog and lunged from the shadows. I screeched and slammed my magic into them. It tore a hole through their chest but didn't slow them down.

"I'm guessing you know what these things are?" I bellowed.

"Mistfits."

"Mist-fits? Is that a joke?"

Exekiel lunged over a boulder. I leapt up after him.

"Is it funny?" He called.

Maybe in other circumstances the name would have been hilarious. Now it only filled me with dread.

My spine burned as a mistfit raked its hand down my back. Scraps of my dress sizzled away.

Fuck.

We had to do something. There were too many to outrun. We'd changed course so many times, I had no idea where we were or where we were headed. Any minute now we could run off the edge of a cliff.

We raced around a large tree with low-hanging branches and thick weighted leaves.

"They must be guarding the keys," Exekiel whispered.

My fingers pressed into the tree bark as I peered around the trunk. Mistfits moved passed us like wraiths. Their gaping maws were wide and their hollows for eyes, cold.

"We need to distract them." I knelt, grabbed the largest stone I could carry and flung it as far as I could.

The mistfits swiveled with a vicious hissing sound and hurtled in the direction the rock landed.

"Let's go."

Exekiel gripped my hand and we ran. Mist gathered around us. It was a few seconds before the creatures burst free and lunged after us.

Exekiel wrenched me against his side as he splayed his wings and shot into the air. The trees were densely packed. We crashed into one branch and slammed into another. Exekiel grunted as his wings were tangled in the leaves and torn by the branches.

The mist only rose with us and the creatures came with it. My gut plummeted.

"Get down!" Exekiel bellowed.

I ducked just as a misted hand punched above my head.

"Fuck!" Exekiel snapped.

His shadows gathered around us. But the creatures easily slipped through his wall. I felt their bite. This time, pain seared down the side of my arm.

We banked left. The mistfits hissed in our wake. Exekiel swooped right. I threw my arms protectively over our heads as twigs snagged in my hair and slashed at our skin.

Unsteadily, Exekiel balanced on a branch with me in his lap. I curled into his chest and searched the distance for some sign of where we were supposed to go to find the keys.

My heart leapt. "I see something," I panted. "I think it's the keys; glowing over there."

Exekiel had his back braced against the trunk but he peered over his shoulder. "You're right."

Anticipation ran trilled me. We had to get over there, but how?

Fog climbed higher. Any minute it would reach us and the creatures would emerge.

"Get ready to run."

Exekiel descended. As soon as my feet struck the leafy ground, I ran. Exekiel pulled his wings back inside himself and raced beside me.

The mistfits came at us like a tidal wave. Exekiel slashed behind him with an errant shadow. Like my power, it carved through the creature, but the mistfits kept coming. Together, we lobbied out blast after the blast but the creatures were closing in.

I gripped Exekiel's arm and wrenched him behind a large boulder. My heart slammed into my chest as the creatures ghosted past. The sounds they made set my teeth on edge. They were searching for us. Soon, they'd find us.

"We need to head East," Exekiel murmured. "As long as we remain hidden, we should be able to reach the keys before they get to us."

I nodded and pulled power into my fingers. Not that it would do much good.

We waited. The only sounds were the rough puffs of our breaths and the distant garbles of the creatures.

When the coast seemed clear, Exekiel and I exchanged a look and we crept from our hiding space.

A mistfit descended from above. I shrieked. I wasn't sure but the creature seemed to flinch back. My stomach clenched. Had my voice done that or did they just not like being yelled at? Exekiel had said the only way to survive them was to outrun them, but he didn't have the gifts I had. He didn't have a voice that could command armies.

I ducked to the side as a mistfit swung for my throat. Exekiel dropped and rolled to avoid being impaled by its clawed hand. His leathers were scorched and the skin along the back of his neck was red and raw.

"Stop!" I shouted. My voice was thick with power.

The misfits froze. It was only a second but long enough for Exekiel to shove to his feet. He blinked at me. There wasn't time to process what I'd just done or if I'd done it at all. He wrapped us in his shadows to make us harder to see. Then together, we ran east.

The mistfits pursued but we were almost there. Up ahead the rainbow of colors gleamed.

Finally, the dense fog began to clear.

"This way!" Exekiel shouted.

I raced after him. The mistfits swarmed in at our backs. My heart rabbited in my chest. We charged into a clearing. Here holograms of keys flickered in the air like coins in a Super Mario game.

I reached for a vibrant blue key that bobbed near my head. My fingers passed through the hologram as it beeped then vanished.

Instantly, the misfits pulled back. However, three now surrounded me. Each had a blue key dangling from its wisping neck. They stretched their hideous gaping mouths into a sneer. Their low groans and growls rattled like nails in a jar.

Shit.

I braced my feet on the ground like I could fight them. But the only weapon I might have had was my voice.

The mistfits pounced. I sang. I didn't know what else to do. I wasn't sure if it would work. These creatures weren't tangible. They were ropey wisps of air.

Still, the melody and language of a world I didn't fully know, sailed from my lips. Power surged from my tongue.

> *I am the unconquered and you will not harm me.*
> *I am the future; the Queen of your sea.*
> *I am the unconquered and you will not harm me.*
> *I am your queen. Now give me your key.*

The song settled over the creatures. Their faces went slack. One by one they removed the chains from their neck and held them out to me. My heart flipped. Three deadly creatures were under my control. Just like that.

That knowledge thrilled me more than I'd expected. A rush that made me feel invincible. I swiped a key from the closest hand and turned to Exekiel.

He was surrounded by at least five of the creatures. Each one carried a red key which must have been the color he chose. His powerful chest heaved as he blasted out orbs of gleaming shadow. Some seemed almost solid and punched through the mistfits that surrounded him with enough force to scatter their particles to the wind. But the effort slowed him down and the others were closing in.

I ran towards him with the song ablaze on my lips. Again, the mistfits froze. Their hands extended to offer up a red key. When Exekiel reached for it, they screeched so loud it grated down my spine.

I stumbled back as the creatures converged to form one giant mistfit. They loomed over him and still emitted that horrific cry. Their mammoth mouth stretched wide.

My stomach lurched. The keys weren't for Exekiel. He hadn't been the one to sing the song. I charged in front of him and held out my hand.

The mistfits settled almost instantly. *What a rush.* I swallowed thickly as they placed a single red key into my hand. My fingers curled around it. I sagged with relief.

"Let's go." Exekiel turned but I didn't follow.

Every part of me wanted to run from this place with him at my side but we'd done what we set out to do. We'd completed Level Seven. Now we'd leave this place and go back to being enemies.

I stood taller and looked him straight in the eye.

"So long, Shadow Saint." I took off.

As I ran, I tapped into my siren's gift and shouted, "Restrain him but don't hurt him in any way."

My creatures heeded my command. Exekiel's eyes widened. He didn't understand what I'd said in the language of a siren. All he knew was that the beasts were gathering around him.

I wrestled down my uncertainty and ran as I tucked both keys in my cleavage. Exekiel was not my ally. If the roles were reversed, he would have done the same. At the end of the day, he wanted to see me with a collar around my neck, my magic stripped and my people oppressed. He was not my friend. He was not my anything.

"Varialla," his voice boomed after me like the crack of thunder. I felt it shudder through my bones and reverberate through the ground.

I stumbled and held my arms out at the side as I raced down the hill. I'd caught sight of the Fall of Fates when we were up in the tree. I didn't know how far they were but I barreled in their direction. I closed my eyes and tried to block the sound of Exekiel's shouts as I ran faster.

It was mere minutes later when his deafening roar raged after me. He'd broken free. Nothing could contain the Shadow Saint especially if they couldn't hurt him.

I cursed and ran harder than I ever had before. I didn't want to risk the time it would take to pull up the map on my phone. I kept my eyes locked on the Fall of Fates and raced in the direction I assumed it was.

Exekiel's shadows found me first. Swirling whips of black slashed at my heels. I screeched and lunged over them. Another swiped for my arm and coiled around my wrist. I ripped free and kept running.

"Nice try, sea-witch!" Exekiel's voice echoed across the open field and sent shivers down my spine. The trees seemed to bend away from it and the grass curled in on itself as his innate power rumbled through them. The power of death.

I had to get out of the open. Frantically, I darted down a path between trees and ran headfirst through the thicket.

"I will find you," Exekiel roared. He sounded so much closer now.

I glanced over my shoulder. My blood froze. A wave of shadows swept towards me. I flung myself to the ground and rolled beneath them then hopped back to my feet and sprinted ahead.

Dry leaves cracked underfoot. Tree bark sliced into the palms of my hands. My makeshift sandals of leaves and twine stuck in pockets of mud, and twigs stabbed my heels.

This was a nightmare. I'd expected the mistfits to restrain him for longer than five flipping minutes.

I shook off my useless shoes and kept running. I couldn't stop. The fucker was hunting me and he wouldn't stop until he got that key.

I pelted down another path and ducked beneath low hanging branches. Exekiel's scent struck me. Sharp and alluring. My stomach pitched. He was close. Too close.

I looked behind me but all I saw were trees that shuddered in my wake.

I swerved down another path. Here, the trees were less densely packed. Slivers of moonlight cut through the leaves and made it easier to see. My gaze searched the skies. I didn't know which direction he was coming from. Was he on foot or had he let loose those violent wings?

"I will catch you, little bud." His voice echoed around me and made it impossible to tell where it was coming from.

"You have to find me first," I murmured beneath my rasping breaths.

The sound of flapping wings beat overhead. Something rustled in the trees at my back. I swiveled one way, then the other. Where the heck was he?

A branch snapped to my left. The earth shook to my right. Fuck. I spun in circles. My heart ratcheted in my chest.

"You know what?" I shouted, "If I didn't know any better, I'd say you were enjoying this."

Something growled right behind me. I spun but saw nothing.

"Run." Exekiel's voice carried towards me on the wind. Then I saw him; veiled in shadows. His teeth were a slash of silver in the night. "Run."

I ran. Despite everything, a smile tugged at the edge of my lips. Who knew the illustrious Shadow Saint had a primal kink? Who knew I had one? It was just another thing that made us infuriatingly compatible.

My feet beat the earth and kicked up scattered leaves as I tore through the underbrush.

The thud of his heavy footsteps followed. The crack as he snapped branches and plowed through the smaller trees.

Exekiel chased me like a starved beast let out of his cage to feast for one night only. He was wild and swift. His long strides devoured the distance between us. Like before, the interconnected squares of *Fadea* glowed silver on his forearm. Only now I was the prey. Something like hunger shone in his gleaming pink eyes.

I raced towards a path on my left, then in the last second, pivoted and shot towards the right, straight into a wall of black.

My heart flipped. I skidded to a stop but it was too late. My feet kept moving and I hurtled into his shadows. I spun and tried to tear free but they latched onto me and held tight. I was stuck like a fly in a web.

Exekiel's low laugh rumbled through the trees. My eyes swept the distance and my throat closed. There, palely lit by the moon, his silhouette prowled towards me.

"Little bud," he purred "What am I going to do with you?"

36

EXEKIEL:
OWNING HER

Varialla strained against my shadows. With every tug, they gripped her tighter. She was suspended between two trees with thick trunks and waxy leaves. Her arms and legs were splayed for me. I curbed a growl. The scent of her pussy was sharper with her legs open like that.

I bared my teeth and drank her in. The pulse that jumped in her throat made me hard. Sweat glazed her russet skin. The swell of her full breasts heaved inside what was left of her dress. After more than a week in the wild, one strap had torn off and the other hung from her shoulder. The beadwork around her middle shimmered like starlight. The lacy hem was now short and shredded. I would only have to curl a finger to feel what was hidden underneath.

I cricked my neck and stalked towards her. The pound of blood rushed in my ears. The thrill of the chase roared in my veins. She had awoken a side of me I hadn't known existed. Now it growled like a beast determined to break free.

There was no taming it. A visceral hunger burned beneath my skin. I craved the feel of her lips on mine. The sweet strokes of her tongue. The warmth of her legs wrapped around me.

"I believe you have something of mine."

Varialla jutted out her chin. "Do I?"

I chuckled and moved closer. "The key sea-witch. You have my key."

I stopped inches away; close enough to see the stars reflected in her hazel eyes.

"Tell me where it is and I'll let you go."

"Let me go and I'll tell you."

I sneered. She matched it. My cock throbbed.

"Always so defiant." I stroked my hand up and over her breast. She arched into my palm as I squeezed. Then I continued my ascent and closed my hand around her neck.

The way her eyes widened and her lips parted in a gasp did something to me. Heat shot through my skin and pumped at the head of my erection.

I curbed a growl.

"Tell me where the key is or I'll search for it myself."

I gripped her waist in my other hand. She tensed. The muscles in her arms shifted as she tried to fight my shadows.

"Considering you're not wearing much, there are only a handful of places it could be."

Her gaze held mine as I trailed my hand up the length of her body. There was a challenge in her eyes. I grinned and slid my hand higher until I grazed the underside of her breast. Her entire body shivered.

"Varialla," I tightened my grip around her throat.

She arched a brow. "Shadow Saint."

I let out a low chuckle and cocked my head. "I am a Saint in name only."

My hand molded around her breast and I used it to yank her towards me.

She half-moaned and hissed at the pain. Her head tipped back. I circled my thumb around her nipple and watched her writhe. Need pulsed in every part of me. I needed to see her break. I needed to see her straining for air. I needed to see her come for me. Only me.

I tore my hand from her neck and pushed it between her thighs.

Her eyes sparked open. She looked right at me. There was no mistaking her primal hunger. The torturous yearning that echoed my own.

"Do you want me, little bud?"

Her nostrils flared but she said nothing as I pinched her nipple between my finger and thumb, and dragged my hand along the wet lace of her underwear.

"Fuck." She quivered.

"Do you want me?"

Varialla gritted her teeth and moved into my hand.

"Aaahh," she whimpered.

I was so hard, I thought I might break.

"Yes, or no?" I rasped.

The need to fuck her was overwhelming. I felt unhinged; maddened from the chase and compelled to claim her, mark her, own her.

She scrunched her eyes closed.

Then finally stammered, "Y- yes. Fuck. I want you."

I dropped to my knees like a man at prayer but the only thing I was going to worship was her. She was my sanctuary; my salvation and her words had set me free.

Goosebumps rippled along her flesh as I hitched up her dress and the chill of the night air bit into her skin. *Fates, save me.* The intoxicating scent of her hit the back of my throat. I pushed my head between her thighs and groaned.

"You're going to be the death of me," I grunted which was ironic because I never felt more alive than when I was with her.

I peeled her underwear down until they were stretched around her ankles then my mouth met her pebbled clit. Varialla sang. Not a moan or a scream but a symphony of sounds that chorused in my soul.

With the backs of her thighs cradled in my hands, I slid my tongue up her hot, wet center. The little beauty moaned and bucked. My shadows pulled taut as they held her in place.

One more lick and she was quaking.

"Shit," she cried.

I dragged my tongue around her clit. "I'm going to devour you."

She made soft, mewing sounds as she looked down at me. Her face was creased in pleasure. Her breaths were heavy and broken. I watched every sweet agonizing sensation play out on her face.

"I'm going to eat your cunt, little bud, and then," I used my fingers to spread her and slurped at her dripping pussy. She spasmed and cursed. "Then I'll come back for seconds."

I licked her again. "Then thirds." My tongue plunged inside her. "Then fourths."

I feasted on her with all the visceral hunger that had plagued me every time she was close. The maddening ache that had tortured me for the last few days. Her taste exploded across my tongue. I drank her down. I sucked and nibbled, and pulled her clit between my teeth. Her cries reached a new crescendo.

Stars burst across my vision. My cock strained against the ties of my breeches. She was destroying me. With every roll of her hips and hitch of her breath, I was undone.

I clamped my hands around the swell of her plump backside and dragged her more furiously into the beat of my tongue.

Varialla tugged against my shadows like she wanted to reach down and fasten her fingers around my head; to tug on my hair and pull me closer.

"More," she panted.

I willingly obliged. I gave her exactly what she wanted just where she wanted it.

"I'm coming!" She gasped.

Her legs kicked against the shadows that restrained her.

"Shit!"

Her pussy pulsed against my flicking tongue.

"I'm coming!" She screamed, "I'm coming!"

A burst of salt and honey spilled into my mouth. I swallowed it down and continued to lash at her until she hung limp from my shadows.

Only when I was certain that I had drained every drop, did I let my shadows lower her to the ground and finally let her go.

Varialla stared dreamy eyed up at me from where I knelt over her. Her fingers tiptoed up my thigh, to the waistline of my breeches.

She pushed her hand inside and ran her hand down my cock.

"Fuck." I bent over her; my fist pressed into the wet earth.

Varialla exhaled deeply as her wicked fingers continued their caress. "On your back. Now."

She sat up and had me pinned to the ground in seconds. Arousal shot through me. Varialla undid my ties and the night air kissed my thighs as she shimmied my breeches half way down. I groaned when her fingers curled around my cock. I was so close to the edge after watching her come. A well-placed breeze could have had me ejaculating.

There was no preamble or teasing. The groundwork had been laid. I needed her mouth on me and my little bud knew it.

She bowed her head and sucked me into her hot, wet little mouth. I bucked and almost came when I struck the back of her throat.

"Fuck!" I grasped the back of her head and held her against me.

Varialla hollowed her cheeks and bobbed up and down. Her hand fastened around the root and squeezed.

"Fuck, beautiful," I breathed. "You look so good with my cock in your mouth."

Her back was arched and her ass pushed up in a way that invited me to fuck it. I clenched my jaw and groaned as I tried to suspend the ecstasy of this moment a little longer. Her tongue ran in circles around the head before she slurped me into her mouth once more. She moaned. The sound vibrated and pulsed down my length.

My fingers flexed in her hair.

"That's it, little bud. Fuck, you're doing so well."

She sucked me harder. Her swollen breasts rubbed against my thighs. Varialla emitted soft moans and breathless gasps that held me captive.

My release burned at the seam of my cock. I was close. A prisoner of her mouth as she worked me.

"Come for me, shadow."

The words were a hot whisper at the head of my shaft.

"Come for me," she begged. "I'm thirsty."

Her tongue stroked over my tip. I erupted. Hot rivulets of come sprang from my cock and spurted down her throat. My head spun as violent shocks of pleasure careened through every muscle inside me.

The little beauty swallowed every drop. She cleaned me off and kept licking.

"Fuck." My stomach tightened. I bucked into her mouth.

Finally, an eternity of ecstasy later, she sat back on her heels. She looked pretty pleased with herself.

I jerked and almost came again when she wiped her mouth on the back of her hand.

She smirked. "Good boy."

"Get on top of me." I grasped her hips and pulled her onto my lap. She squealed. Her breasts juddered. I didn't give her chance to breathe. I yanked her down until her tight, wet cunt soaked my cock. I hissed through clenched teeth as she moved.

"Fuck, little bud. Look how you've blossomed."

I bolted up and flipped her onto her back. Her hazel eyes sparked. I withdrew from inside her and the head of my cock teased her drenched hole. Her eyes rolled.

"Fucking beautiful."

I thrust back inside her. My roar rattled the trees around us. Her own cry sirened through the night and sang in my soul.

I plunged into her silken depths and lost myself entirely. She was so tight. So perfect. So fucking made for me. I buried my face in her hair and inhaled. She smelt like sea salt, strawberries and sin.

I groaned, "I can't get enough of you."

I planted one hand on her hip and pinned her to the ground. Then I looked down and watched myself fuck her. Long furious strokes in and out.

"Look at you." My pelvis met hers over and over. "You take this cock like such a fucking good girl."

The beauty mewed beneath me. Her head thrashed from side to side and she clawed at my waist like she was trying to climb inside my skin.

There was an urgency between us that was unmatched. Like we knew that if we thought too long about what we were doing, we would be forced to stop and dear Fates, I couldn't stop. Nothing could pull me away from her. Not wyrd-worms, not mistfits, not all the fucking sense in the world. I railed into her; rammed my cock right down to the fucking root.

"O god! O god," She panted.

I bowed my head and sucked her nipple between my teeth.

"I'm your God now."

There was nothing gentle in my motions nor in the way her nails sliced into my back. I hissed at the sharp sting of pain and ploughed into her harder.

Her hips rose and fell in tandem with mine. With every upward thrust she tightened around me. I welcomed the vicious tug.

She was insatiable. A drug I couldn't get enough of. Nothing could sate this addiction. The slap of flesh on flesh was backed by my grunts and her rising moans.

My cock hardened to the point of painful—a bite of sweet agony. My thrusts doubled and I fucked her into the ground. It sank and shifted beneath her. Mounds of earth gathered around her arms and legs, and clung to her dark, sweat-glazed skin.

"You feel so good."

"Shit. You're—Aaahh…" She couldn't get the fucking words out. She was gasping for breath. "Exekiel," she panted, "Exekiel!"

Her legs shook. Her eyes rolled back in her head. Fuck. She was a goddess.

Unable to hold back, I brought my mouth to hers. The heavens sang. Our tongues explored each other. My cock stiffened. My vision glazed over. Almost instantly, I was overcome by unending rapture. My body jerked on top of hers and Varialla repeatedly screamed my name.

37

VARIALLA:
PANDORA'S BOX

Exekiel consumed me; body, mind and soul. We'd gone another three rounds on that forest floor before we'd finally been able to pry ourselves away from each other long enough to find a cave for the night. There, Exekiel had slammed me up against the wall and roughly fucked me from behind.

Today was more of the same. One mind-bending orgasm after another. I hadn't even known I could orgasm before him. Not really. All I'd known was a small rush of pure satisfaction that lasted half a second then fizzled out. With Exekiel the sensations were endless and the aftershocks lingered longer than I could keep count.

Now, for at least the eighth time today, I rode my mate's thick cock. Despite all common sense, I bounced on his erection like it was a pogo stick. Up and down. Faster and faster. My tits jumped wildly. If I'd been more blessed in that department, they would have smacked me in the face. I was a woman possessed and I rode my mate like a monster made for fucking him.

We'd officially opened Pandora's box. Instead of freeing all the worlds evils, we'd unleashed ravenous sex beasts who couldn't get enough of each other.

Now everything hung in the balance and I wasn't sure which way I wanted it to tip. This didn't change anything between us. We still wanted different things. Yet, at the same time, it had changed everything.

My inner walls clenched and violently spasmed around Exekiel's hard cock. He reared up inside me with a roar. Pleasure spliced through my entire being and ricocheted across my skin.

An unknown amount of time later, I finally reentered my body and collapsed on top of him.

My head rested on his chest and I breathed him in. Woodsmoke, warm apples and him—his very essence that felt like coming home.

We were so screwed.

Exekiel's fingers trailed shivers up and down my spine.

"Well," I forced a laugh. "That was unexpected."

His voice rumbled through his chest. "Not really. I knew I'd have you moaning for me again."

I looked up at him. "Cocky sod."

He grinned. My heart stopped. Fuck, he was stunning. The thick column of his throat. The square cut of his stubbled jaw. The curl of his lashes. Everything about him was made to lure people in. To leave them paralyzed by his impossible perfection that they had no choice but to succumb.

Oh, how I'd succumbed.

My cheeks heated and my toes curled at the memory of all he'd done to me last night and again this morning, and all I'd done to him. There was so much more I wanted to explore but this was a fleeting moment in time. Time, we didn't technically have. The clock was ticking and we had to move.

I snuggled closer and drew in a breath. We couldn't stay here. As much as I wanted to remain like this forever.

I inhaled and braced myself before I said, "We should probably…make a move."

The words stung but I forced them out. It was for the best. The longer I stayed here with him, the more I felt like I would never be able to be without him. But this was about more than me—than us. This was about righting the wrongs he'd committed and about setting the Outer Isles; my friends, free.

There was a drawn out beat of silence before he murmured, "It's late. We'll head out in the morning."

I couldn't hide the relief I felt. I nuzzled into him. His arms encircled me. We both knew this couldn't last but we would savor every second we had.

"Okay," I whispered and kissed the area over his heart, right on top of the scar the obsidian dagger had left. "Tomorrow."

Tomorrow turned into the next day and the day after that. We spent every moment exploring each other. We discovered new ways to make the other moan and played a Game of: Does this make my little bud, wet?

When Exekiel wasn't ruining me for other men, he made subtle comments about my relationship with Loch and the corruption of the Royal Court.

He had a theory that they'd been working with the sirens the night they'd attacked Shifter Springs. The night that had marked the Brutal War as brutal, and led to the barrier and almost two hundred years of oppression. I hadn't wanted to hear his theories then. I didn't want to hear them now, but I couldn't pretend that doubt hadn't niggled at the back of my mind ever since.

I'd learnt the hard way that Loch wasn't the heroic leader he claimed to be but a power-hungry asshole who would stop at nothing to have his way. His hatred of all Inlanders ran deep. It wasn't impossible to believe that he would slaughter an entire cast of them if it served his needs. It was possible that the attack at the banquet had been for the same reason. Not to help the Outliers, but to help himself get whatever they'd promised him in return.

Anger I hadn't fully confronted filled my lungs. The memory of Loch pawing at me, the way he'd spread my legs during the attack, and worse, the way I'd liked it, burnt inside me.

"Everything alright?"

I blinked at Exekiel. He sat across from me by the fire and used his dagger to skin some fish.

I inhaled before I said, "Just thinking about Loch."

The air around Exekiel darkened. Wisps of shadows curled from his skin.

"Oh?"

I rolled my eyes. "Not in that way."

Although in a way it was. Again, I relived the moment Loch had me spread on that table. The way he'd moved his hand between my legs and pulled down my panties—the things he'd promised to do to me. Arousal I didn't want to feel mingled with my disgust.

I'd trusted Loch; blindly followed him because I was so desperate to belong—to be wanted. Deep down I'd known something wasn't right about him. Lucinda had tried to warn me but I hadn't listened. Now the asshole owned a piece of me and he'd tried to fuck me on the puke-covered bodies of the dead.

"I'd prefer if you didn't think about him in any way," Exekiel's tone was dry as he sliced his dagger along the fish's flesh.

I snorted. "What if I was thinking about killing him…slowly?"

Exekiel's brow lifted. "Then for the first time, I'd say we agreed on something." He dragged his hand along his jaw. "And when you get tired, I will take over."

A smile played around the edge of my mouth. I gathered up the edible leaves and berries we'd found earlier and placed them on a large leaf.

"I won't get tired."

Exekiel's gaze darkened. That thought seemed to excite him in a wholly different way than what I'd meant. My body flushed. I was so turned on. I had to look away. I'd have thought I would have had enough of him by now but that didn't seem possible. I would never get enough of this devastating Fae with his powerful thighs and bruising thrusts.

Exekiel's nostrils flared. I pressed my legs together and slowly exhaled. He'd warned me about my scent. The pink of his eyes glimmered. I grabbed my waterskin and took a deep pull. If only we had something stronger.

"What brought these murderous thoughts to your head, little bud?"

My mind played off like a reel. Loch, my father cradling me in his arms. He rested my head on his chest, sang me lullabies and read me stories. Then Loch the man with his tongue in my mouth, his fingers shoved inside me. His teeth against my throat. Then Loch, the monster. Who siphoned my power, stripped my control and punished me with pleasure and pain.

Not for the first time, I considered telling Exekiel about the Ceremonial Bind between Loch and I. The one inflicted on me before I was old enough to think. But I couldn't face his reaction, and a part of me felt like admitting it made it real. Here, I could pretend the connection between Loch and I didn't exist. Here I could pretend that Exekiel and I had a future…Maybe we did.

"His attack at the banquet," I finally snarled which was partly true, and my anger was real. "Loch said he wanted peace in the Isles but that attack was anything but."

I picked up the leaf of berries and headed towards the river to wash them.

"Nothing the Rebel Leader says or does can be trusted," Exekiel growled.

I snorted and knelt by the water's edge. "I noticed."

"Now do you see why going along with his plans could backfire?"

I rolled the berries in the cool water but glanced back at Exekiel. Something in his tone said he was trying to make a point.

"Do you see why it may not be a great idea to free your people if that's what Loch wants?"

My shoulders tensed. "What?"

Exekiel's gaze searched the skies. He was looking for camera-orbs. He did that a lot.

When he looked back at me, his eyes shimmered on the cusp of red and rose.

"There is only so much I can say here, but trust me, little bud. Freeing your people now could damn the entire Realm."

I got to my feet. Half the berries fell and floated away.

"Trust you?" My brows lifted. "Trust *you?*" My laugh was cold as I gathered up the remaining berries in the bottom of my dress. "The Fae who ran me out of the Realm when I was a child. Who exiled my people. Spied on me for the Council. Who seduced me to get inside my mind?" With each accusation, I strode towards him and jabbed a finger at his chest. "The Fae who's threatened to kill me more times than I can count, who imprisoned my mother and who recently left me tied to a tree?"

Exekiel grabbed my hand and pulled me towards him. I pulled away.

When I came back into the Games, I vowed that this time, I was trusting myself. No Exekiel. No Loch. No Council. No bullshit. I had a plan: Win the Games. Free the Outer Isles. That plan hadn't changed.

I couldn't let Exekiel use my doubts about Loch to turn me away from what I came here to do. I couldn't let him warp my mind so that my people stayed in exile.

I folded my arms across my chest. "Tell me something, Exekiel; if you win the Games, do you still plan to force my people to their knees and strap a collar around their necks?"

He hesitated. That hesitation said it all. "Varialla—"

"Save it." I stalked back to the fire and dumped the freshly cleaned berries onto a large leaf. "I don't need to hear anything from the man who would put me and my people in chains."

"For good reason."

I spun to face him. "There is no good reason!"

Gosh, I'd been an idiot. This was never going to work. No matter which way I twisted this or how much I wished things were different, Exekiel would always be my enemy.

I swallowed the knot of sorrow in my throat. "Let's just forget it." My hands balled into fists. "Whatever this is between us only exists here and now. Not outside these walls. This is not an alliance or a relationship." Tears stung my eyes. I blinked them away. "This is nothing more than this."

It couldn't be more.

A rare hint of anguish flickered in Exekiel's piercing pink eyes before it died and turned to stone. "Fine."

I stepped away from him and fought the urge to let him curl me in his arms and give me the comfort only he could.

"Fine."

38

VARIALLA:
TICK TOCK

Exekiel woke me with his tongue. Last night, the conversation had been awkward during dinner and we'd eventually gone to sleep side by side but not touching.

Now, it was like our argument had never happened. Sleep clung to the edges of my mind as brisk thrusts between my legs stirred me all the way awake.

My eyes shot open and I gaped down at the hulking Fae whose wings arced behind him as he feasted between my thighs.

I moaned and jerked beneath his tongue's lashes.

"Shit." I grasped a fistful of his soft, dark locks and pressed him closer.

Exekiel growled and sucked me into his mouth. My legs clamped around his head but he pushed on my thighs and spread them.

"I want you splayed for me, little bud." His wet, shiny lips slanted in a way that made my heart beat faster.

"You can have me anyway you want," I promised as his thumb rubbed my clit.

The sensation was overwhelming. A cry burned in my throat. I flung my arm over my face and bit into my forearm.

"Eyes on me," Exekiel commanded.

My insides spasmed. I lowered my arm and looked down at his wickedly handsome face as he pumped two fingers inside me and flicked my clit with his tongue.

"Mmmm," he groaned. "I love the smell of you in the morning." His tongue slid from his mouth and Exekiel lowered himself to deliver a slow, languid lick from my anus to clit.

I thought I was going to combust.

As he continued to lick me, he breathed me in. His eyes rolled. "Like fucking salvation."

His tongue plunged back inside me. His thumb continued to work my clit. Fuck. If this was makeup sex, I would fight with him more often.

His stubble grazed my thigh as he altered his direction. Pleasure speared through me sharper than I've ever known. My cries bounced off the cave walls.

Sweat slid between my breasts. My breath choked in my lungs.

"Such a good girl," he praised. "Such a delicious little creature."

I writhed into Exekiel's wet, hot strokes. My vision spotted. I was coming undone. Unravelling on the edge of his ministrations.

"Fuck," he breathed. "You're everything." His fingers dug into my hips and faster than I could focus, he rolled us so I was seated on his face.

I lifted my hips. My hands braced in the flaky dirt.

"What are you doing?" I gasped.

His nails bit into my ass. "Eating your sweet little pussy." His hot breath brushed across my sensitive skin. I shuddered. "Fuck my face, little bud. Come for me. Now." He yanked me down and buried his mouth deeper. His tongue struck every sensitized spot inside me.

My cells shattered. My body shook. I arched back. My hands braced on his chest. I felt as if my lungs were on fire. As if power had replaced my blood. My hips undulated. I trembled uncontrollably. Then scarlet wings born of flame surged from my spine and glorious euphoria gripped my heart.

"Fuck!" I shouted.

Exekiel's eyes darkened. He fed on me more greedily as he took in the birth of my wings, my horns; the blaze of my inner dragon set free.

My toes curled in the dirt. My mind spun. Then my strained release surged out of me. The sounds I made were ineligible; barbaric, as I helplessly convulsed on my mate's relentless tongue.

We had to go. There was no way around it. Every second I spent here, I risked my rank and the future I'd promised my people. Now, nestled on the ground between Exekiel's legs, I told him the same thing.

"I know," he murmured from where he sat behind me with his fingers in my hair.

Earlier, midnight-horns had appeared right where his fingers were. But like my wings, they'd faded as soon as I came down from the high of my orgasm.

Now, Exekiel was trying to pull my hair into a French braid but so far, he'd only succeeded in pulling it.

"We'll go as soon as I'm done."

I yelped. "You're supposed to be braiding it, not yanking it out."

He grunted, "Easier said than done, little bud. Are you aware of how thick your hair is?"

I snickered. "I've been styling it for twenty-five years, Fae-boy. Can't you handle it for twenty-five seconds?"

"Careful." His fingers curled around my neck. My pulse skipped. "I might just take my blade to it."

I glared up at him. "You wouldn't dare."

"I would," he purred. "If I thought my blade could actually get through it."

A cackle rolled out of me. "Shut up."

He chuckled and planted a kiss on my forehead. "You'd look beautiful either way."

I swallowed thickly. I wasn't used to this side of him. It felt more dangerous than when he was threatening to kill me.

I tilted my head back and his lips met mine. Warmth spread from my fingertips down to my toes. I would never get tired of kissing him. My heart beat faster and every part of me came alive.

His kisses were pure heaven dipped in hell. As scorching and as damning.

Before I could stop myself, I turned and straddled his lap. His hands quickly found their way to my ass and he moved me against him. His lips trailed a path of fire along my jawline and down my throat. I gasped and gripped his shoulders; drew him closer. I held onto him like driftwood in a shipwreck. But I couldn't get swept away; not again.

Exekiel pulled back and breathed, "Fuck," as if he'd had the same thought. He gripped my jaw in one hand and forced me to meet his conflicted stare whilst his other hand hitched up my dress. "Why can't I get enough of you?"

A piercing alarm cracked through my rising desire and the holographic map of the Fields surged from the phone screen. It was twice our size and an arrow flashed over Level Eight.

I blinked and tried to clear the heady rush from my mind.

"It's flashing," I panted.

"Fuck, we're running out of time."

My stomach dropped. How was that possible? We had ten days to finish each level. How many had we sacrificed for this time together?

I sprang to my feet and tried to hide the dread that pulled in my gut.

The fairytale was over. It was time to head back to the real world of sabotage and secrets.

"I guess this is it," I said as casually as I could, as I quickly tied the shoes I'd crafted out of folded leaves and twine. My voice was almost swallowed by the alarm that refused to stop. "We can go back to hating each other and forget this ever happened."

Whatever this was, we'd agreed it couldn't exist outside of the Games. We still wanted different things and we would still take each other down to get it.

Exekiel's shadows rippled around him as he turned towards me. The heat of his gaze was intense and unshakeable.

"I will never forget this." His shadows wrapped around me and drew me to him. "You are forever imprinted on my soul."

He kissed me; a passionate, desperate kiss as if he knew it would be our last. As if he was saying goodbye. My heart squeezed.

"I love you," he whispered against my lips.

I froze. For a single second, I forgot about everything outside of this moment.

His fingers ran along my cheek. I briefly closed my eyes. "The air I breathe is sweeter when it tastes like you. I never sleep as deep as when you're in my arms." He pulled me closer and rested his forehead on mine. "For so long my shadows have been my sole companion, but with you, I can see the stars."

I tasted the salt of my tears when his lips met mine again. Too soon they were gone.

"I love you, Varialla. I always will."

He kissed me a final time, winked and whispered, "Bye."

Then he was gone.

39

VARIALLA:
THE FALL OF FATES

There wasn't time for wishing and regrets. Exekiel left and I choked down the surge of emotions that rose inside me. I could relive every bittersweet second of this when the Games were done. When I sat on the Eternal Throne with only my memories of him beside me. Because he was it for me. I would never want or love another man the way I loved Exekiel V'alin. But he and I could never be more than the moments we stole in this Game.

With my gaze fixed on the map, I raced in the direction of the Fall of Fates. The arrow above it had started out a deep black but was now a searing red.

The alarm peeled louder. My pulse spiked.

"Shit, shit, shit!"

I'd been so stupid; so selfishly lost in a fantasy that I'd almost fucked everything up. The Poisoned Heart on my side burned sharper than it ever had before. I almost felt it spread; felt it sink its toxic claws into my breast.

I skidded towards the rocky shore of the fall and quickly realized that level eight required me to dive in. I didn't hesitate. I plunged into the bitter frozen depths that almost caused my entire body to seize up. I wasn't sure how anyone had survived these frigid waters but with gritted teeth, I forced my muscles to move.

Keys shimmered on the silted riverbed. Fighting off the shivers that wracked my body, I swam the endless distance towards them.

I used my siren gifts to fend off the worst of the water that crashed over me, then I used the heat of my inner dragon—which responded more easily lately—to warm me from the inside. My limbs eventually relaxed. I pressed on.

The alarm blared. This time it was so shrill, pain splintered through my teeth. Any second now the door to Level 8 would shut and I would be out of the Games.

A figure moved lower down. Even within the mass of churning water I knew it was Exekiel as he made his way to the exit.

I swam faster.

The earth shook. The alarm screamed. The keys vanished.

I froze. For what felt like an eternity, I gaped up through the ripples of the river and into the falls. The level was over. I hadn't made it through. Piercing pink eyes met mine through the water. Neither of us had.

Before I could fully understand what this meant, the scene faded away.

Drenched and shivering, I was once again dropped on the sands of the arena. Like before, the remaining contestants stood beside me with an audience hollering around us.

It was close to sunset and the sky was shades of orange and red. Banners waved in the bleachers and people chanted our names. Goather commented on the champions—those who had found their way into the top ten. Exekiel was now at number eight. I wasn't even on the list.

It all passed me in a daze. There were a few heckled shouts and mocking taunts of how Exekiel and I had been so lost in each other that we'd lost track of the fucking time. Now we'd have to compete in the Jousting Tournament. If we wanted to get back into the Games, we would have to fight for our place.

The pillow barely muffled my scream. How had things gone so epically wrong? How had I plummeted to number seventeen in the ranks? And how was I supposed to survive the jousting tournament taking place in three fucking days when I'd never jousted a day in my life? I groaned and slammed my fist repeatedly into the mattress.

"Go into the joust like that and you're sure to win."

I sat up and blinked. In the doorway, Maximus and Lucinda waited with their arms folded. A bottle of wine hung between Max's fingers and Lucinda twirled three chalices in her hand.

I bowled off the bed towards them and flung my arms around their shoulders. They pulled me close and squeezed. Some of the tension eased from my posture. I'd missed them more than I realized.

"I messed up," I whispered.

Maximus patted me on the head. "How can we learn, if we never make mistakes?" We separated and he sashayed into the room. "That's why the Fates created wine."

He popped off the cork and Lucinda was there to catch the bubbles that frothed over the lip.

I had so many questions. I didn't know where to begin.

"Here." Lucinda pressed a chalice into my hand. "First, drink, then talk."

I drained the drink in one long gulp then held it out for Maximus to refill.

His brow lifted. "We're going to need more wine."

I collapsed on the bed. "We're going to need a miracle. I don't know what happened out there. It was like the world stopped spinning with him."

"It's common between mates, especially ones with a bond as strong as yours when it's finally given permission to flourish." Lucinda took a swig from her own chalice.

I swallowed another mouthful and fell back on the mattress. "It doesn't need to flourish. It needs to die a quick and painful death."

I sighed and propped myself up on my elbow. "Have you had any more news on Odus and Eudora? All I've been told is that they're in the sick beds of Evermore."

Unlike the nobles, they hadn't been granted care at the palace infirmary. Nymphs and other apparently lower-class beings weren't worthy of the beds. That would have pissed me off but, at the time, I'd just been so relieved to hear that Odus was alive.

Lucinda climbed up on the bed and curled her legs under her. "According to High Priestess, Azalea, they're both going to make a full recovery." She grimaced. "However, Odus was in a coma until a few days ago and Eudora's leg was cut off. She's currently going through rehabilitation."

My hand flew over my mouth. Tears sprang to my eyes. They'd taken her leg?

Lucinda looked down and swirled the goblet in her hand. "Apparently Odus watched the replay of level five on orb vision."

Level Five was the quicksand round. The level where his girlfriend had sacrificed herself to save the rest of us. It'd been almost a month since then, but every time I thought about it, the agony was fresh.

My throat thickened and I scrunched my eyes closed. Jia had killed herself just so I could fuck my mate into oblivion and get thrown out of the Games.

Another frustrated cry tore out of me. "How was I so stupid?"

"It wasn't your best decision," Maximus agreed from where he sat crossed legged at the foot of the bed. "However, when you're done hating yourself for your sexplosion, I want to know every little—or not so little—detail." He waggled his brows at me.

I snorted. "Sexplosion?"

"What would you call it?"

Lucinda snickered. "Didn't you get enough of them from what the orbs broadcasted? It's been on replay all day."

I groaned. Once or twice, I'd noticed the perverted camera-orbs filming me and Exekiel but I hadn't been able to stop. My mind had officially left my body. All I'd cared about; all I'd craved was him.

"They blur out all the good bits," Maximus whined. "The most they showed was her tits."

I scowled at him from beneath my arm. "Don't sound so disappointed."

"They're lovely, really. You should be proud. But they're not what I was there for."

I laughed. Despite everything, I felt a bit better after a few minutes with them, and the wine, of course.

"What I'd like to know is how the two of you ended up like that in the first place?" Lucinda added with a wry quirk of her lips. "I thought you were done with the Shadow Saint."

"I was—I am." I shook my head.

"Then how, pray tell, did he end up with your pubes in his teeth?"

I laughed so hard; it became silent. I couldn't breathe. Maximus spewed his drink across my quilt. Tears streamed down my cheeks. Lucinda cackled.

"I'm serious," she cried between laughter. "How did we get here?"

I crossed my legs at the ankles convinced I was about to wet myself and sat up; causing the scarf I'd tied around my head to slip. "We'll get to all that later." I dabbed at my eyes. "First, I want to know what happened to you in level five."

Maximus clapped his hands. "That's exactly what I asked on the way over here. I was told I had to wait until we were all together." He nudged her with his foot. "We're all together."

He refilled our glasses and we drank as Lucinda told us that she'd been taken to some camera pod by Exekiel.

My heart thumped against my ribs.

"What?"

I'd spent so long with him and he hadn't said a word.

She grimaced. "He had a video of me getting off with my source and used it to…" she considered her words, "*Negotiate* my cooperation."

My mouth dropped open. My skin crawled. Exekiel had told me to trust him but this was exactly why I couldn't. Shit like this didn't add up to the Fae I loved but they were one and the same.

"What did he want?" I asked. My throat was dry.

Lucinda's mouth twisted to one side. "He wanted me to arrange a meeting with the Giants. I assume it has something to do with getting them to sign his so-called Petition of Peace."

"Boo! Petition of Peace, my ass," Maximus jeered and slugged from his chalice. "More like Petition of Poops."

The wine had clearly hit him.

I felt numb. Exekiel and I had agreed that we were still enemies in this but how did he slip so easily from villain to friend and more than that? How did he tell me he loved me and at the same time, use my friend to help him cage me?

Lucinda cocked her head and poured more wine into my cup. "I'm guessing you have questions?"

I didn't know where to start.

"I have questions." Maximus grunted. "Who the fuck is your source? I can't believe the Shadow Saint knows before us."

I laughed. That was a much better question than the ones spiraling through my mind.

Lucinda's answering smile was the most delicate thing I'd ever seen her show. "Evangeline Degalos."

My eyes bugged out of my head. Maximus choked on his wine.

"What?" he spluttered.

Evangeline Degalos; second primary and mate to Adir Degalos. During my awkward dinner with Exekiel the other night, he'd claimed that she was supposed to have won the Games but they were rigged. Apparently, a siren had been disguised as a nymph on her styling crew and had convinced her to lose in the finale and let Adir take the lead.

At the time I'd been too irritated with him to listen and in the end, we'd agreed to drop it.

Now, I couldn't help asking, "Is it true that everyone thought she would win the Games?"

"She was incredible!" Maximus enthused. "Unstoppable until Phase Three." He shook his head. "I'll never understand what happened there." He took a swig of his drink and snickered. "Some people say she deliberately threw the Game so her mate could win." He rolled his eyes.

Lucinda narrowed hers. "Strange question, Varialla."

"And an even stranger explanation of why I asked."

I gestured for Maximus to refill our chalices then told them everything Exekiel had told me. I hadn't been sure if I was going to say anything. Partly because he could have been lying and partly because

I felt like I was breaking his trust. However, after what he did to Lucinda, I didn't know what to think. I clearly couldn't trust my judgment when it came to him and if I had to choose between him or them, I trusted them.

Maximus and Lucinda didn't seem as shocked by the allegation as I'd been.

"After the injustices I've seen from the noblemen and women of this Court, nothing would surprise me." Maximus raised his cup and drained every last drop.

Lucinda's gaze was thoughtful. "I did always wonder how so many sirens managed to get past the guards."

I straightened. "You think he was telling the truth?"

"I hope not," she rushed to say. "But..."

"It's possible," Maximus concluded.

My gut turned. They were supposed to tell me how ridiculous I sounded for even considering it. That Loch Orqanz would never ally himself with the Royal Court of the Five Isles. That the Court wouldn't consort with Outliers. But what did I know? Those assholes had been hiding the truth from me since I got here. But if Exekiel was right...fuck.

I covered my face in my hands.

"This is so much bigger than I thought, isn't it?"

For so long, I'd been clear on my goal. When everything else had been murky and going to hell, I'd had a plan. Win the Games, claim the Throne, tear down the barrier to free the Outer Isles. Nothing else had mattered more. Now freeing them could mean condemning them and the rest of the Isles.

I shook my head. "I won't let him collar my people whilst he plays caped crusader."

"Of course not," Lucinda snorted. "But I think you agree that something has to be done."

I swallowed. "Like what?"

She grimaced. "I can't answer that. You have to trust your gut on this one. Follow your heart."

I scowled. My gut was telling me to run far and fast but my heart was firmly in the Shadow Saints grasp.

40

EXEKIEL:
YOU DIDN'T LISTEN

It was hard to put what happened between Varialla and I behind me and focus on the Games when every time I looked at an Orb-vision, we were plastered across the holo-screen. Our bodies writhing; her perky tits bouncing. Fates, she was my everything.

"I never stood a chance, did I?"

My gaze flicked to Vivienne who sat beside me in the tavern's booth.

She jerked her head at the screen. "Against perfect Sea-bitch over there."

My lips twitched. "I thought you said you liked her now."

Vivienne's thin eyebrows shot up into her hairline. "I said I was grateful to her for saving your life from those barbarians," she spat. "Although I still don't understand why she did."

I pressed a hand over my heart. "You wound me. Would you have preferred she let me die?"

Ever since Vladimir had confronted Varialla, the truth about that night was out. It hadn't impacted her inside the Games since players were cut off from the outside world. However, upon our return, it had been plastered across every holo-screen and in every issue of Goblin's Gab.

Headlines read:

The Sea's Savage saves Mortal Enemy.

Hated or Fated?

Foreign Temptress takes human vows "til death do we part" to a new level

That one was a bit wordy for my taste but the readers seemed to like it.

Vivienne rolled her eyes. "You know what I mean." She tapped her nails on the side of her metal goblet. "If she'd let you die, the barrier would have fallen. The Outer Isles would have been free. She would have gotten her war." Her frown deepened. "Without you, her powers are basically unmatched. The sea-witch could have had everything she wanted." Vivienne looked at me. "So, why did she choose you instead?"

I took a swig from my cup. "Hard to say."

Vivienne let out a shrill snort of laughter. "Or maddeningly obvious."

"She did it because you are everything she truly wants."

Vivienne and I turned to Kraxus who now stood beside the booth with a handful of darts and two pints of ale. "Maybe if there was no war, no duty, no honor, she would choose you every time."

He slid into the booth and handed a pitcher to Vivienne.

I grunted. "Who knew you were such a romantic, Kraxus?"

"I did," Vivienne scoffed, but she said it with less loathing than she usually would when referring to him.

Apparently the two had found each other in the maze and spent a considerable amount of time together. Nothing had happened between them, but earlier, Vivienne admitted that she didn't think the shifter was a complete idiot anymore.

I was starting to wonder if all mates had been put together in that level. To see if there was anything beyond physical between them. A trial within itself. Particularly for those who were already involved with another or who saw the mate bond as a chain on freedom.

"So, what now?" Vivienne sat taller and took a sip of her drink. "Will you attach a leash to her collar and walk her like a bitch when you take the throne?"

My shoulders tensed. I slid my stare to hers. My eyes cold. I didn't have many friends and even less since the Brutal War. Vivienne had always been one of them. Her unwavering loyalty and vicious streak had been what stood out to me. Now, they pissed me off.

She sensed she'd gone too far. Her nostrils flared and she pursed her pouty red lips. She would never apologize and I didn't blame her. I wasn't just fucking our enemy; I'd fallen love with her. Neither of us knew how to navigate this territory.

For now, I had to remain focused on my mission. To avenge my family and see the true villains brought to their knees before they had a chance to strike again. I hated that what I had to do would hurt Varialla and her people but the barrier could not fall until our enemies did.

Vivienne sighed. "I don't know what's going on with you and the sea savage and I can't say I agree with it." She held up a hand. "But whatever you decide to do, I will try to support it. You know I've always wanted you to find someone who makes you happy."

I looked at her. She waved me off. Vivienne and I had ended our tryst nearly a century ago, but she'd never quite gotten over it. For me, it had been purely physical but for her it had turned into something more. Eventually I'd ended it to keep from hurting her. I wasn't sure I'd succeeded.

Kraxus cleared his throat. I shot him a grin that made the veins in his neck jump.

Vivienne squeezed my shoulder. "Just…be careful."

"I second that," he grumbled. "Don't make the same mistake her father did. Or us Bravinore's will be the next cast to be wiped from existence." His words sent a sliver of ice down my spine.

I lifted my glass in a toast. "Never."

Like me, Prince Thraxen, heir to Shifter Springs had fallen in love with the enemy. It had cost him his life and the lives of his entire cast. His identity was the one thing I hadn't revealed yet. The second I saw Varialla's flames—a mix of teal and blood-red—I'd known who her father was.

It made sense that her mother had seduced the next in line for the throne. They say she truly loved him in the end. Perhaps she thought there was a way out that didn't involve mutiny. I supposed we'd never know the truth since the Council had cut out her tongue and ripped out her teeth. They said it was part of her punishment but I knew it was a way to keep her quiet since she let herself get caught.

Nikolai, Atlas and the others joined our table with more drinks, and nymphs who liked to hang around Inlanders. With us, they could go to places they couldn't, sit at the best tables, drink the best liquors. I wouldn't pretend it wasn't a fucked-up system we had.

"I'm going to the Fates Cathedral," I eventually murmured to Vivienne.

She gave me a knowing look and nodded. Vivienne was the only person I'd told about Satrialla. Most assumed she'd died with her family. I never bothered to correct them. A Fae like me had a lot of enemies. Satrialla was a weakness I wouldn't let them use against me.

Outside, the air was cool. I pulled up the collar of my trench coat and strode through the streets.

The din of debauchery died down the closer I got to Cathedral Lane. I jogged across the square where the last café was closing up for the night. All other establishments; bakeries, book stores and such were closed. The crowd thinned to a few lone stragglers. Eventually, it was just me.

A figure descended from the rooftops. I was ready. I always was. My head snapped up and my fist shot out. It collided with my assailant's gut. He fell to his knees. I got behind him and had my forearm around his neck before he could rise.

He clawed at my arm and tried to twist out of my grip.

"What do we have here?" I let him go and kicked him in the back. There was the satisfying snap of his spine.

He bawled and faceplanted. He tried to crawl away on his elbows but I stood on the vertebrae I'd just shattered. The fucker screamed.

"You're not leaving so soon, are you?"

The Fate-stain sobbed. Snot dribbled from his nose. Tears tracked his cheeks. I was mildly insulted they'd sent such a pathetic squib to ambush me. Then again, they wouldn't.

I spun too late. Another fucker was right behind me. He stabbed a needle into my shoulder.

The air shifted behind me. I swiveled and knocked aside the dagger that had been about to ram through the back of my skull.

"*Ulius*," I hissed and squeezed the wrist of my would-be attacker. His bones turned to dust in my grip.

The fucker screamed.

More came at me. Figures cloaked in hoods to hide their faces charged from the alleys. Lit by the silver hourglass symbol of Zorsch, my shadows rushed to meet them. Death found its mark. Four bastards hit the stone. Their skin charred and flaking. Their bodies were nothing more than empty husks.

"Shit!" someone gasped.

"Do not run." The familiarity of that voice sent rage to the ends of my teeth.

I spun and surveyed the cloaked cowards that closed in around me. There were at least two dozen of them. My gaze zeroed in on the one in the middle.

"Alexov," I purred.

His teeth flashed but he didn't lower his hood. "Attack!"

On his command, they did. Those on my right, charged. Three in the form of beasts; two large wolves and a fucking bear. Magic pummeled me from another direction. Brutal blasts that I barely dodged as I caved in the skull of one wolf and tore out the fangs of the other.

His howl echoed through the square. I rolled beneath the swinging paws of the bear and rammed the wolf's fangs through the soft flesh between its neck and jaw. Blood sprayed over me. His body juddered then returned to a large fucker with tattooed cheeks. I recognized him. He was a soldier of the Royal Guard.

I used his corpse to cover me from the blows of magic as my shadows rose and tore through the square.

I couldn't unleash them like I would on a battlefield. The risk of them seeping beneath the cracks of someone's door and claiming innocent lives was too great. The Royal Court knew that. It was why they'd chosen here to attack.

Despite Alexov's order, those my shadows pursued, ran screaming. I caught several around the ankles and dragged them to their knees as they pleaded for their lives. So at odds with the murderous shits, they'd been a few moments ago.

My shadows sank inside their flesh. Their skin split and black trails of blood seeped from the cracks. That was one thing I loved about my shadows—each death could be different. I never knew what I was going to get.

Something sharp struck the back of my neck. I swiveled only to have another come at me from behind. A bite of pain sliced into my side. I trapped the bastards head in my hands. He'd barely squeaked before I twisted and broke his fucking neck.

"Meet me like a man," I shouted at the one I knew was Alexov.

My head spun. Chunks climbed up my throat. Telltale signs that they'd injected me with the same poison Loch Orqanz had used on me a few months ago. Back then I'd been caught off-guard; so lost in my mate I hadn't heard them approach. They'd ambushed me, beaten me bloody and somehow, with the aid of the toxin, the Rebel Leader's magic had overpowered mine. Given him the opportunity to ram a blade through my heart. Tonight, would not end the same.

"Very well." Alexov lowered his hood.

The shits around him did the same. On his left was Pre-Primary Knox. On his right, Primary Adir, backed by a few other members of the Court.

The last time I saw Adir he'd been choking on his own vomit. Now here he stood; the only one to make a full recovery from the poison that night. According to the Royal Court, Adir was too powerful to succumb to the effects of toxin. What they really meant was that he'd been given the antidote. His near-death experience had just been another ploy; a way to convince the people that he'd suffered as much as they had. To make them believe he couldn't have possibly been behind the attack.

Alexov sneered. "You just couldn't listen."

I lunged for his throat. Their magic came down on me like an avalanche. My knees threatened to give out but through sheer will, I held my ground. Two of them grabbed my arms and pinned them behind my back.

"I told you not to visit the Outer Isles," Alexov paced towards me. "You didn't listen."

My vision spotted. I fought through the haze of the toxin and flung my head back, shattering the nose of the guard behind me. He screamed.

I heaved on my shadows. Their ascent was slow. The other guard gripped me tighter. I twisted out of the other ones hold and punched him in the throat. He retched and staggered back.

More came at me. I took them down. But with every strike, my bones felt heavy. My aim was off.

"I told you to stay away from the girl." Alexov spoke louder as I ripped apart his men to get to him. "We had our own plans for the siren."

He sneered over his shoulder at Adir who fisted his cock.

"Plans that kept me on the throne and that siren bitch on her knees." The First Primary waggled his brows.

The Fate-stained fuckers around him laughed. Spit sprouted in my mouth and I spat it to the ground. A cold sweat crept across my brow.

I pulled on my power but now it barely rippled.

"But you," Alexov barked. His eyes were cold and vicious. "Didn't listen!"

My head tipped back as his fist crashed into my jaw. My shadows rose aimlessly, outside of my control.

My vision blurred. I shook my head to clear it.

"I will kill you." I snarled.

It wasn't a threat. It was a promise.

Alexov glanced at the syringes that littered the ground.

"Not likely," His grin sharpened. "With the amount in your system, you'll be dead within the hour. When you're discovered in the early hours of the morning, everyone will believe that a strange plague is sweeping through the Isles." He chuckled. "If they want to survive, they must do everything we say."

The others laughed. My stomach tightened with painful spasms. My head throbbed. Now the fuckers weren't restraining me, they were propping me up.

Alexov nodded and they flung me to the ground. Pain exploded through my gut and cracked across my skull as their boots came down on my flesh. But their blows were minor compared to the agony of the poison that ripped through my insides.

It was worse than the last time. Under the weight of their magic, I was crushed. My power stuttered in my lungs and the symbols of the Fates flashed across my skin. They were sporadic and fleeting.

Rage rattled through me. With the last vestiges of my strength, I pulled on my shadows. Determination became my blood. My shadows rose and I lassoed them around a councilman's throat. His eyes widened with horror as they tightened and choked the life out of him. He decayed right before my eyes then crumpled to a pile of dust.

The others lurched back. I pushed to my knees and swayed. This was not my end. I wouldn't fall until they did.

As I staggered to my feet, some of them ran. Others looked anxiously at Alexov, waiting for his command.

He looked like he might tell them to restrain me, but his eyes darted to my shadows that coiled around my arms.

"Leave him," he spat. "He won't be our problem much longer."

Adir sneered. "And his siren bitch will die with him."

Their laughter rang in my ears as they pulled up their hoods and disappeared down an alley. Rage seized my lungs.

"*Thesona*," I whispered.

The healing effects of the Fate slid through my veins. It wasn't enough to nullify the poison but it could slow its progress.

Spit filled my mouth. My legs gave out. The cold concrete ground cut into my fevered skin.

With trembling fingers, I gripped my Five Isle's phone and tapped the symbol of the ear.

Its hologram emerged.

I rasped, "Connect: Vivienne."

She answered on the second ring. Terror instantly filled her eyes when she took in the state of me. I knew that, like my hands, black veins had spread across my neck and face.

"Cathedral," I choked.

Then the phone clattered from my fingers and everything went dark.

41

VARIALLA:
SAY SORRY

My bath chamber filled with clouds of steam and the air was perfumed with jasmine and rosemary. I inhaled as I slid into the water's warm embrace. This was my second bath today but I still felt the filth of the Games caked into my skin.

I perused the scented oils that lined the rocky edge but froze when something moved beneath the water. I spun and raised my hands as two figures emerged. Power shimmered around my fingertips but promptly fizzled out.

Colette and Loch stood before me. I ignored the icy blue eyes of the man who thought he owned me and turned to Colette. My first instinct was to run to her but the anger in her eyes kept me planted.

"Look me in the eye," she snarled. "And tell me that you killed Konch, Viktor and Reed."

Shit. I knew this day would come. I'd been anticipating and dreading it.

I held her stare and said, "I killed them. They threw me into a well then attacked my mate."

That familiar thrum of fire burned in my throat just like it had that night. When it came to Exekiel, I would burn the world down to save him. It was a truth I'd finally accepted and I wasn't going to apologize for it.

Loch scoffed. "So, you're saying he means more to you than us. Than our freedom!"

I spun on him. Water sloshed around me. "I'm saying don't touch my fucking mate."

Venom burned in his gaze as he dragged it over me. It lingered a little too long on the water that lapped beneath my breasts. I probably should have cared that I was naked but I didn't. Right then the only thing stopping me from mauling the bastard was Colette. I noted with some satisfaction the scar I'd carved across his face.

"Reed was Aya's brother." Colette's voice doused some of my fury and I turned back to her. "Konch would read to the children in the infirmary every night."

My jaw clenched. If I hadn't killed them, Exekiel would be dead and I would be a prisoner of the Coral Court. I'd be at the mercy of Loch's twisted bullshit and the Isles would be at war. I didn't regret what I'd done, but I hated that I'd hurt her. Hated that I hadn't been able to tell her in a better way.

She shook her head. "They were the good guys."

"There are no good or bad guys, Colette. There are only people and the choices they make in each moment. One bad choice doesn't mean you've never been good or kind. And one good act doesn't mean you've never done bad things."

Konch may have read to the children but according to Exekiel, he'd also coerced a dragon shifter to slaughter his entire family. Reed was Aya's brother but he'd helped concoct the poison that they'd unleashed at the banquet.

There was no good or bad here. The villain in one's story was often the hero in someone else's.

"I had a choice to make and I know it's hard to understand but I chose the lesser of two evils." My gaze slid to Loch.

Behind Colette's back, he sneered.

"I am sorry that I hurt you but I'm not sorry for what I did."

Colette scrubbed a hand down her face. The enraged devastation in her eyes carved me in two. "I don't even know who you are."

Without waiting for Loch, she ducked beneath the water and swam through whatever grate or pipe they'd come through. No Danimous was required this time.

Come to think of it, how had they gotten in? How had nobody noticed? Unease crept up my spine. I wrapped my arm across my breasts. With Colette, I hadn't cared that I was naked. Without her, the atmosphere was different; almost sinister.

"Now, do you see why I told you not to tell anyone?" Loch drawled.

I instinctively stepped back. "That wasn't for me. It was because you didn't want people to know that they died by dragon fire."

His eyes flashed.

"*My* dragon fire."

Loch had tried to make me believe that he kept that side of me a secret so that I wouldn't know how strong I was. In fact, it had been so that nobody knew. So that they looked to him as their savior and me as the tool he used.

His jagged teeth glinted. "You mean, mine."

My breath caught as I felt the bind tighten between us. My nostrils flared. I tried to fight its pull but Loch wrenched tighter. He held me and my power captive.

"You cannot access that side of you without me."

He was wrong. Recently, I'd tapped into my dragon gifts more easily. Especially when I was around Exekiel. Especially when he was inside me.

"And I cannot take the Realm without you." Loch shrugged. His hold of the bind slackened. "Which is why I've come to apologize."

"Shove your apology," I snarled.

There was nothing he could say or do that would make me forgive the things he'd done.

It was strange but if Exekiel hadn't run me out of the realm as a child, I wouldn't hate Loch right now. I would have spent my entire life being groomed for him. Trained on how best to bind our power when the time came. I would have known from a young age, that I would wed the man I saw as my father and I would have been taught that my duty was to him and his needs only.

In a weird, dysfunctional way, Exekiel's desire to kill me had saved me.

"I don't care what you have to say," I hissed. "The only reason I haven't killed you for what you tried to do to me in that banquet hall is because you are the leader of my people. For now."

He chuckled through tight lips. "This is exactly why I have to apologize."

He waded through the water towards me. Unlike Colette he'd morphed his tail to legs. He wore a deep beige loincloth around his waist.

I stepped back and narrowed my eyes.

"I've been going about this the wrong way. You see, in order for our bond to solidify, it must be consummated."

He took another step towards me. I took another step back. Magic burned at my fingertips. I didn't want to kill him. After what happened with Konch and the others, if I took Loch, my people would never trust me. Never follow me. But I would kill him if he forced my hand.

"I'd hoped we could come to that agreement naturally. I wanted to be patient with you." He grimaced. "But by being patient I've just made it harder for you to accept the inevitable."

He moved closer. On instinct, I waved my hand and a blade of water glinted above my fingers. It looked as sharp as ice. For a brief second, I was too stunned to do anything then I looked back at him and hissed, "Don't touch me."

Loch hung his head and sighed. A fucking heavy sigh as if he was a victim here.

"I truly am sorry but I promise once we do this, you'll feel differently about everything."

He closed the distance between us and had me pinned against the side of the pool in seconds. I wasn't surprised when his rough hand closed around my neck. I didn't even flinch.

"Centuries I have put this plan in place," he dragged his thumb along my jawline. "Decades, I have maneuvered the pieces and manipulated the people." His grip tightened around my neck and he pressed closer to my naked body. "I have worked too long and sacrificed too much to let you ruin this for me." Loch's other hand fitted around my breast. I gasped; struck by a violent bolt of lust. "You may not love me, Varialla. But you will obey me."

His lips descended on mine. I reeled back as his tongue plundered my mouth. A surge of sensations swirled in my core. Loch ran his thumb in tight circles around my nipple. My knees shook. It was only him that was keeping me above the water.

"As soon as I make you come," he growled and bit down on my neck. "You'll never want me to stop. I promise."

O god. I blinked and fought to get a hold of myself. His touch commanded me more completely than it ever had. He'd clearly been holding back before but now he was going in for the kill—for everything.

"I'm going to make you feel so good, Princess."

He already was, as much as I wished he wasn't. I didn't have the same mad craving for him as I did for Exekiel but the need was undeniable. I wanted him inside me. I gasped when he lifted his loincloth and I felt the rough stroke of his swollen cock between my thighs.

Fuck!

Water slapped around us as he moved. The sharp contact made my head spin but it also brought me back to my fucking senses.

His mouth captured mine. I felt the tug in my chest. That familiar and infuriating twist of our bind as he yanked on my willpower and tried to make it his own.

Not today, asshole.

I brought my hands out of the water and slammed them into the side of his head, hard enough to rupture his eardrums. Loch bawled and rocked back. His hands were cupped over his ears.

"You can't stop this," he bellowed.

It was like he didn't care that someone might hear him.

I vaulted out of the bathing pool and raced towards my bed chamber where I kept the enchanted dagger from the trials that never missed its mark. He could use my magic against me but he couldn't control my weapons.

I flung a silk robe around myself—a flimsy attempt at a barrier between our bodies—and rummaged through the drawers of my dresser. His footsteps thudded behind me.

Before I could turn, Loch's hand was on the back of my head. He slammed me face down on the dresser. His fingers yanked on my hair as he wound my braid around his fist. His other hand gripped my hip and held me in place. He pressed himself against me.

"This will all make sense once I'm done with you."

I bucked and struggled to break free. Makeup powder plumed up my nose. The sharp edge of my compact mirror cut into my cheek.

Loch bent over me. "Once I come deep inside you, you'll understand."

His magic wrapped around mine and flooded my system. My eyes shot open and a scream stuck in my throat. It was a blend of agony and earth-shattering bliss. Need thundered between my legs but for once my mind was clear.

The bastard's cock stiffened and prodded my backside through my robe.

"Do you feel it?" He rasped. His breath was hot on the back of my ear as he pushed my legs apart. "Do you feel me breaking you? Bending you to my will?"

He straightened and yanked on my hair, forcing my head back as he rowed his hips hard. Pleasure sparked through my skin. Fuck. I wanted him. I wanted him so badly it hurt. But he was insane. It wasn't me—it was the bind. Some manipulation of my self that they'd inflicted on me at birth.

I squirmed as Loch rubbed himself against me. My hand fumbled for the dagger in my drawer but he had me pinned. He had no intentions of letting me go.

"Stop fighting." He sounded unhinged. "Let Fate run its course."

Loch hitched up my robe and stroked his hand across my bare ass. I was instantly wet. I stopped fighting. His fingers slid up my body and brushed the side of my breast. Hot tingles rippled through me. I moaned.

He was right. I couldn't fight the bind. I couldn't fight him. He wanted me to give in so that's what I would do. I was going to give the asshole exactly what he wanted.

"Do you get it now, Princess?" he growled. "I am your master."

His touches were almost loving which was laughable considering this bastard didn't have a loving bone in his body.

I nodded as much as I could with his hand gripped in my hair. "You are my master."

He paused then flipped me onto my back. Perfumes and powders toppled off the dresser and smashed across the tiles. Nail polish bottles dug into my spine. Loch grasped my thighs and dragged my legs up around his waist. I bucked when I felt the press of his erection through his loincloth.

His eyes danced with wild fervor. "You feel it."

It wasn't a question but I panted, "yes."

I let my body be overcome by the hunger I felt for him. The need that pulsed within. It was easy to give that part of me over to his command. He grinned and I knew he smelt it on my thighs.

Loch bent forward and his lips hungrily captured mine. I returned it just as eagerly. I met his next thrust with a roll of my hips. Only a thin scrap of fabric divided us and I felt every hard inch of him.

He groaned and the kiss deepened. His pelvis struck mine harder and my head repeatedly thumped into the base of the mirror.

My body warmed. My heart raced. Thanks to the bind, I would probably always want this man that I'd once thought was my father. A part of me would always value this connection between us. But not as much as I valued myself.

I rocked into him and let him run his hand up the back of my thigh. I let him lift me off the dresser and carry me to the bed. I let him think he'd won.

Loch grinned against my mouth as he settled on top of me. He pulled on the ties of my robe. It fell open and the asshole drank in my curves and the slope of my breasts.

"I knew you'd see sense," he breathed as he knelt between my legs and undid his loincloth.

His penis glistened at the tip as it sprang free. He dragged his thumb over the head and slid his slick thumb down his length.

I gripped his hand. "Let me, Master."

His eyes widened. The fucker threw his head back and let out a breathless laugh as I stroked his cock.

"Oh yes," he breathed. "Please me, princess. While I please you."

He leaned over and pushed his fingers inside me. A reluctant moan was shorn from my throat. He worked my core like a sex demon. His thumb assaulted my clit and I struggled to catch my breath.

Fuck! Focus, I chanted to myself even as my body burned beneath his touch

His hips pumped into the stroke of my hand. Once. Twice. He lost himself in the rhythm. With each stroke, his grip loosened on my power and I felt it rise in me.

"Yes," he grunted as he furiously fucked my hand. "I'm going to come in your mouth. Would you like that, princess?"

"Please!" I begged.

He groaned and fingered me to the point of no return; to the precipice where I knew I was about to fly off the edge.

Just like with Exekiel, my inner dragon reared its head. Loch didn't notice the horns that crested from my crown or the wings that scored from my back. He only felt the heat I pummeled into my hand. Not a ripple but a wave of fire.

Flames of red and teal shot from my palm and wrapped around his swollen dick.

The fucker screamed. His blue eyes were bright as he scrambled and fell off the bed. I bolted up onto my knees and watched as Loch stopped, dropped and rolled. The flames didn't go out. Dragon fire wasn't so easily snuffed.

I cackled. *Cock flambé, anyone?*

"Fuck," he roared and hurtled towards the bath chamber where he flung himself into the pool.

I lunged off the bed and raced after him.

When Loch finally emerged from beneath the water, I stood over him with my robe securely tied and my hands on my hips.

"I told you, you'd regret putting your hands on me again."

He glared; his teeth bared. Shivers racked his body and his hands were cupped over his goods.

"You're a fucking fool," he gritted out.

"No." I stepped closer to the edge of the water. "I am the last dragon shifter. I am Queen of the Coral

Court. I am a pissed off woman and I am taking my power back from every fucker who said I couldn't have it."

"The Outliers will never accept you without me." he spat.

"That choice is theirs. It's called free will. Get used to it."

Magic sang through my veins. If he was trying to take it from me, I didn't feel it. I let it burn in my eyes and tipped my chin higher. I dared him to challenge me as my scarlet wings rimmed in teal thrummed at my back.

"You have no idea what you've just unleashed."

I leveled him with a glare. "Neither do you."

Loch sneered, sank beneath the water and swam back the way he'd come.

42

EXEKIEL:

REVELATIONS

I imagined it was a strange thing to find the man you thought you'd killed sitting across from you at the dinner table. The look on Alexov's face was almost laughable if I could find any part of this fucked up situation remotely funny.

There'd been no doubt in my mind that I was going to survive last night. That I would outlive every single one of these Fate-stained shits just to see them fall beneath my wrath.

Thesona had slowed the spread of the poison which gave me enough strength to crawl to my hands and knees and drink the vial of antidote I'd had tucked in my cloak pocket. The antidote had been a prototype that Ilbryen and I were working on.

It hadn't been an exact cure but it was enough for me to walk with my weight shared between Kraxus and Vivienne as they got me to a healer who purged my blood with herbs and the rare healing magic of certain elves.

Now, I smirked at my attempted-assassins and swirled my goblet in my hand. Now we played the game of politics and civility. There were too many players involved in this for me to go carving them up willy-nilly. My strike had to be precise and where it could do the most damage.

A large figure slumped in the chair beside me.

"They did it, didn't they?" Kraxus folded his beefy arms across his chest. His voice was a low rumble.

I glanced at him from the corner of my eye.

Last night, he and Vivienne hadn't believed me when I'd told them that certain Court members had tried to have me killed. It had been much easier for them to accept that a siren had corrupted my mind and made me think I'd seen council members.

I didn't press the point. Vivienne had grown up in a household that had tried to convince everyone to wipe the sirens from the face of the realm. To blow the Coral Court from the depths of the sea and scatter its remains and its people to ash on the wind.

"What gave it away?" I drawled.

Kraxus scratched the back of his head. The movement caused the veins in his biceps to strain against his skin.

"I've always suspected there was something off about that night. When we heard the commotion, my father had run out to help." His leg bounced beneath the table.

"I was supposed to be hiding, but I snuck to my window and peered out. My father had been about to take down a siren that was controlling a little girl dragon shifter but a Royal Guard attacked him…killed him." His brow creased and he drummed his fingers on his thigh. "My mother was convinced I was seeing things because I was traumatized but I know what I saw."

I turned to face him fully. "You were quiet about this last night."

He grimaced. "I didn't want to say anything in front of…" He jerked his chin at Vivienne.

I snickered. "Pretending you agree with her isn't going to do you any favors. You're mated for a reason, bunny boy, regardless of your differences."

He grunted. "That's easy for you to say. Your mate's as batshit crazy as you are. She hates your guts yet still can't stay away from you."

My lips quirked. "You've got me there."

The next time Alexov looked my way, I raised my cup, brought it to my lips and drained it in one long pull.

Kraxus noticed the exchange. His lips barely moved when he murmured. "What's your plan?"

I nodded my thanks to the nymph who refilled my goblet. "To let my shadows, do what they do best."

Kraxus snorted. "Do you think they're all just going to line up for you? In an open area; a safe distance from any spectators?"

I swallowed a mouthful of my drink. "They will when I give them a reason to."

I didn't mention the weapon. Kraxus seemed loyal enough but that kind of information wouldn't be given freely.

The guests over by the door cheered. I turned as Camal Silverhound strutted into the ballroom. He was now ranked at number one with his lackeys coming in, in the top five.

Behind him, more nobles than usual crushed through the double doors that were flung wide and jammed with reporters and floating orbs. Each one was desperate for a glimpse of the next potential champion of the Games.

The finale was just days away and would take place right here in the city. The air hummed with speculation and placed bets.

I felt her before I saw her. Varialla's power was more potent than usual. It thrummed through the earth and called to mine. I straightened. My gaze zeroed in on the doors just as my mate strode into the hall.

Maximus, Calder, Kylin and Lucinda flanked her like bodyguards. Each one held their heads high. I didn't know if they'd coordinated their outfits, but they were dressed from head to toe in black, blue and chains of silver.

Varialla was the only one I truly noticed. She wore a low-cut black lace dress that dipped below her belly button and revealed the swell of her perfect little breasts. The hem of the dress was jagged and fell halfway down her thigh but mounds of blue and silver fabric puffed from her hips and cascaded around her bare legs.

Heavy silver chains tapered from the thin straps to hang down her arms and slash across her breasts. But what was most captivating about her were the scarlet wings tipped in teal that beat at her back, and the horns that arced from the crown of her head. Thin silver chains dangled between them.

My hand flexed around my chalice. My heart took a little longer to beat.

The crowd went from the deepest quiet to the roar of thunder. Varialla was instantly surrounded. The orbs flashed and moved in dizzying circles above her head.

Microphones were thrust in her face and question after question was lobbied at her.

I didn't know whether to laugh or throttle her. This was how she chose to reveal who her father had been?

"Ms. Hastings, why did you never share that you were a dragon shifter?" One reporter called.

"Have you known this entire time?" inquired another.

"Should we still call you Ms. Hastings or will you be going by your father's name?"

"Varialla, over here!"

Chaos blazed around her but Varialla moved through the crowd as if she barely noticed.

Some of the questions she answered. Others she ignored as she and her allies made their way to their assigned seats. The reporters tried to follow but the Royal Guard held them off. They weren't allowed beyond the doors. Though the orbs stayed with her as she greeted every new adoring noble.

The commotion escalated as more people noticed her appearance.

"She's the last dragon shifter!" A noblewoman screeched.

Her lithe form pushed to the front of the crowd and she dropped to one knee before Varialla. Her eyes were wide and her pale cheeks flushed.

"You truly are here to unite the Isles," she gushed. "To return that which was taken from us. You were sent here by the Fates."

More of the audience fell to their knees and bowed at Varialla's feet.

"Look at her wings!" A male Fae shouted. "They are the colors of Prince Thraxen."

"She is a royal," someone else bellowed.

My stare swung in the direction of every voice. I hadn't given much thought to how the people would react to Varialla's dragon half but I hadn't considered they'd be on their knees.

In Phase Three of the Games, the People's votes would count for forty percent of each player's rank. With this kind of reception, her chances of winning went up. The sight of my mate being worshiped like the goddess she was, filled me with a possessive sort of pride. But if she won, the divide between us would only grow. No matter what, I wouldn't let her free the Outer Isles. Not until the corruption had been purged from our streets.

A quick glance at Alexov and the others told me that not even the Council hadn't known Varialla's true identity. It seemed the Rebel Leader had been keeping that piece of information to himself. Probably because he planned to use it against them. The irony was delicious but I couldn't savor the taste. If Varialla won the Games, that deranged bastard would be that much closer to the Eternal Throne.

Varialla's stare hit mine. My heart punched in my chest. Fates, she'd always been stunning, but now, in her true form, she was regal. Powerful. Beautiful. The way she commanded the room. Commanded me. I'd never felt so willingly undone.

"Open your eyes!" Count Victus boomed as he shoved his way to the front. He was twice her size. My shadows stirred in response to the threat. "Her family killed the dragons so she could take their place!"

Others shouted their agreement.

"She is a product of perverse power and coercion. She is an Unblessed." He thrust a meaty finger in her face. A growl rumbled in the back of my throat. "A Fate-stained shifter slayer! She shouldn't be praised. She should be slaughtered for the abomination that she is."

I was on my feet before I could consider otherwise. I gripped the fucker's hair in my hands and pressed my foot into the arch of his back as I shoved him to his knees. Around me, guests gasped and shuffled away from my writhing shadows.

"Watch what you say about my mate in my presence, Count Victus," I snarled. "I would hate to turn this celebration into your burial."

The elf had the good sense to keep his mouth shut. I trailed my shadows along his cheek. I'm pretty sure he pissed himself. With a chuckle, I let him go. He fell forwards in the awkward semblance of a bow.

"That's more like it." I glanced at Varialla. I'd expected to see her smiling, instead, she scowled.

She raised a brow and pouted her lips in a way that made me want to push my cock between them. "Not everyone settles their disputes with violence, Shadow Saint."

I sneered. "Of course not. You prefer to sing."

A smile played around the edge of her beautiful mouth. It took everything I had in me not to grab her and claim her lips with mine.

Varialla said nothing as she turned and continued on through the gaping crowd that rushed around her.

Others hung back with lethal glares but were careful not to say anything within range of me.

Eventually, she settled in her seat at the head table between Evangeline and Camal. She was immediately hounded with questions. It was more like an interrogation than general conversation.

I reclaimed my seat on the opposite side of the table. I tried to pretend otherwise, but my attention was solely fixed on Varialla. I tracked every move she made and every breath she took. Not for the same reasons everyone else did, but because being this close to her without touching her was a new kind of Hell.

I'd spent so long with her during the Games, these few days without her were torture. Last night, I'd barely resisted the urge to go to her rooms and demand that she sleep beside me.

Someone cleared their throat. I pulled my stare away from Varialla and found Lucinda watching me. The witch dipped her head. This sufficiently had my interest piqued.

After a quick glance around the table that told me no one was watching, I returned the gesture and slipped from my seat. Hands tucked inside my pockets; I strolled out onto the terrace.

It was a cold night. The sky was bright with stars. The air was fragrant with spiced liquor and fresh water flowers.

I did a quick sweep for orbs. There weren't many places for them to hide save for the fountain in the center of the terrace, but I wasn't taking any chances.

When every corner had been searched, I rested my elbows on the rail and stared across the glittering expanse of the Eternal city. From up here, I could spy the other Isles dotted across the sea. The four that converged around the Isle of the Eternals and those that existed beyond the shimmer of the barrier.

The snow-capped mountains of Fae-reef were spectacular. Even from here I could make out the gardens that jutted from the mountain face and the waterfalls that spilled off their ledge.

The tap of her heels moved closer, then the witch came up beside me.

"Ironclaw," I murmured. "Do you have something for me?"

43

EXEKIEL:
PIECES OF ME

Lucinda stood close and kept her voice low. "I'm told it arrived a few days ago." The witch subtly slipped a rolled-up piece of parchment about the size of my little finger into my hand.

It seemed so small and insignificant yet there were few things that ever felt this profound. My fingers ran across its rolled edge. I had hoped for a response but I didn't realize just how much until now.

My gaze was out to sea when I asked, "did you read it?"

Lucinda scoffed. "No and not from lack of trying."

I grinned. The parchment, as expected, was blank to those who didn't know how to reveal its secrets.

"What are you up to, Shadow Saint?"

My brow lifted. "What do you mean?"

She turned to face me.

"When you asked me to put you in touch with the giants, I assumed you wanted to bring them to your side to sign your stupid petition," she murmured. "But Enrique says you didn't mention it. That you simply wanted him to send a message."

"That's right."

"To who?"

"A friend." I couldn't stop the curve of my lips.

For so long I'd wondered if he'd survived that night. If he had, would he answer when I finally called. This bit of paper had returned a part of me, I'd buried with my brothers.

"A friend?" she glanced around us, "In the Outer Isles?" Lucinda practically mouthed the last two words.

"Is that so shocking?"

She huffed a laugh. "Not really."

I frowned.

She snickered and headed back towards the glass doors. "I've always known you weren't as bad as everyone believed."

My eyes narrowed and I cocked my head to one side. "You can't prove that."

She grinned and slunk inside.

I was on my way inside the hall, when Vladimir sauntered onto the terrace with a pipe in hand. He lit it with a match and sucked on the pipes end.

"Dragons and poisons." He let out a cloud of smoke. "What will the next banquet bring, I wonder?"

I surreptitiously tucked the message into my shirt pocket. "Only time will tell."

The elf snickered and took another drag on his pipe.

"I presume you heard about Demetrius." The elf raked a hand through his silver hair.

I didn't give a shit about the Shifter Council member who'd lost his life during the banquet to the very poison he'd help bring into this land, but I did my best to appear regretful.

"I heard."

Vladimir shook his head. "And to think I was supposed to be sitting in that seat."

"What?"

He sighed heavily. "I wanted to be next to Gwendoline so when no one was looking I changed the place setting." He dragged a weary hand down his face. "I survived and Demetrius died in my place."

I reined in a bark of laughter. I'd always known Vladimir's hostility towards the sirens was too genuine for him to be secretly working with them. But this confirmed it. The poor bastard didn't know that the very Court he served were responsible for the lives he mourned. He didn't know the depths of depravity that festered within these very walls.

Unlike the other Council members, Vladimir had been voted in by the people after I'd flung the previous members chariot from the sky. That death, like all the others I'd taken care of over the years, had been written off as some freak accident. Not only that, but Vladimir's signature hadn't been among those on the plans for the weapon. That was why they'd tried to kill him. He was a liability; a risk they couldn't tolerate as the Games drew closer to the finish line and them to their end goal.

I doubted I could ever trust the elf to join me in taking down our true enemy but I was glad he wasn't one of the fuckers I had to destroy.

Common sense told me to stay in my rooms. It was late. The jousting tournament was tomorrow. The best thing I could do was get a good night's rest. Yet, all sense failed when I thought of her.

Instead of lying in my bed, I paced back and forth through my chambers. The rug was worn beneath my feet. My calves grew hotter the closer I came to the fireplace. I couldn't settle. Not when I knew Varialla was so close. Not when I'd gotten used to the feel of her body against mine whilst I slept.

With a grunt of exasperation, I stalked towards my bedside table and poured myself a glass of water. I drained it in one gulp and raked my hands through my hair. I had to get a grip.

Whatever existed between Varialla and me had been a glimpse of a life we couldn't have. We'd agreed it wouldn't extend beyond the Games. I couldn't fall apart every time I missed her. I shouldn't even miss her, and not as much as I did.

I glanced at my bed. All I had to do was climb inside. Instead, my feet moved towards my door. I had to see her.

I was halfway there when light flickered beneath my door. A shadow moved. My eyes narrowed and I peered closer. The amber glow danced like a candle flame. The energy that came through the wood was familiar and warm. My breathing slowed as I padded towards the door. The person on the other side paced as much as I had.

I wrenched on the handle and yanked it open. Varialla spun towards me. A flame flickered in the palm of her hand. She'd been about to walk away.

"Where the fuck do you think you're going?"

She opened her mouth to respond but whatever she was going to say, I swallowed. With her face cupped in my hands, I drew Varialla's lips to mine. Her fingers curled into my chest and she opened her mouth for me. I stroked my tongue across hers and groaned when her teeth grazed my bottom lip.

Fates, I'd missed this.

With each passing second, the kiss grew more urgent. Her nails scraped over my bare chest and elicited sharp tingles down my spine. I lowered my hand from her cheek to cradle her neck whilst my other hand slid to her waist and pulled her up onto her tiptoes so our hips aligned.

Varialla gasped and pulled her lips from mine. I almost choked her just to bring them back to me.

"I saw Loch."

I froze. The Rebel Leader was the last Fate-stained fucker I wanted to think about right now, especially in regards to being near my mate.

"And?"

"He won't be bothering me again, anytime soon." She half smiled but the look in her eyes said she had more to say. Varialla licked her lips that were swollen from our kiss. "I had to lure him into a false sense of security first." She didn't look at me. "I had to lure him into my bed."

White hot rage scorched through my veins. A haze of red settled over my vision. He'd had his hands on my mate. He'd touched what was mine. Shadows rose from my shoulders and arced around my wings. I'd always planned to kill the bastard. Now his death was owed me twice.

"We didn't have sex," she quickly added. "Hand stuff only." She laughed awkwardly and shook her head. She was clearly nervous.

I could have put her out of her misery. I could have told her that even if she'd fucked him, I'd still want her. There was nothing she could do that would make me want her any less. Nothing she could say that would stop me from loving her—needing her the way I did. But I let her squirm.

"I just—I just thought you should know." She frowned as if wondering why she felt compelled to tell me at all. Technically, we'd agreed to be nothing to each other. She shouldn't even be here right now.

Yet, the thought of her being anywhere else was impossible. I pulled her closer and dragged my thumb across her bottom lip. Lips that were made for mine.

"When you say, he won't be bothering you…"

She half smiled. "I set his balls on fire."

My eyes widened. "You truly are a savage."

She laughed. I kissed her again, hard. My hand tightened around her neck. This was not a kiss of longing but one to remind her who she belonged to.

"I forgive you," I snarled. "But never again. No man but me will ever taste these lips or feel this skin." I stroked my finger down her neck. "You are mine, Varialla. From this point until the end of eternity."

She trembled. "You're the only one I want."

The stark relief I felt at these words was overwhelming. I claimed her lips again, for now and forever. Varialla whimpered and staggered back until I had her pressed against the wall. Our lips never parted as I lifted her and wrapped one of her legs around me. We moved as one. The friction was intoxicating. My little bud moaned. For the brief second our lips parted, her breaths came out of her in soft helpless pants.

"You're so fucking sexy." I sucked her tongue into my mouth.

Varialla squeaked and pulsed her hips against mine.

Fates. I'd never been so unraveled by one kiss. I couldn't get her close enough. I grasped her soft ass and squeezed. The little beauty arched into me like she was offering me her perfect tits. Her nipples were hard beneath the silk fabric of her night shirt that matched the soft ilk of her skin. It made me want to tear it off with my teeth.

"I'm going to fuck you so hard, beautiful."

I dragged her mouth back to mine. With our tongues still entangled, I walked her backwards into my room and used my foot to slam the door. Tonight, I wasn't going to ravish her. I was going to own her; mark her in every way that mattered so she would never forget that she was mine.

As we moved towards my bed, her little fingers pushed down my trousers and I peeled off her night dress. Our mouths parted for the second it took to get it over her head before I claimed her lips again.

Varialla fell back onto the mattress that bounced beneath her. Her weighted breasts fell to the sides. Her knees were bent and her legs were open as she shuffled further back onto the mattress.

A low growl simmered in my throat. I exhaled through my nose. This woman was going to be my undoing.

"Fuck me," she breathed and trailed a finger around her breast.

I groaned. "Do you want my cock, little bud?" My hand closed around it and I tugged.

Varialla bit her bottom lip. "Yes." Her fingers slid down her quivering torso and pushed between her thighs.

My blood roared. She didn't look away from me as she teased and touched what was mine.

"I want it right here."

I stroked my cock harder and watched my mate writhe on the bed. "I'll put it anywhere you want it, beautiful."

Her head tipped back as her fingers sank inside her tight cunt. *Fates, fuck me.* She was a vision. Firelight danced across her deep brown skin. The flames highlighted the pulse that jumped in her slender neck. The way her stomach shuddered with her breaths. And that delicious wet that glistened between her thighs.

Fuck. My cock went painfully hard. I lowered myself on top of her and dragged her hand away. I pinned it at the side of her head.

"You can touch yourself when I tell you, you can," I growled into her hair. "Got that, little bud?"

I rowed my hips. She gasped as I stretched her on just the tip of my dick.

"Shit," she panted. Her fingers interlaced with mine. "How do I keep forgetting how big you are?"

Her words only made me harder.

"You can take it." I stretched her further; pushed deeper. Her eyelids fluttered. "You can handle anything can't you, little bud?"

A delicious moan sailed from her lips and she moved to match my motion. Her tight cunt sucked me in deeper.

"Fuck. I've been going mad without you."

Varialla ran her fingers through my hair. Her body undulated beneath me as she tried to take in more of me.

"I'm sorry it took me so long to get here."

Our eyes met. I shook my head. "I would have waited until the end of eternity so long as I could share this moment with you."

She swallowed then jerked as I pushed deeper. Her tight wet hole lubricated my cock. With each thrust our bodies came together easier.

"One kiss from you is worth a lifetime."

Braced on one elbow, I pressed on her thigh with my other hand to force her to widen for me. Then I thrust harder, faster. We both cried out when she took me down to the root.

"Look how perfect you are." I bowed my head and kissed her; deeply, thoroughly. "I knew you could do it."

"Fuck," Varialla cried as I repeatedly impaled her on my cock.

"It's always you," she stammered. Her brow was creased in pleasure. "I only ever feel this way with you."

"Because this is where you belong." My fingers dug into her thigh and I pumped inside her. She bucked. Her sweet little pussy wept around my cock. "You can stop searching, little bud. Your home is with me."

44

VARIALLA:
COMING HOME

Exekiel's words crashed over me like a wave breaking at shore. I couldn't think. Couldn't breathe. I was paralyzed by his touch; by his fathomless devotion. I didn't realize I was crying until he kissed a tear from my cheek. I turned my head so our lips met.

Our fingers intertwined. My body bloomed.

Exekiel moved into me. This time was different; deeper in every way. His firm cock penetrated my body; whilst his soul tangled in mine. There was no end or beginning. Only us and this moment.

I was consumed by the lure of his vibrant pink gaze. The puff of his breath that shuddered across my cheek. The flutter of his hair as it fell over his brow.

I brought my hand up and traced the angles of his face; the outline of his mouth.

"I am yours, Exekiel. For as long as you'll have me."

His eyes held mine. "Then I will take forever," he vowed.

Exekiel brought his mouth to my breast and sucked. His tongue dragged around my dark, peaked nipples. I gasped and pushed into him. Every graze of his finger; every lash of his tongue ignited me.

I rocked into him. His grip tightened around my fingers and he moved faster and faster. I was increasingly aware of the deep, burning throb between my thighs.

Soft yips slipped from my lips as Exekiel struck a new part inside me. I coiled my other hand around the back of his neck. Mouth open, I panted his name.

"Exekiel…Exekiel…"

This wasn't fucking. This was finding myself in him and him in me.

"Fuck. You're so hot," he grunted.

His rhythm intensified. My back bowed off the bed. He was so deep inside me; he pushed my soul from my skin and urged it into another plane. A realm of pure blinding ecstasy.

And him; his powerful thrusts and perfect cock were the only things that tethered me to a fragment of reality. The only thing I could make sense of as he struck multiple nerve endings that sparked and fissured with each fierce thrust.

"O God!" I screamed, "Exekiel!" I juddered beneath him.

"I know, beautiful." Exekiel kissed me as he continued to pummel me into the mattress. "I know."

The slap of his hips beating mine was deafening. The creak and thud of the bed as it struck the wall. I thrashed wildly; caught up in every intoxicating beat.

My head spun. The earth moved. My inner walls tensed and spasmed around his hard, pulsating cock as he reared up inside me and together, we came.

We went another three rounds before we finally collapsed in each other's arms. Of course, my wings and horns had made an appearance. But now that I had better control of them, I'd retracted my wings inside myself. I still wasn't sure how to comfortably move with them. I left my horns out.

The air smelt like sex. Sweat dripped down my skin. I was well and truly satisfied and yet still craved him.

I groaned into the crook of my elbow from where I curled on my side. "This need for you is getting out of hand."

He chuckled into the back of my head. "Then by all means, put me in your hand." Exekiel curled his fingers around mine and guided my hand to his still erect length. I squealed and yanked my hand away.

"Not until I do some stretches," I scoffed.

He laughed and held me closer.

My fingers ran along the fine hairs on his forearm. "Exekiel?"

"Hmm?" he murmured.

"What happened here?" I gestured to a puncture wound on his arm, and rolled over to face him. There were others along his skin. His leg, his back, his chest. I'd meant to ask him about them earlier but he'd efficiently distracted me.

Exekiel stroked a finger down my cheek as if he couldn't help but touch me. "Certain members of the Council have decided I've outlived my usefulness."

This time I didn't tense or try to deny the truth I'd fought for so long. "The Council did this."

"Yes." Exekiel studied my reaction like he expected me to roll my eyes. A few weeks ago, I might have. But Lucinda had told me to follow my heart and that's what I was doing.

I already knew Loch was a self-serving prick. It wasn't so hard to believe that he would work with our enemies if he thought it would get him ahead. He would do anything for power. Why not slay the innocent? Work with his mortal enemy? Or try to fuck his supposed ally against her will?

I inhaled deeply. "Tell me everything."

I hadn't been ready to listen before. I hadn't been able to trust him nor accept that I knew even less than the little I thought I knew. Now I was ready. Now I wanted to know exactly what we were up against, so we could make a plan to tear it down.

"Everything is power," Exekiel murmured. "For centuries, the Games dictated that when a new Primary was crowned, the old stepped down and became a whisper in history." He leaned over and popped open a hidden panel in the back of his bedside table.

"However, the current Court and Council have not been willing to relinquish their seat."

Exekiel pulled out a scroll. Its color was a tawny brown like it had been stained with coffee. He unrolled it and revealed a diagram that looked like an old gramophone connected to chairs and a large glass tube. The image was surrounded by arrows with instructions and names beside signatures.

My stomach flipped. I recognized some of those names. Signatures of sirens beside members of the Royal Court. Loch Orqanz was among them. I'd already decided that I believed Exekiel but seeing it written plainly carved something open inside my chest.

Across the top were the words: *Sonu di Carghel*, which translated to the Song of Change. It was the song Loch said all sirens would sing once the Outliers were free. Now I wondered if he'd meant something else. I wracked my mind trying to think of every time he'd mentioned the song and what he'd said.

"What is this?" I whispered.

"A weapon they plan to use to seize control of the realm."

Horror blew through me and tangled in my web of rage.

"They want to brainwash the entire realm?"

"To some degree." Exekiel's tone was rough; an undercurrent of fury brimmed beneath it. "They plan to make us more agreeable and accepting of their changes."

My hands balled into fists. My tongue tasted sweet and the urge to sing a song of savagery clung to the back of my throat. "How far are they along with it?"

He scrubbed a hand through his hair. "I don't know but they seem to be going faster now. It's like they're running out of time."

I stared down at the parchment. My mind lagged as it struggled to make sense of what it was seeing.

Once again, my world had been upended. Apparently, finding out I had magic and being taken to a supernatural world hadn't been enough. Now, I'd been flung into a world of espionage, chemical weapons and corrupt governments. Governments that wanted to turn its people into play things.

I still couldn't understand what Loch got out of this. Not only because I couldn't ignore his borderline-obsessive loyalty to the sirens, but because he could get everything he wanted, through me.

"What if they are running out of time?" I cocked my head. "Or at least, the Council are."

Exekiel lifted his head from where he'd leaned it back on the headboard. His arm rested on his bent knee. "What do you mean?"

I gestured to the parchment.

"When the sirens agreed to take down the dragon shifters and when they signed this, they didn't have me." I hopped up onto my knees. This made sense. "My mother had no claim to a throne so they'd agreed to do the Court's bidding in exchange for Shifter Springs."

A way to get in the Inlands and get their revenge.

Exekiel nodded slowly. "But now they do have you and you have access to a throne. The only throne that truly matters."

"Exactly. What if the Royal Court are trying to speed up the process because they know that if I win the Games, Loch will go back on the bargain?"

The corner of Exekiel's mouth twitched. "You don't think the Rebel Leaders given up on you since you scorched his testicles?"

I laughed and flopped beside him. "No." I hugged my knees to my chest. All traces of laughter gone. "No, I don't think he's given up."

If I became the First Primary of *De Cinque Istrovos*, that bastard would never let me go. He would twist that toxic bond around my neck and choke me with it until I succumbed to every pain and pleasure, he wanted to inflict on me.

"There are three things in this realm that Loch Orqanz wants. Revenge, power and me."

Wisps of shadows curled from Exekiel's skin. "He will never have you."

"He won't." I agreed. "But with me on the throne, I could give him two of those and the hope of all three."

Exekiel turned to face me. His eyes turned a crimson red. "What are you saying, little bud?"

I drew in a breath. "There are ten winners of the Games. One becomes Primary. Nine become Council. But there is a tenth seat on the Council reserved for the right-hand of the Primary and chosen by the Primary."

Exekiel's nostrils flared. He knew where I was going with this.

"If I sat on the Eternal Throne and put Loch as my right-hand, he would never give them what they need to use that weapon. Sirens."

"No."

"No?"

Exekiel slid off the bed and pulled on his shorts. "No." He scooped up his tumbler of *Volgiskey* and took a swig. "You think if that bastard gets near you and the throne, that he'll settle for two out of three?"

I sat up on my knees. "He won't have a choice."

I sounded more confident than I felt. The truth was Loch had a hold on me. It was powerful and overwhelming. Every time, I was around him, its intensity terrified me.

It grew stronger over time and it had already had almost two hundred years to strengthen. That asshole had ways of slipping into my mind and altering my thoughts. The Ceremonial Bind made me burn for him in ways that left my soul cold but my skin hot.

"I will give him his revenge on those who cast us out. I'll let him have a say on the running of the Court. So long as he helps me destroy the weapon."

I put on Exekiel's shirt and padded across the room to where he stood staring at the flames that danced in the fireplace.

"Once he helps me destroy it, we will destroy him." I pressed a hand to Exekiel's cheek and forced him to look at me. "My heart, my body and my bed are yours. Only yours."

"I don't trust him." I hated the turmoil in his eyes; the memories I knew he struggled to suppress. "How can I leave you alone with him?" He tightly grasped my waist. "You are everything to me."

My throat thickened. I blinked back tears.

"Exekiel," I whispered.

He looked at me and I ran my thumb across his lips. "I love you."

He tensed. My heart raced like I'd just run a sprint. I'd never said those words to anyone unless I was being sarcastic. Now I was ensnared by the weight of his gaze.

His eyes darted between mine and the pink seemed to swirl before it settled on a warm ruby red.

"Say it again," he murmured.

I smiled. "Greedy, much?"

Exekiel gripped my chin between his thumb and forefinger. "Say it again."

"I. Love—"

Exekiel tugged on my chin and guided my mouth to his. The kiss was as sweet as sin. My toes curled and I pressed up to meet the warmth of his lips. Exekiel took my ass in his hands and squeezed.

I moaned. My fingers curled around the back of his neck where I teased the soft strands of his hair.

"Fine," he panted when our mouths parted. "Sweet-talk your way into the Rebel Leader's good graces."

His lips claimed mine again, in a possessive, hungry kiss that I felt down to my toes.

As his tongue stole my senses and ravaged my mouth, he walked us towards the bed until we fell onto it.

"But I will continue to look for the weapon," he murmured against my lips as he spread my thighs. "If I find it before the finale, I will end this."

I pushed my hands down the back of his shorts and felt the muscles of his ass shift beneath my fingers. He moved into me.

"It wouldn't be us if you weren't working against me in some way." I laughed, breathlessly.

Exekiel arched a brow as he hooked his thumb in his shorts and pulled them part-way down.

"Shut the fuck up, little bud, and take this dick like a good girl."

My mouth dropped open. My heart raced. A part of me thought I should be offended. Before I could decide, my mate plunged his iron cock inside me, and reminded me exactly why my soul called his name.

I woke to the feel of Exekiel's morning wood pressed into my backside. I gasped and instinctively pushed into him.

He gripped my hip. "Careful, little bud. We don't have time to go another round."

I rolled my ass up and down his perfect cock, despite how tightly he held me. "Are you sure about that? The joust doesn't start until this afternoon."

"Yes," he panted as he moved with me. Shocks of pleasure rocked down my spine. "But we need to get you back to your rooms. The nymphs will be waiting to style you before breakfast. Although," his voice dropped an octave. It became a deep baritone that rumbled through me. His hand crept lower and pushed between my legs. I moaned. "Right now, there's only one thing I want to eat."

I shuddered. His words caused my inner walls to flutter in search of him.

"Fuck me, Shadow Saint. And make it fast."

Exekiel chuckled. Then he was upon me. I wasn't wearing any bottoms but he hitched up his shirt that I'd pulled on when I got chilly during the night. I rolled down his own loose shorts and his delicious cock sprang free.

His pink eyes flashed. His lips curved into a wicked smirk. "Brace yourself," he murmured then rammed his cock inside me all the way to the fucking hilt.

"Shit!" I shouted.

Sparks burst across my eyes and I was immediately undone. Each rough and reckless stroke drove me closer to the edge. I hung onto his shoulders. My nails scraped his back. The Shadow Saint wrecked me from the inside out.

He was feral. Wild on lust. Wild for me.

"Fuck beautiful, I like to think of myself as a sane man, but when it comes to you," he growled. "I lose my fucking mind."

Without severing the connection between our bodies, Exekiel knelt and elevated my hips in the same motion so my ass was off the bed. He grasped my hips tightly and used the new angle to yank me up and down his hard cock.

"Holy shit!" My heart couldn't keep up with the pound of his thrusts that rattled in my soul. The new angle stole my breath. There was a wet squelch as I soaked his cock.

Shit!

We went round after round. Each one was fast and filthy. A mess of sweat, spit and other bodily fluids that Exekiel massaged into my breasts, sucked from between my thighs and pumped into my mouth.

By the end of the fifth time, I was sticky with the remnants of him on my skin. His back was a canvas of scratches that I'd carved into him. And we were both thoroughly exhausted.

"Okay," I panted from where we lay tangled in his sheets on the floor. I had no idea when we'd moved from the bed. "Now we really have to stop."

Exekiel was sprawled beside me. "Agreed." He propped himself up on his elbow and kissed me. My heart jumped. "You have a throne to win, after all."

He rolled firmly on top of me. As sore as I was, I welcomed the gentle rock of his hips.

"We," I corrected and coiled my arms around his neck. "*We* have a throne to win."

My eyes rolled as Exekiel's impossibly thick girth nudged me open. He hissed and his brow rested on mine.

"And a weapon to find," he breathed, pushing harder. "And blood to be repaid."

45

VARIALLA:
THAT'S NOT MY NAME

From the wings of the arena, I looked out across the sand field that shimmered in the late afternoon sun. In the center, a group of Pegasus pranced and played. Eighteen, in total. One for each contestant that would be competing in today's tournament.

They kicked up clouds of sand and affectionately headbutted each other like they didn't have a care in the world. Their hearts weren't slamming against their ribs like mine was. Their mouths weren't desert dry.

Overhead, the stands were packed more than usual, and others still flew in on chariots. It was the beginning of the end. After tonight, the final competitors in the Games would be decided. One of them would be crowned the new ruler of the Five Isles. For the sake of everyone, it had to be me.

I shook out my hands and practiced some of the moves Maximus had gone through with me yesterday. All I had to do was stay on my Pegasus longer than fifteen of the eighteen contestants and I would be safe. Easier said than done.

Goather's voice bounced off the stone and echoed around the arena. One by one, he bellowed the contestants' names and they stepped out of their wing. I let out a breath and adjusted the swathes of fabric tied around my palms. According to Maximus, they would make it easier to grip the lance. I hoped he was right. I'd need all the help I could get.

"Varialla Zairenyth; formerly Von Hastings."

I felt like I'd been punched. I'd only recently discovered that my father was Prince Thraxen. Now he had a last name. *I* had a last name. I wanted to scream above the cheers that I was a Von Hastings. It was the only thing I'd ever really chosen for myself and I wasn't going to lose it. Especially not to some man I didn't even know. Someone who possibly hadn't wanted me.

With a deep inhale, I stepped out onto the sanded arena to thunderous applause. I'd retracted my wings since I still wasn't used to their weight and they threw off my balance. My horns, I kept visible and the girls had capped them with silver tips of iron.

I smoothed a hand down my chainmail armor and leather corset. The sleeves were fitted slabs of metal that surprisingly didn't restrict my movement and the neckline climbed up to frame my jaw.

On my lower half, I wore black leather leggings with steel shin guards, and a weighted belt that had a swath of silver fabric hanging from its sides and back like a cape.

The other contestants watched me with murder in their eyes as we each mounted our assigned Pegasus. They hadn't been too pleased since I'd revealed my dragon half. There were no other sirens or dragon shifters in the Games and they felt like I had an unfair advantage. Maybe I did but I wasn't complaining.

I met the cold stares of each one of them and sat a little taller.

But another set of eyes burned into me from the right. I glanced in their direction. My heart beat faster. Exekiel sat astride a large black Pegasus with pulsing black wings rimmed in silver.

He'd been fitted in black leathers that had armored shoulder-plates. Lethal metal spikes arced from his forearms and shin protectors. The leather vest left his bulging biceps exposed and the veins stood out when he gripped the reins.

Leather straps and buckles crisscrossed over his chest and he wore a navy-blue half-cape that draped down one side of his body and made him look both regal and deadly. His eyes seemed brighter as if they reflected the first rays of sunset. His dark hair shuddered in the breeze.

I sucked in a breath. I would never get tired of looking at him.

The white Pegasus beneath me splayed its wings. I pressed my thighs into its flanks as it surged into the air.

The crowd roared. A medley of instruments that sounded like trumpets, drums and symbols echoed through the arena. Once again, banners for each competing cast waved from the stands.

Goather waved us forward. He stood in the back of a gold chariot wearing a tartan jacket. He had a blue bow tied around his orange goatee and what looked like blue pompoms hooked to the end of his horns.

"It is time for the final joust of the season," he boomed.

The crowd cheered, wildly.

"Remember, players, that this is a test of your strength, skill and endurance. Magic may not be used to wield your blows," he called.

Feet thumped against the stands; a rhythmic beat that thundered in my soul. I tried to draw strength from it but cold prickled up my spine. There was something off in the energy. An unease that trickled down my spine. Something salted coated the tip of my tongue. Was that the magic of a siren? I turned to scan the stands when Goather brought a conch shell to his lips.

"May you go with the brave and the blessed," he called.

The shell's horn blared across the arena. The jousting tournament began.

46

EXEKIEL:
ABOVE THE CLOUDS

The skies were a blur of anarchy. From the first cry of the horn, the contestants blazed into action. They formed two groups. Half went for Varialla. The rest came at me. I flipped the lance in my hand and prepared for the first blow.

An obsidian tipped lance whistled past my ear. I leaned out of range then pivoted and slashed upwards. My lance speared through my attacker's jaw and came out the top of his head. His body went limp.

I roared as I wrenched my weapon free and was met with a violent shower of blood. The metallic scent hit my nose. Red painted my skin. The shifter's body fell. His Pegasus bolted.

The next blow came from the left. Pain shot through my side as a lance punched through my armor and into the meat of my back. My shadows plumed but I couldn't unleash them. If I did, I'd be out of the Games with no chance of getting on the Council. I'd lose my title, my rank, and the access that went with it. Varialla could only vote in one member, and, in order for our plan to work, that had to be the Rebel Leader.

I swiveled and blocked the strike of another attack and another. The players moved like a machine. They'd planned this. A way to get us out of the Games. As a siren, Varialla was their greatest threat. At number one, I was their greatest competition.

Overhead, Varialla rode on a powerful silver-bred with red-tipped wings. It easily followed her direction and swerved around the glinting weapons. Her counter blows were clumsy but she swung that thing like a feral demon.

I kicked my heels and thundered towards her.

"Not so fast!" A female Fae shot into my path.

Her movements were stiff and jerky, like she wasn't in control of her skin. Her eyes were unfocussed. When she thrust for my throat, her arm twitched. The lance bounced off my armor with a spark.

I maneuvered around her next fumbled attack and took off. With every furious gallop, a fresh stream of blood pulsed from the wound in my side. I gritted my teeth and pressed on. Since the gash had been carved with obsidian glass, I couldn't use the healing of Fate *Thesona*.

The other players pursued. Each one had the same glassy expression as the girl. It was the same look I'd seen on Drax's face when he'd gone after Satrialla. The same look those in the Games had had when Varialla had coerced them.

This was no ordinary attack. This was the work of a siren. I wheeled my Pegasus around and searched the stands.

Pain sliced down my arm. I spun and came face to face with Edmund Dench; one of Camal's right hand men. His name hadn't been in the bottom rank of the Games, so what the fuck was he doing in the joust? Unlike the others, his eyes were clear and sharp. His face half hidden by the helmet he wore.

"Your reign is over." Edmund thrust at my middle.

I gripped the end of his lance and wrenched it forwards. His eyes widened as he was ripped from his steed.

"Fuck!" he bellowed as the Fae plummeted to the sands of the arena.

Another strike slammed into my back. I hissed and twirled the lance above my head despite how my side throbbed and arm protested. I slashed three fuckers across the neck. Their throats opened.

The audience howled. No one seemed to notice the jittery way the players moved.

"Remember the aim is not to kill," Goather shouted from his chariot. "Only to dismount your opponent."

The players couldn't hear him. Under the command of a siren, they vaulted towards me like they were possessed.

"However, if they should die in the process…" The audience laughed and I heard the amusement in Goather's voice, "So be it."

I swerved through my opponents and urged the Pegasus to fly faster. Its wide wings beat wildly. Its feathers were ruffled by the wind that shrieked around us the higher we climbed.

Blood pooled from the gash down my arm and slipped over my fingers. My grip on the reins slackened. It was getting harder to hold on and wield my lance at the same time.

The other players pursued. The sounds they made were inhuman. Their eyes rolled.

Something disturbed the air at my right.

"Get on," Varialla shouted. She brought her Pegasus up alongside mine.

Her hair, that was pulled into two braids, whipped behind her. Her lip was split. Her bronze armor was dented and backed by sunlight.

Varialla shuffled backwards. I dropped my lance and wrapped my arms around her Pegasus' neck. Once my grip was secure, I swung my leg over and pulled myself up onto its back. The skin at my side stretched. A fresh bout of pain wracked my body. I felt the warmth of my blood soak into my shirt. I gritted my teeth and sat as straight as I could.

"They're being controlled," I shouted.

"I know," Varialla bellowed. "I can taste it."

We took off. Her silver bred was fast but it wouldn't be enough. We had one lance and one Pegasus between us. The only way to end this was to find the sirens behind it.

"You know," Varialla panted as we soared upwards into the cover of the clouds. The others were on our heels. "I'm getting really tired of saving your ass."

I grinned at her over my shoulder. "And yet it always ends with me between your legs."

Varialla's nostrils flared and she smacked me in the back of the head. "Eyes on the sky, Fae boy."

I chuckled and relieved her of the reins. She'd need her hands to fight.

"Ready?" I called.

Varialla adjusted her grip on the lance and wrapped her other arm around me. I winced when she brushed the wound.

"Ready."

I pressed my thighs into the Pegasus flanks. The creature responded beautifully. We descended from the cover of the clouds and veered towards the stands.

The other players were upon us. A warlock with red hair thrust a lance at my face. Varialla swung out with a battle cry. Her lance slammed into his and knocked it from his hand.

She yelped triumphantly. "Did you see that?" she squealed.

I shook my head and grinned as I urged the Pegasus on. We picked up speed and crushed closer to the stands as our opponents closed in.

"Shit." Varialla shoved her free hand into a small pouch at her waist.

"What are you doing?" I shouted.

She pulled out a handful of Pegasus crunch.

I scoffed, then winced and cradled my arm around my seeping side. "You can't feed the animals."

"That's the good thing about being a newbie," Varialla shouted as we swept closer to the stands. "You read all the rules and find every loophole."

She sat taller and watched the Pegasus behind us approach. "There's no rule on helping an opponent and there's no rule on feeding the animals."

The nine remaining riders surged towards us. Varialla flung the Pegasus Crunch into the air.

Eight of the nine creatures swooped down to get it. Four of the riders tumbled from their mounts. The audience went wild. They stamped their feet and bellowed at the sky.

Egron Makaw, the rider of the only Pegasus that hadn't been duped by the treat and the fucker whose Achilles tendon I'd slashed, bellowed, "She's a fucking cheat."

"Interestingly enough, there is no rule against this," Goather's voice echoed over the arena. "Perhaps the Gaming Council should have reviewed their guidelines."

Laughter rang up from the stands. I blinked through the pain that built in my side and peered closer at the smiling faces. Somewhere a group of sirens were singing a song.

"There," I nudged Varialla.

Three cloaked figures stood together. They were the only ones not cheering or waving banners. They were doing all they could to go unnoticed but that only made them stand out.

Varialla followed my gaze and nodded. "Let's go."

47

VARIALLA:
Unleashed

We flew towards the cloaked figures as the other players righted their steeds and thundered back up towards us. They were already out of the Games but they were determined to take us with them.

My body tingled. Prominent black scales spread across my skin. They climbed from beneath my armor and covered my hands, my neck, my face. Scarlet wings born of fire plumed from my back. In seconds, they shimmered and hardened; their sharp edges rimmed in teal and gold. Onyx horns curved from my head and heat burned in lungs that felt too full to contain its air.

I gasped. For the first time, I felt the essence of my inner dragon fuse with the core of who I was. Our cells knitted together until it no longer felt like a separate entity. It was me. A side of me that had been buried and begging to burst free for a long time. I'd just been too afraid to embrace it.

Now I drowned in it. My eyes burned and I instinctively knew they'd transformed to the slitted eyes of a dragon. I knew they glowed like amber fire.

The sirens' heads snapped up when they saw us coming. Their eyes widened. The audience screeched as Exekiel and I reared to a stop at the edge of the stands.

"Run!" My voice rang with an echo of power. I raised my hands that were wreathed in fire.

Everyone sprang from their seats and bolted. The sirens included.

Exekiel shuddered in front of me, then his shadows surged forwards like whips of smoke. They swept through the stands and lassoed around the retreating sirens. The three figures struggled as they were wrenched into the air and held aloft before me. I didn't wait.

As the other players hurtled towards us like they were possessed and the siren's song touched my ear, I tipped my head back. Flames of red and teal sprang from my throat and turned their writhing forms to ash.

All except one. The female siren with pale skin and sunken eyes yelled something and gestured at the Royal Box. Every head turned to where the Court members raced towards their chariots. Adir murmured something to Knox and the two pushed their way to the front. There was no sign of Alexov.

It was hard to hear the woman over the chaos and shouts of the people. Exekiel moved closer and I kept my lance aimed at her throat.

An arrow speared through her skull.

My heart lurched. "No!"

Her eyes widened.

I reached for her. "What did you say?" I shouted. "What did you say?"

She twitched and her unfocused gaze swung to me. Her frail voice ghosted past my ear. "We are the distraction."

48

VARIALLA:
THE EDGE OF ELF BAY

As chaos swarmed through the arena, Exekiel and I scanned the skies that were congested with chariots. We pursued those marked with the royal emblem of the Five Isles. We had no idea where Adir and the others had gone. But if the sirens were the distraction, it must have had something to do with the weapon.

"Shit, shit, shit."

My arms wrapped tight around Exekiel's waist as we bolted through the night sky. He grunted when I pressed down on his wound. My arm was instantly soaked with his blood. He needed a healer.

Exekiel pushed the Pegasus harder. With the symbol of *Fadea* aglow on his cheek, he hunted those who had taken everything from him. There was a lethal glint in his eyes that spoke to centuries of rage and ruin. To pain I couldn't begin to process. Now the ones responsible for it were on the verge of doing it again.

I unsheathed the dagger I always kept strapped to my thigh and slashed off two strips of his cloak. I tied the larger one around his middle and the other around his arm to stem the blood flow. It wasn't much but it was the best I could do in the time we had.

Eventually the chariots around us veered off in various directions. They took with them the shouts of excitement and fear that rang through the audience. Until, only one black chariot glinted in the distance. Exekiel thundered after it.

The familiar thrum of the ocean skittered down my spine. They were headed towards the barrier.

The chariot started to descend. We did the same. Keeping our distance, we landed further back, in an area that looked like a royal's seaside getaway.

The usual cobbled streets of the Isles were now polished deck wood and a row of colorful shops and cafes stretched along a promenade. In the pale light of the moon, I could tell that the sand was pure white.

"Where are we?" I whispered as the tinkle of shell windchimes merged with the crash of waves.

"At the edge of Elf Bay," Exekiel murmured.

He turned and stroked our Pegasus. They seemed to communicate with their eyes. The animal whinnied then shot back into the sky; returned the way we came.

I blinked at Exekiel. "Are you an animal whisperer, now?"

He grinned and flicked his head. "Come on."

Long narrow steps led down from the deck to the beach. There countless figures gathered on the sand and moved across a glass bridge beyond the barrier. It was narrower than the one Colette and I had used to enter the Five Isles.

Exekiel crouched low and crept across the sand on his elbows. I dropped beside him.

"It's an emergency exit," he explained with a nod to the bridge. "Kept hidden for obvious reasons."

I couldn't help thinking that the ones it should have been hidden from were the only ones who knew about it.

We slithered closer. I made out the heads of people in the water as they swam towards the shore. They didn't need the sanctioned boats that Outliers who paid toll or had an invitation used because they all had tails. They were sirens. It was the First brigade of the siren army. According to Loch, that was made up of at least three thousand men and women.

My mind reeled. "Shit."

"My thoughts, exactly," Exekiel grunted.

I knew, after doing some digging, that Exekiel could take down over a hundred men in the blink of an eye but this was more than a hundred. And each time he did it, took its toll.

Hidden behind small dunes and willowy shrubs, we prowled towards our enemy. There was no way we could attack but maybe we could learn something to help us when the time came.

A part of me still hoped that Loch would slow their progress. I'd been one of the final three remaining in the sky when the tournament ended tonight, which meant I was back in the Games. Surely, he wouldn't give up his one shot at the Eternal Throne to settle for less.

"Why do they need this many soldiers?" My voice was barely a whisper.

"Because it takes a lot of power to control an entire realm." That voice wasn't Exekiel's but Adir's.

I didn't get chance to scream before the Primary and his men descended. Not one. Not ten. But hundreds. They pounced on Exekiel and drove him into the ground. Whilst more tackled me and wrenched my arms behind my back. Iron clamped around my wrists. My dagger was ripped from my hand.

"Get off me!" I screamed. The force sent those who held me, hurtling back.

"Let me—" My voice choked off like it was snatched away.

"Don't yell, Princess. It's rude." Rage and horror coated my tongue as Loch Orqanz stepped between the soldiers with a shit-eating grin on his face.

Behind him, Exekiel continued to brawl with hundreds of men that came at him at once. He unleashed the Fates. His shadows rose but just like my voice, they flickered and died. They bloomed again and swept the guards aside but lacked their usual force.

My stare shot to Loch. He hadn't just taken my voice. He'd used our twisted bind to take my power and turned it on my mate.

"How could you work with our enemy?" I croaked.

Loch laughed bitterly. "That's rich," he snarled, "Coming from the whore who's fucking one of them."

His knuckles struck the side of my face. Blood filled my mouth. My eyes stung.

"I think I'll leave you to it." Adir winked and sauntered back to where Alexov, Gwendoline, Knox and other Pre-Primaries gathered to welcome their army at the bridge.

"Don't do this," I hissed as Loch prowled around me. I wanted to scream and yell in his face, but he still held my voice in a vice. "I can win the Games. I can get us the Eternal Throne."

He sneered. "Us?"

He hit me again, so hard I struck the ground. The chains clanked around my wrists and made it impossible to break my fall.

"I don't have to be your Queen for us to be allies." I struggled to my knees.

My voice was a little stronger now. It was like he'd loosened his hold to hear me out.

"You'll be my right-hand; have input on the running of the kingdom. On how our enemies are handled."

Wasn't that what he wanted most? Revenge and power?

Exekiel roared as one of the soldiers drove a blade through his shoulder. Chunks climbed up my throat. He ripped the blade free and ran it through the soldier's skull. He didn't stop as he spun to face another opponent. And another.

I forced my stare back to Loch. I had to get him on our side. The soldier's followed his command. One word from him and this could end.

Loch squatted in front of me. "Tell me, Princess," He grasped my braids in his hands and yanked my head back. "How stupid do you think I am?"

He gripped my jaw. His webbed fingers dug into my cheeks. "Empty promises to save yourself or maybe," he glanced over his shoulder, "to save him."

I bucked as Loch siphoned more magic from inside me. Exekiel shouted. The sound tugged at my chest. It wasn't just my magic that overpowered him. It was the wounds that he'd sustained during the tournament and the magic of the other most powerful beings of the realm that pressed down on him.

The Royal Court members continued to let the soldiers in but I felt their power pulse in the air. Felt it close around us.

"Don't you see, Princess?" Loch kept one hand fisted in my hair but trailed the other down my neck.

"You're going to give me everything I want. This realm, your power, your body. They'll all be mine." His hand closed around my breast and squeezed. "Under the control of the device, you'll be much more agreeable."

Fear and fury choked in my lungs. "You wouldn't." I tried to wriggle out of his grasp.

Loch leaned in and ran his cold tongue up the side of my face. I recoiled.

"I would." He growled in the back of his throat. "I can't wait to fuck you, Princess." He pushed his hand down the front of my leggings. I jolted when his fingers ran over my clit.

Pleasure and rage tore me open.

"Get off me." My voice was no better than a breathless gasp.

Like Exekiel, I was being buried beneath the power of hundreds; thousands. It was like they'd banded together to coil a cage around us.

Loch rubbed me hard and fast through my underwear. I groaned and wrestled with the chains around my wrists. I tried to tear them free. To keep a clear head as that fucking bond manipulated my emotions. It made a part of me want to open my legs. To let him take me.

Loch groaned and I knew he'd felt the damp spot that spread between my thighs. "I'm going to fuck you raw, Princess."

"No," I panted as he pushed his fingers lower. "No."

I brought my arms up over his head and crossed my wrists in front of him. The chains tightened around his neck. His eyes widened with wrath and the promise of pain.

"Loch!" Adir barked. When had he returned? "Leave your doll. We need to move before the guard change."

Loch grinned despite how tightly I squeezed and how his eyes watered. Then he turned his head and sank his jagged teeth into my arm.

I screamed; my voice fully returned to me. The pain of his bite was unreal. He shredded my flesh; cut down to the bone in seconds. It was like he was part piranha, which according to the history's I'd read; he could be.

Desperate, I pulled free. My stomach roiled. There was a hole in my arm and a chunk of my skin hung from his blooded lips. Loch spat the flesh to the ground and hopped to his feet.

I wanted to curl in on myself but I cradled my arm, and forced myself to stand. I looked to where they'd restrained Exekiel. He was surrounded, on his knees with confusion and fury in his eyes.

Had he seen where Loch's hands had been and what he was doing to me? Had he seen how a part of me had wanted to give in? Did he feel the pressure of my magic amongst all the others that held him down?

Fuck. I wanted to explain. I should have explained before but I'd been afraid of how he'd react if he knew that I would always be bound to the Rebel

Leader. It was nothing like the connection he and I shared, but it was powerful enough to shatter my world if I let it.

"One more thing," Loch sang. His pale eyes were bright. His lips still stained with my blood.

He shoved a hand into his waistcoat and pulled out a metal collar that pulsed with a toxic energy. The earth tipped beneath me. Exekiel tugged more violently on those who held him. His shadows rose, but again, were echoes of what they usually were.

"Don't you just love the irony?" Loch skipped towards him. "You wanted to strip me and my people of our power. Instead, I'm going to take yours." His sneer was pure predator. He stopped before Exekiel and grinned back at me. "Then I'm going to fuck your mate, until the only shape of a cock inside her, is mine, and she forgets you ever existed."

Power levels be damned. At those words, Exekiel became a creature of the night. Not the son of the Fate of Death but death itself. His eyes gleamed like beads of fresh blood and his shadows claimed the world.

49

VARIALLA:
FLAMING HEART

Every nearby soldier went down. Their screams barely passed their lips before their charred bodies withered and fell.

Loch wrenched on our connection so tightly, it was like he'd choked the air from my lungs. I wheezed and gripped my chest. He used my power to create a shield around himself that blocked Exekiel's shadows. They thrashed around him but never touched his skin.

I had to concentrate on breathing as I got on my knees and fumbled in the dirt for some way to break these fucking chains. A rock, a dagger; anything.

Commanders of the army bellowed orders but they turned to frenzied shouts when Exekiel splayed his wings. The Fates lit up on his skin and his shadows surged over the soldiers like an ink-stained sea.

At least a hundred of them fell, whilst the rest fled. Exekiel moved through them like the ghost of death.

"Don't let him close the barrier," Adir bellowed.

That was clearly what Exekiel planned to do. He was headed right towards it.

"Fuck!" Loch took off after him but he was nowhere near as fast.

Exekiel carved through the soldiers like a blade through warm butter. He was terrifying and magnificent. A vessel of destruction and eternal rage.

"He's too strong!" Someone shouted.

"Unleash the arrows!"

Arrows with flaming tips soared through the air. I gave up on breaking the chains, shoved to my feet and raced towards Exekiel. We would have to fight our way out of this and we would fight it together.

Ahead of me, Adir lifted a bow and arrow and took aim. I pounced. Together we fell. Sand plumed around us. He tried to stand. I grabbed his ankles and held him down as I climbed up his body.

"It's too bad you refused to join our side, Princess," Adir grunted as he flipped onto his back and conjured a shimmery silver dagger in his hand.

That was his affinity—to create items from raw magic.

"And what side is that?"

He swung for me. I gripped the chain that bound my wrists with both hands and slammed it down on his chest.

"A side where power is kept in capable hands and not handed off due to a popularity contest."

This time he slashed for my throat. I dodged the blow and rammed my thumbs into his eyes. He barked. The dagger faded. Adir fumbled to smother my nose and mouth but I gnashed my teeth and pressed harder.

Dragon's heat filled my hands and warmth rushed through my fingers. The Primary's cries turned tortured. Wet coated my thumbs. He screamed as I dug deeper. Magic swirled at my fingertips. The sea sung in my veins. A song of war.

Something slammed into the back of my head and I was knocked sideways. I rolled in the sand and hopped to my feet with my fists raised. Fire bloomed around my knuckles and melted through the chains. I really had to get used to using this dragon fire.

"Varialla, stop!"

My heart lurched when mahogany brown skin and deep mocha eyes caught my attention. Nile. My stomach flipped. When had he joined the army? His brow was creased and his eyes flared with confusion.

"What are you doing?" he gasped. "Loch struck a deal with the Royal Court. We're on the same side."

"The only side they're on is their own," I shouted over the carnage.

"Not anymore." Nile smiled. It was full of hope and innocence. "They're going to put us on the throne of Shifter Springs so long as we help them keep the peace in the Isles."

"Bullshit!" I thrust a finger at Adir who crawled away. His eyes were swollen shut and blood dribbled down his cheeks. "Whatever he's told you, is a lie."

"It wasn't him. It was Loch."

I scoffed. "Even worse."

Nile's face hardened. "What?"

"It's all a lie," I shouted, begging him to understand. "Have they told you how they plan to keep the peace?"

"We're their army."

"You're their weapon," I cried. "Exekiel and I are fighting to stop it."

"Exekiel? The Shadow Saint?" His tone was sharp. He shook his head. "I knew you were sleeping with the Fate-stained shit, but I didn't realize his dick was so good you'd turn your back on your own people."

"That's not what I'm doing." I stepped towards him but he stepped back.

"Collette tried to warn me." Sorrow filled his eyes. "I wish it didn't come to this, Varialla."

Nile bowed his head. Blinding pain burst straight through my spine and into my heart.

I gaped, wide-eyed at the blade that now protruded from my chest. My knees buckled. Blood spurted from the corners of my mouth. Nile choked back a sob and scrubbed a hand down his face. His horror-struck expression darted from me to my attacker. I couldn't even look them in the eye. The coward had stabbed me in the back.

50

EXEKIEL:
UNDYING

Agony sliced through my chest. My vision swayed. With a hand pressed to my heart, I searched the sand. It was soaked with blood.

I turned in the direction I'd felt Varialla's magic sputter.

Where are you little bud?

I doubled over and clutched my side as a fresh wave of pain cleaved through my insides. Varialla's agony was my own. My breaths became heavy and my steps were sluggish. I didn't even care about what I'd seen pass between her and the Rebel Leader earlier. I just needed to get to her. Needed to find her.

My knees buckled. I held my hands out to catch my fall but they slipped and I struck the ground.

Don't die, little bud.

As the son of Zorsch, I knew our chances of surviving this were slim. But as long as there was a chance, I wouldn't give up.

Varialla couldn't die today. Our story couldn't end here. I hadn't found her now, only to lose her to the same fucking monsters who'd taken everything else from me.

My chest tightened. The life bond pulled and strapped around my neck like a noose. Pain split my skull. I hunched over; my head pressed into the grainy sand.

I tried to stand but my body wouldn't move. The Fates had saved me once. Not this time. My arms shook until I finally collapsed. Flat on my back, I stared bleary-eyed at the barrier that pulsed and shimmered in the distance. I felt the fine cracks that webbed across it. Soon it would be gone completely and everything would have been for nothing.

My shadows flailed. Their deep black was now a pale grey. It was a weak warning to any who thought to attack.

"Exekiel!" A familiar voice pierced my thoughts.

Someone clutched my hand and shook my shoulders. I groaned.

"Thesona!" They screamed.

Through a haze, I saw an outline of a face. A flash of dark hair and bright blue eyes. Vivienne was hunched over me. She shouted something in my face.

"Use your dying breath and save yourself!"

Her pale cheeks were flushed and tears tracked her cheeks. Fuck! Did this mean I'd reached my end before I could dismember the bastard that had harmed my mate? I'd planned to take his body in pieces before this moment came.

A different kind of pain pierced my heart. Varialla was dying. The only comfort was knowing that I was going with her.

"*Thesona*!" Vivienne shouted. She slapped me across the cheek. "I knew I should never have left you with that siren."

It took my mind a moment to process what she was saying as I felt the sweet tug of the abyss calling.

"Use your dying breath."

I fought to stay conscious. To fight. But it was an enemy I couldn't see.

I clung tighter to Vivienne's hand and tried to piece together what she meant.

Understanding trickled in. In one of the articles recently printed about the life bond between me and Varialla, it had said that no one could break it except for *Thesona* herself. However, the power of *Thesona* flowed through my veins. There was no guarantee this would work, but I would use my dying breath to try.

My body sagged into the earth as I dredged up my last ounce of strength. Life evaded me as easily as the breeze passed through my hair.

"Do it," Vivienne urged. "Save yourself." She nodded. Her teary eyes pleading.

My own eyes closed as my shadows cut through the people and surged towards Varialla. I felt each breath tighten and fade in my chest.

With only one left to give, I whispered, "*Thesona.*"

My shadows fell over Varialla. As they healed her fatal wound, I died.

51

VARIALLA:

This is What Nightmares Are Made Of

Every part of me screamed. Agony had replaced my blood, my skin, my lungs. Pain was all I knew. Somewhere somehow, I heard Exekiel's voice; carried to me on the wind.

I thought I told you not to get us killed.

My fists curled in the sand that clumped around my fingers. My heart struggled to beat around the blade that carved through it. Everything was happening too fast.

In the last few weeks, I'd felt more alive than I had in my entire life. Maybe this was why. Because the Fates knew I would end up here. Tears stung my eyes. There was still so much I wanted to experience. Opportunities I wished I'd taken.

Someone held my hand and murmured, "I'll miss you."

It was Nile. His forehead rested on mine.

I tried to warn him about Loch and the weapon. I tried to say something, but my mouth refused to work. A sour tang danced on my tongue.

The pain became excruciating, sharp then vanished entirely. I was numb and falling into the abyss. I tumbled off the edge of the end, but something wrenched me back.

A rush of power flooded my system. A single word in a voice I would always know whispered, "*Thesona.*"

Exekiel's shadows fell over me. They seeped into my skin and wrapped around my broken heart. I screamed as the dagger was forced from my chest. The blood soaked into my clothes receded. My mind spun. Nothing made sense except one truth I couldn't face.

Exekiel was healing me. He'd brought me from the brink of death. But if he was saving me, who was saving him?

Panic took root in my veins. Life poured into me but I still felt like I was dying. I gasped for breath and forced my eyes open. Maybe I was wrong. Maybe we'd both survived. I blinked across the blood-soaked beach.

Dawn was approaching. A fraction of the soldiers lay dead. Even more of them had run. But some remained on the beach and stared up at the barrier that groaned in the distance. It pulsed like a beating heart; a thud within the earth.

One…two…the shimmering structure shattered into a million glistening shards of black. My heart punched in my chest.

Exekiel was gone. This time, I couldn't save him. I screamed inside my soul. I begged the stars to change his fate. They didn't listen.

I watched in muted horror; my vision blurred, as the fragments of power swirled towards their master and merged with Exekiel's shadows.

They wrapped around his limp form like writhing snakes. My chest felt like it had been torn open. Moments later, a bright light cleaved through the sky. It bloomed brighter and carved through the shadows. When they finally cleared and the light faded, Exekiel was gone.

Maybe his sacrifice had gotten him one thing he wanted; the glory of being a true Fate. I tried to take comfort in that thought but it only left me cold. I couldn't move, couldn't think. Then, at last, the sweet bliss of unconsciousness claimed me.

I jolted awake. Clashes of figures and memories of faces swirled across my mind. I was no longer sprawled in the sand but in a bed staring up at a shell encrusted ceiling.

I bolted upright and almost hurled from the pounding in my head.

A hand rested on my shoulder. "Steady."

I jerked away and blinked wide-eyed at an unfamiliar face. Although there was something I recognized in those piercing blue eyes. As clear as the water that surrounded me.

He was a siren. He appeared to be a few years younger than me. Though in this realm, that didn't mean much. His skin was the golden brown of dawn on tree bark, and he had wavy golden locks that framed his oval face.

I wrestled with the sheets as I tried to climb out of the bed.

"What are you doing?" he hissed.

There was only one place I could be with a siren at my bedside and surrounded by water. The Coral Court. Loch's Court.

"Getting out of here." My voice was raspy. It felt like it hadn't been used in days. "Don't try to stop me."

My words were more threatening than I felt. I was drained. My tongue felt fuzzy and my head ached.

My legs got tangled in the sheets. I almost toppled from the bed but the stranger caught my arm and steadied me.

"Of course, I won't stop you. I'm here to get you out." He grunted, "I would never leave Exekiel's mate in the hands of the Rebel King."

I froze. My heart tightened at the sound of his name. I stared up at the stranger. Into those impossibly familiar eyes.

"What do you mean?"

He glanced over his shoulder then bit into his finger until it bled.

"Ex recently sent me a message." His blood dropped onto a piece of folded parchment that he'd pulled from beneath a scale. The blood spread like spilled ink as it met the water and stained the sheet. Words in Exekiel's familiar handwriting appeared. My heart leapt. I leaned in.

"Maybe you can tell us what he wanted to do next."

I blinked from the page to him. "Who are you?"

The siren's mouth twisted ruefully and he raked a hand through his golden locks. "They call me Aquarius."

EPILOGUE

EXEKIEL

I awoke in the in-between. In a cocoon of white light and wisps of gray. I wasn't in Fatevale and I was no longer on the shore in the midst of a battle. I'd died. I'd traded my last breath for Varialla's. And yet I hung in between living and not.

A figure cloaked in shadows moved beyond the light.

From his statue in the Archway of Angels, I recognized the breadth of his shoulders, the sturdiness of his stance and the angle of his bearded jaw.

"You have done well, Exekiel." Zorsch's deep voice—my father's voice—spoke inside my mind. "By sacrificing your life to save another, you have shown the mark of a true Fate. Why did you not meet me at the Gates of Fatevale?" His silhouette shifted closer beyond the light. "Is there something holding you back?"

"Yes." Like his, my voice came from inside my mind.

A lot of things tethered me to the Isles. Things I'd never truly thought I'd have again. Friendship, family…love.

"You wish to return."

"Yes."

The figure hesitated. "Do you understand that if you go back as a true Fate, your legend or lack of it, will follow you in life but not in death. You will be giving up your seat beside me in Fatevale. The next time you die, you will do so like everyone else".

There will be no ceremony waiting for me at the gates. No statues erected in the Hall of Fates in my likeness. I would simply fade into the unknown.

"I understand."

The veiled image of my father shimmered. For decades I had dreamt of this day. To prove myself worthy of Fatevale and return. To meet the man who sired me with a woman who never knew I existed. Now no dream was complete without Varialla in it.

"You still wish to return?"

I didn't hesitate. I simply said, "Yes."

DID YOU ENJOY

THE ROYAL GAMES?

If you enjoyed this book, please leave an honest review on Amazon, Bookbub and/or Goodreads.

Reviews and ratings are extremely valuable for indie authors like myself. It helps new readers decide if this book is something they would enjoy, and it gives me some invaluable feedback to keep writing the books you love.

I cannot wait to hear what you think and I truly thank you for taking the time to read this series.

To join my newsletter, stay up to date on my upcoming releases, & more, scan here:

Special Thanks

S. McPherson

I would like to send out a humungous thank you to
all my lovely readers, from my incredible ARC
readers to all those who have read the book since its
release and to those who are yet to come. I would
also like to say a special thank you to my beautiful
mum for the constant support along the way, and to
my incredible audiobook narrator and friend,
Angelique Franklin of Phoenix Rises Media for the
back and forth's and great laughs.
Thank you to everyone who has reviewed and/ or
shared some love for the Fit for the Throne series
on social media or via word of mouth so far.
I cannot express how much I appreciate you and I
hope you stick around for what's coming next.

I love you in this realm & the next x